Kent Harrington is a native of San Francisco, and the author of two previous novels. He lives in Northern California.

PCP (8|11)

SE

THE AMERICAN BOYS

Alex Law is lost; more than twenty years of secret wars and spying have left him numbed and spiritually bankrupt. An alcoholic womanizer and veteran CIA 'genius', Alex is now a comic anachronism in the world of espionage. Hopelessly, he longs for his estranged wife, Helen. Enter a gang of bent CIA men, with a plan to run the world. When an old company friend identifies Alex as the only remaining solution to a national security problem, Alex becomes embroiled in a drugs scandal of monumental proportions that requires him to dredge up all his old self-respect and courage in order to save his wife and son.

KENT HARRINGTON

THE AMERICAN BOYS

Complete and Unabridged

ULVERSCROFT
Leicester

First published in Great Britain in 2001 by
Robert Hale Limited
London

First Large Print Edition
published 2003
by arrangement with
Robert Hale Limited
London

British Library CIP Data

Harrington, Kent
    The American boys.—Large print ed.—
    Ulverscroft large print series: adventure & suspense
    1. United States. Central Intelligence Agency—Corrupt
    practices 2. Intelligence officers—United States—Fiction
    3. Suspense fiction 4. Large type books
    I. Title
    813.5′4 [F]

    ISBN 0–7089–4771–9

Published by
F. A. Thorpe (Publishing)
Anstey, Leicestershire

Set by Words & Graphics Ltd.
Anstey, Leicestershire
Printed and bound in Great Britain by
T. J. International Ltd., Padstow, Cornwall

This book is printed on acid-free paper

To Susan Harrington, even more
beautiful than Paris on a rainy day . . .

Power corrupts. Absolute power is kind of neat.

— John Lehman
Secretary of the Navy, 1981–1987

Que el canto tiene sentido cuando
palpita en las venas del que morira
cantando las verdades verdaderas . . .

Victor Jara

MEXICO CITY

Present Day

He had a desire to be near women — white ones, black ones, yellow ones, red ones, old ones, young ones, as long as they were female, with female ways, brilliant or stupid, nuns or perverts, it didn't matter to Alex. He craved his opposite. He wanted to hear female voices: hear them chit-chat or climax or even be angry with him. Alex imagined it was why he spent so much of his time in bawdyhouses. He liked women. *Any* kind of female was preferable to what he saw around him: a café full of male intelligence officers. He wanted to smell the perfume of a woman's long hair on a summer evening, or the scent of his wife on her sweaters (before

1

she left him), or the towel of a whore who had wiped her mascaraed face and left it on his sink. Yes, of course he was lost after twenty years of war and spying. What did anyone expect he would be — certainly not *found*. Oh, god, yes, he was lost. He'd admitted that *long* ago. Women, Alex thought, through his withering hangover, made being lost a lot less important and tiresome. They were the treasures you hung onto in the night, some bit of underwear and a smile you remembered when you were told to start counting your ammunition. For civilians, who never got down to the grit and bloody end of things, it was different. In the civilian world, women had been reduced to *colleagues* or *friends*. God, he thought, how ridiculous. He, for one, would never hold a woman and think of her as anything but the opposite of death. *Lost, all right*, Alex thought, *but not dead yet. I'll be dead when I call you a 'colleague.'* And then he smiled one of his famous Alex special smiles that was, despite everything, charming and made all the difference. People liked Alex Law, they always had, at Yale and before and after, despite everything he'd done over the years to make it hard for them to like him. But some people are charming and, at the bottom, decent in a way that isn't perfect or *nice*, or sometimes even pleasant, which would spoil it. Perfection spoils anything. And, as someone once said, beauty and charm in themselves make the world at least bearable.

To try to clear his head, Alex sniffed at the air. It smelled of coffee and, under that, there was the smell of damp suits suddenly thrust into a warm room and, under that, the smell of after-shaved men who live very well. There was a constant clatter of plates and the sound of men's brassy voices, and a loud hissing from a cappuccino machine behind him across the café. Each bang of grounds being knocked loose on the bar was a horrible prelude to the next, like pistol shots. He tried not to flinch.

Alex calculated, carefully putting down his beer glass, that he'd spent the last twenty years alongside spies in most of the major cities of the world, and he was tired of their haunts, their second-rate suits, and their second-rate morals. All their haunts were some variation of the Café Montserrat, some better lit than others, that was all.

Despite his hangover, which was excruciating, Alex decided, lifting his glass, that he would never again step into the place. *I'd rather be shredded by a Zapatista bomb*, he thought to himself, swallowing the last of his beer. He would have to find a new place, he decided, turning around. If he were lucky, maybe he'd be blown into the past when things had made more sense. Maybe they will blow me all the way back to Yale, preferably summer time, he thought, finishing his drink.

Alex stared at the glazed and sweating bulletproof window and tried to recall the best years of his life — his golden years at Yale. Images rolled by in his mind, like bits from a student film. He was mesmerized as he recalled a much younger Alex parading about in the past. *Alex, the Yalie, walking into his private apartment with doorman. Alex, the Skull and Bones member, in jeans and striped blue and white shirt, looking slightly nautical, on the steps of his fraternity. Alex with his elite circle of friends, whose families owned so much, standing together arm-in-arm in the summer at one of those unimaginably glamorous house parties in the Adirondacks. Alex's sun-bleached hair combed neatly to the side, his grin boyish and distant, his upper body college-student scrawny but tanned to perfection. Impromptu trips to London with his girlfriends, the tremendous bills paid by his father without ever a mention. Yes, he'd been bright-eyed and beautiful then.*

'Hey, Alex. Getting much Mexican pussy?' Glad said in a bristling tone before he'd even

4

gotten to Alex's table. 'I've heard it's a real tonic.' The doctor's voice cut through Alex's daydream like scissors. 'The darker the meat, the sweeter the treats.' Glad's voice climbed over the considerable café noise.

When he looked up, Alex's face was still boyish and very handsome but much tougher-looking now. He was furrowed around the eyes. Everything he had experienced while in the CIA, including the Battle of Cuito Cuanavale in Angola, registered in those piercing eyes, which were, oddly, a feminine blue. They were the kind of eyes people get who have seen too many things they shouldn't have and carried the secrets, cataloging them all. Whores often have the same damaged look. His eyes held no more illusions and shunned intimacy because of the pain. Alex had made a point of not wanting friends now. Not having friends helped him get through life.

'I like them *slutty*, Alex, and underage of course. I know *you* can fix me up. And don't lie about it, Alex. You nail them everywhere you go. I'm looking for ones who take to *older* gents, ones with exotic tastes, mysteries of the Orient if you know what I mean. You bang them like a gong, don't you.' Alex shut his ears to Glad's voice. He had one last private thought before he was completely

5

overrun by the doctor's ugly fantasy: *I need Helen again. I've always needed her. Have I lost her for good?* A frightening realization hit Alex with a physical force: *You've been a fool if you think you can get her back. Why should she come back to you? Divorce papers aren't valentines. It's the cock of the gun, I'm afraid.*

Dr. Glad offered his hand. Alex was forced to stand up, something he'd avoided with his hangover. *They were fellow officers. They would shake hands he supposed.* Alex ordered himself to reach out and respond in an appropriate manner. Alex animated his face with a template smile he used when running one of his agents which was neither friendly nor indifferent. He loathed Glad but he believed in decorum. They shook hands. It lasted too long. There was physical contact which Alex hated; he had to bear Glad's anthropoidal sweaty grasp and the phony camaraderie that spilled out of him — *the whole truckload of ape shit,* he thought, smiling.

Glad had spotted Alex sitting alone, shunned by the mostly younger CIA officers taking their morning break from the embassy. Alex looked just as Glad remembered him from their days in Lisbon, terribly handsome in that English, Jeremy Irons way — a blue-eyed lanky patrician. His good looks were marred by a bad hangover, but still, even now in middle age, he had a charming elegance and economy of manner as he stood up. When you spoke to Alex Law you always got the feeling you were climbing onto his yacht, Glad thought, shaking Alex's hand. Alex pulled his hand away first.

'I heard you're on your fourth embassy in as many years, old boy,' Glad said chortling, his hand still stretched out as if it hadn't had enough. The Montserrat's hubbub was exaggerated by a low, dark ceiling that seemed to amplify every harsh male sound. The doctor sat down at Alex's table first, uninvited. 'I thought you'd be running your family's empire by now,' Glad said. 'Still in the game, I see. I never understood why you weren't in some corner office, smooching secretaries and playing golf by *now*.' Glad's voice was overbearing and too affable to be anything but obliquely hostile. The doctor was from CIA's psychological warfare operations directorate (PSYWOP) and looked remarkably like David Letterman. He had the same hollow-eyed expression of a farm boy who's burned down the barn, the same mismatched body parts, the head too small and the arms too long. His face was made uglier by a ponytail and white hair. The doctor was almost as tall as Alex. He was a miscreant even by the CIA's peculiar and generous standards of behavior, Alex thought, looking at him.

'It's always good to see you, Ted. Really it is. You're a little far afield, aren't you?' Alex said, ignoring the remark he'd heard a thousand times about his family's banking empire.

'Odd jobs . . . hocus-pocus stuff. No more needles and pins.' The smile crawled larger over the doctor's face.

Alex managed a second weak official smile that said nothing and sat down. 'Are you with us long? When was the last time we had a chance to talk?' Alex said, hearing his own voice. He tried to sound as if he cared, acting the part of *fellow officer*. Alex wanted to bolt from the table but he forced himself to face the doctor. Their eyes met for a moment. Glad's eyes were watery and unfeeling, the creases of his mouth smug and ugly as if he'd been taught to smile at school. Alex realized he'd always been right about Glad. *He was a monster.* Alex looked away and out the big picture window of the café to the great simulacrum of Paris, Mexico City, hoping his head would clear. *But he's one of our monsters.*

'I have to talk to you about one of the

American Boys, Butch Nickels. I'm afraid he's off the reservation. We're looking for him. We've heard he's been living in Cuernavaca since he left us. Of course, if he should contact you, you'll let us know, won't you. I know you two were great pals back in the old days,' Glad said, smiling. 'I'll stop by your office when you're feeling *more alive*. We can have a real chinwag about the old days.' Glad winked at him and nodded toward the American embassy across the street, aware now that Alex was nursing a hangover. 'How's the wife and kids?' Glad leaned in close, into that space that one cherishes in the morning, and took Alex by the elbow, violating it. 'Us old-timers got to stick together.' Then, *sotto voce*, 'I'm afraid Butch might have tread on the other side.' He had a conspiratorial glint in his eye. 'Bad business, whoring around. But then Butch was never much for making the right moves, was he? Any bobble would attract Butchy boy,' Glad whispered, straightening up and retreating. Alex, stunned by the assault of mouthwash and aftershave, tried to hang on and not lose the little bit of breakfast he'd managed to get down.

'I didn't even know he was out of the business,' Alex lied, trying to reach for his coffee, forgetting it was cold, but Glad's arm had blocked it. Glad feigned a smile and scrutinized Alex. Glad's eyes were penetrating, like two little whirling dentist drills now, as he watched Alex steady himself.

'Well then,' Glad said and stood up suddenly. 'Good to see you, Alex. I'll stop in. Don't forget my girls.' The doctor got up, disturbing the creamer that had been overfilled. Long white fingers of cream ran over Alex's folded *New York Times*. The doctor moved back into the noise and took an adjoining table with a group of well-dressed younger men from the embassy. The young faces were free of anything but ambition and exhibited that special cruelty that smolders in the eyes of young men who have more authority than experience. Glad glanced back once, as if he had been thinking about Alex's little lie, and smiled. He knew Butch Nickles had, in fact, called Alex.

Alex's generation — the ones that had come up with him in Africa, in Central America, and even inside Cuba — for all their faults, for all their outrageous sins (and there had been many sins), would never have laughed at a fellow officer in the dignity-robbing way that Alex was snickered at as he stood up to leave his table later. Alex felt physically the younger mens' derision like an enervating force behind him. He ignored it;

10

he understood he was utterly useless to what he thought of as the 'smart bomb' set who were taking over. At forty-five he was a relic, an old cannon left in the sun to rust and stare out at the sea. He got up and decided to show them, almost marching out, still a little drunk. It only made them snicker more. He remembered as he wound his way past harried waiters what Mobutu Sese Seko had once said to him on a reviewing stand: 'I owe it all to you, Alex, to you and your American boys.' Things had been different then. *Much different then. I had a wife then.*

Alex strode through the café managing not to bump into anyone, clutching his past triumphs, his alcoholism, his private income, his physical beauty and his ruined life. He carried them all like a soldier going over the top who has very little time left for anything but dignity. *I'm not a drunk . . . am not a drunk, he thought. I am not past it.* Their silent laughter — he could feel it — propelled him. For the first time in his life, he was struck by the realization and the fear of what he'd become: a glorious has-been.

In the men's room, Alex pulled on the worn cassock that he'd used for so many years, pulling it down over his smart casual clothes, and left. Like magic, he was no longer the debauched polo player on the make but now a Catholic priest.

Glad, who had enjoyed Alex's humiliation at the hands of the young men at his table, watched Alex push through the big swinging doors of the café out to the street. He had no intention of sharing the truth about Alex with the young men at the table, no intention of telling them that in the old days Alex and a group of young men had changed the face of Africa. He listened to their ugly derisive jokes and enjoyed them. Glad, like so many who had started out with Alex, was jealous of him, so the laughter was a relief. Glad knew the young men at his table were pathetic fops who relied on computers instead of what it really took in their business — what Alex had in spades: a talent for corrupting people and for fighting on the run. It was what had made Alex a leader in his day, especially those two days in Angola when Alex was to distinguish himself. Glad's jealousy of Alex was acceptable now because Alex was washed-up. Glad remembered Alex on his best day in Africa at the battle of Cuito Cuanavale, the Cuban troops overrunning the town and their special branch looking for CIA agents to shoot. Glad's jealousy had been born there. Drunk or sober, Glad thought, wiping his lips with a napkin, Alex had shown something that day that these well-muscled young men sitting around him now with their smart military-style brush cuts would never know.

Glad had been in the room in Nairobi Station when Alex had radioed, hidden in a Catholic church in Cuito with the others — Wyatt, Butch and Claymore. Everyone in the air-conditioned room in the CIA's Nairobi Station could hear the fifty calibers in the background and the chaotic sounds of war coming over the radio. Someone was ringing the church bell for no apparent reason. It provided a strange background to Alex's unflinching voice.

'Imperative that you leave,' the head of station had said into the radio. 'Repeat. Imperative that you leave Cuito. Alex, it's finished. Leave.' There had been a long pause, filled only by the harsh static on the line and the sound of that church bell tolling, as if the answer coming back, across all that war, and all that jungle, and all those dark, silent rivers, took time.

'No. We'll fight,' Alex said finally. It had stunned everyone in the room, as if it were the jungle itself speaking, or some throwback English officer at the Somme. All their impressions about Alex were corroborated that afternoon. He was someone you had to respect. Glad looked at the young intelligence

13

agents around him, all cocksure bed-wetters every one of them. *They wouldn't have stayed in Cuito that day one minute. They would have run over their mothers to get out.*

Through the dirty bomb-proof windows, Glad caught a glimpse of Alex flagging a taxi in the rain, the ridiculous cassock making him look like a plaster Dresden saint. As Glad tasted the brandy's bitterness, a line from somewhere came to him. *He is no more and, impudently brave, the loathly rats sit grinning on his grave.*

2

Langley, Virginia

His briefcase hitting his thigh, his fifty-year-old body struggling to command two steps at a time, his face bright red from the excitement and the adrenaline, Richard Claymore gasped for air. His gray hair was wild-looking from his run across the chaotic parking lot where three of his friends had just been gunned down. It was an odd moment to realize he'd gotten old. All the 'American Boys' were middle aged now and probably wouldn't survive this time, the way they had survived the Cold War, Africa, El Salvador.

Claymore had been in the CIA too long to kid himself or believe in miracles. He knew, stopping on the second landing of the stairs that would take him to his office at CIA headquarters, that they intended to kill him, too.

Claymore had seen the killings close up. He'd phoned Kregan that morning and told him he would not be car-pooling and would drive himself in because he wanted to buy some new tires at Sears after work. He had

15

been three cars behind them. The gunman, a clean-cut Latin in his thirties, had waited for Kregan's white Cadillac to pull into the line of queued cars waiting to turn left into CIA's main entrance. Then he stepped off the island and slid a machine pistol out from under his overcoat, but that was not at all what the police would be told later.

The shooter opened fire on Kregan's car at point-blank range. He was methodical, firing a full clip and then putting in another. Kregan, at the wheel, shuddered horribly from the impact of the bullets. Kevin Ford was riding next to Paul Kregan and tried to get out but was cut down too. Claymore heard the screams from nearby cars. The gunman paused a moment and made sure they were dead. Then he walked down the line of stopped cars toward Claymore. He fired here and there indiscriminately. He'd looked right into Claymore's eyes and moved on, shooting a lone woman in the next car. The gunman trotted calmly to a motorcycle waiting for him on the other side of the street and was driven away. It couldn't have taken him more than three minutes.

Claymore bent over to catch his breath. He slid his hands onto his knees. His shirt was sopping with sweat. He realized, staring at the floor, that they'd all been fools. They were using Corsican rules: if you got in their way you died. He stood up and looked behind him. The staircase — not normally used — was empty. He went on, but was only able to manage one step at a time now.

They shouldn't have met. They shouldn't have said anything. They had acted like amateurs. The three of them, Kevin Ford, Head of Counter-intelligence Directorate, Paul Kregan, who handled disinformation and the press in Washington, and himself, Clandestine's Internal Affairs Officer, had been asked the night before to join a special operation headed by top people at the agency, including the Director of Central Intelligence himself, at a safe house in Langley, Virginia. They were told it would ensure the future prosperity of the agency and entail a wholesale change in the executive branch, including the presidency. They would receive ten million dollars a piece for their part in the operation. Would they support it? When they pressed for details, none had been given. Their jobs, they were told, would be to manage the crisis as it developed in their respective departments.

They had left the safe house in Kregan's car stunned by the audacity of the plan. They stopped for coffee at a pizza parlor and, talking together, realized that they had just been asked to participate in a coup d'état. They should have known better than to talk at all. Kregan said he was going to call the FBI in the morning. Somehow, they had been monitored. Claymore had said nothing but had gone out later to an all-night copy center and sent a very short fax to Red Bowles, the president's security chief, asking for a meeting.

★ ★ ★

Claymore held up his photo ID and tried not to shake. He was breathing hard from the fear and the adrenaline. The guard nodded, gave him a perfunctory good morning and asked him what was going on outside. Claymore ignored him and went on into the hallway. His hand shook as he put down his briefcase and punched in the office code. His office door unlocked. He was trying to keep his mind from being overrun with fear. His secretary was on the phone. She stopped speaking and held the receiver as he came in. Had he heard the news? He nodded solemnly. 'Are you all right, Richard?'

'Shook up, that's all.'

Claymore slipped into his office. He closed the door behind him and leaned against it. It was cool inside his private office and quiet.

He could think here. He glanced at his watch; it was less than fifteen minutes since the shootings. They would realize soon that he hadn't been killed, that he hadn't been in Kregan's car. They would be calling his wife to see if he'd come in to work. He had ten minutes at the most before he would have to leave the office, they would be sure to look for him here, too, of course.

They want to use Alex, he realized now. That's why the Director's office had opened the phony investigation on Alex and why they'd sent Glad to investigate Alex over Claymore's objections. He'd reminded the Director's office that Glad wasn't even part of his staff and had no business working an Internal Affairs case. He thought for a moment of calling Alex directly at the embassy in Mexico to warn him. But that would be impossible now. There would be a record of the call. He realized he was talking to himself and it shocked him. He picked up the phone and dialed a number for Butch Nickels.

'Hello, Patsy.' He had no idea what time it was in Mexico.

'Richard, is that you? Richard Claymore?'

'Patsy, is Butch there? I have to speak to him, it's a bit of an emergency.'

'Sorry, he's up country,' she said. 'Richard,

19

is everything all right?'

'Fine. Could you tell him that? Tell him that. Tell him that Alex is fine. Tell him that we should have a reunion. Alex just called and said he was fine. Tell him that, will you?'

'Richard, something's wrong, isn't it. What do you mean Alex is fine?'

'Just tell him that Alex is fine. He'll understand. Have to run now, dear.' Claymore put the phone down.

Our only hope now is Alex. Talking to himself seemed to help, as if there were someone to share the fear with him. *If anyone can stop them from taking over, Alex can.* Claymore said it aloud; the sound of his own voice was strange. He wanted to run from the office and stopped himself. *We'll have none of that.* Claymore walked across the office and carefully put his briefcase in its usual spot. He sat down at his desk.

Get going!! Time is running out! You're dead, whatever happens, but you might help stop them. Claymore felt the need to say something to his wife. He looked at the phone . . . *say goodbye?* That would be cruel. They had planned a trip to California to see their daughter. *I must stop them.* Claymore checked his watch — three entire minutes wasted. He swung his chair around and turned on his computer and ran the cursor through the list of ongoing Internal Affairs investigations. He stopped when he saw Alex Law's file.

'Mr. Claymore . . . ?' Claymore jerked involuntarily, the way a man might jerk when he was shaken awake. He turned and looked at his secretary. She looked concerned.

'Are you all right, sir?' He nodded. 'You seemed upset.'

'I'm sorry. The shootings . . . ' he said.

The young woman nodded. 'It's awful. It could have been any of us.' The girl thought the shootings were random. Claymore knew better.

'Security would like us for a debriefing on the floor. People from Security want to interview everyone who might have seen anything this morning,' she told him.

'I'll be right there. Where are they having it?'

'Cafeteria, third floor.'

'Fine,' Claymore looked up. 'Save me a seat, Ms. Cruz, won't you.' Claymore forced a tight smile. His secretary smiled back at him and left. He looked at his watch — *seven minutes gone.*

At least he was in the enviable position of picking the agent of his revenge. Claymore opened Alex's Internal Affairs file. He entered a second password and his computer gave

21

him the numbers he would need to operate a locked file cabinet which contained the hard-copy files that were part of ongoing investigations. He crossed the office and entered the code and the file cabinet popped open. He found Alex's hard-copy file and took it out and put it on his desk. He went to the typewriter and wrote Alex a note and put it in the file. He couldn't delete Alex's name from the list of pending cases, but he could hide it so that only an authorized person who already knew what he was looking for could recover it. He hit the necessary keys and watched Alex's name deleted from the list of investigations. Satisfied that he'd thought of everything, Claymore put the hard-copy file in his briefcase and turned off his computer. It would buy Alex time at least.

The phone started to ring. Claymore nearly picked up, then thought better of it. The voicemail was on. He turned on his speaker and listened to his own calm, sleepy voice tell whomever was calling that he was away from his desk. He waited for the message to come on.

'Hello, Richard. Just checking to see if you are all right,' the rough gravelly voice sounded earnest. Claymore fought back the kind of fear that makes you want to either get up and run or get sick, and listened to the voice

22

carefully, going back over twenty-five years worth of voices. He knew *that* voice, he told himself. He gathered up his briefcase and walked out of his office for the last time. It was Wyatt's voice. And he knew that Wyatt Anderson hated Alex most of all.

3

Washington, D.C.

Captain Red Bowles of the Texas Rangers was suddenly an important man in Washington. Coming in with the new President, his face had been in all the news magazines. Sun-worn, it was the kind of round East Texas face that people didn't recognize easily. A journalist once told Bowles he looked like Garth Brooks's older brother. Red Bowles' job was protecting the newly-elected President of the United States, Neal White. He had protected White for the last ten years while he'd been Governor of Texas, and White saw no reason for Bowles to stay in Texas once he had been elected President.

Since coming to Washington, Bowles had stayed up nights worrying about a city he didn't really understand and that he'd felt, from the very first day there, was hostile to the President. The President had put him in charge of his personal security. The Secret Service had rebelled against the idea of Bowles and his Texas Rangers interfering. The President had told the head of the Secret

24

Service that if they didn't like it, he would formally appoint Bowles to the head of the Secret Service. Take it or leave it. The Secret Service had decided to back off and allowed Bowles and his team of Texas Rangers to act as the inner circle of security for the President and his family. When asked why by the press, the President said the Texas Rangers had never lost a game. When asked to explain the remark, he declined.

A bachelor, Bowles had grown up in a family of cowboys and still liked country music. He'd been listening to Merle Haggard's *Tulare Dust* when the fax machine started up in his stylish new apartment in Alexandria. Bowles went to the machine and read the message.

— Grave threat to the President. Meet me Library of Congress — outside benches west wing tomorrow ten A.M. Come alone. I'll know —

Bowles re-read the message slowly and thought it was a joke. He got up and turned off the music. Probably a reporter trying to get an interview, he thought. Then he thought better of it. There had been so much hostility since the day Neal was elected from the major newspapers and the staff at the White House. Everywhere they went, it seemed as if they were the country cousins and the real people in power were the ones in the hallways, the ones who had been there for years, the ones who came to the meetings and bobbed their heads and listened, and then went out and talked to the press and called Neal every kind of dirty name. Now, with Neal threatening the drug cartels with an all-out war, the tensions felt worse.

Bowles looked at the message again, and that part of him that would always be a suspicious East Texas cowboy decided to go. After all, that's what he was paid for, he told himself.

★   ★   ★

The next morning, Bowles left the White House in a taxi and rode to the Library of Congress. He'd never been there before. The benches on the west side of the building were empty that early in the morning. Bowles looked at his watch. He was early. He went to one of the benches and read the paper and watched the government workers file into the library. At ten-fifteen he began to wonder if he'd been a fool for coming.

'You're Red Bowles, aren't you?'

The Texan looked up. He'd about given up. It was almost ten-thirty. 'Yes.' The man who'd spoken to him was about his age, in his early fifties, had gray hair and one of those expensive dark wool overcoats that seemed to be the uniform in certain parts of the capital. Bowles thought the man in front of him looked frightened. The man, an accountant type, stopped looking at Bowles and was keeping an eye on the parking lot below them.

'I don't have much time . . . You're going to have to believe what I'm going to tell you,' Claymore said. A group of women office workers walked by. Claymore looked at them carefully.

'You heard the news this morning?' Claymore said turning back to Bowles.

'Yes . . . the news is a big subject. What in particular?' The Texan was about to conclude that the man in the overcoat was some kind of nut, someone in or out of government who had gone over the edge.

'About the killings at CIA headquarters . . . '

'Yes.' Bowles had heard the story at the White House — something about a gunman on the street shooting down CIA employees as they waited to turn into the agency's parking lot.

'And?'

'The story you'll hear on the news is a lie. I don't know what it will be . . . a cover story, but it will be a lie. *They* did it. People in the agency did it. People in the director's office, top people. I think they have gone over to the drug cartels.'

'Who are you?'

'I'm head of Internal Affairs at Langley,' Claymore said. Bowles' face was no longer passive now. All his experience as a lawman had risen to the surface. He thought the man was telling him the truth. It was a sixth sense earned after so many years on the street, and he'd learned not to cross it. Claymore nodded his head.

'Do you want to go somewhere and talk about this?' Bowles asked.

'There's no time for that. They're going to kill me.'

'*Who's* going to kill you?'

'The same people that murdered my friends this morning,' Claymore said.

'I can protect you. You'll be all right,' Bowles said, trying to reassure him.

Claymore smiled at him as if he were a child. 'I'm afraid you're out of your league.'

Claymore had stopped looking at him again almost as if he were anticipating what Bowles would say to him.

'I'm a Texas Ranger. I can help you. We'll sort it all out. But tell me what this is all about and who you are.'

28

'They're going to take over somehow. They didn't give any details. But I'm certain they want to kill the President. My guess is that the drug cartels have somehow gotten to the Director's office,' Claymore said.

Bowles felt something turn in his stomach. He was surprised to hear it said in so many words, despite the fact that they'd been warned that the cartels would strike back. Bowles looked around the beautiful open space by the library. He hated Washington suddenly, hated everything about it.

'Are you saying the director of Central Intelligence has gone over to the drug cartels?' Bowles said.

'Yes; enough money will buy anything. We were going to get ten million dollars a piece for our parts. God only knows what they're paying the Director.'

'You have proof?'

'Of course not . . . nothing in writing. They wanted us to be part of the conspiracy. We met after the offer at a restaurant and tried to figure out who we could tell. I decided that you were our best chance.'

'Do you have any names?'

'You don't understand, do you? You're not in Texas now.' They both heard the sirens start up in the distance, coming from downtown.

'My name's Claymore. You'll need to know that. Alex knows me.' Claymore set his briefcase on the ground next to Bowles. 'It's all in here. You have to contact Alex Law; tell Alex that the director had my office open an investigation on him. I know it's bogus. Tell him that I think they're setting him up, and that they've sent Glad down to phony things up. Alex Law can save your man, I know it.' The sound of squealing tires turning into the parking lot made them both turn and look. A score of Washington police cars had turned into the parking lot. Bowles watched two unmarked cars turn in behind them.

Claymore looked at Bowles again. 'Tell Alex it's all the people we started with. Tell him it was Wyatt who called me to see if I was OK this morning. Tell him they're using Corsican Rules . . . He'll understand.' Claymore wasn't looking at him anymore. He was looking at the action on the parking lot below. There were too many policemen to count. 'Can you repeat that?' The policemen began climbing the stairs to the library, fanning out.

'Alex Law. Something about Corsican rules,' Bowles said. Claymore started to back away. He was speaking very slowly, methodically now, turning up his collar as he spoke.

'They'll probably kill me here. There won't be any more contacts, the rest are dead. Do you understand? It has to be Alex. It's all in the briefcase.' Claymore was walking backwards, his hands shoved into his pockets, watching the advancing policemen. 'Whatever you do, don't get up and follow me.' Bowles looked into the man's eyes and nodded. 'There's nothing you can do for me now, so stay the hell away.' Claymore turned around and hurried up the sidewalk toward the library.

Bowles grabbed the briefcase and watched the policemen running toward them. He looked again at Claymore. He had gotten to the edge of the library and was walking quickly. The first of an army of policemen rushed the bench. One of them looked at Bowles, stopped, then went on. A few minutes later he heard the shooting. Each shot caused him to hold the handle of the briefcase tighter.

★　★　★

Later, in his office at the White House, Bowles watched the TV news with real horror. The CNN reporter was standing in front of the Library of Congress and said that the man suspected of killing several CIA employees had just been found and shot dead outside the library. He was reported to have been carrying the assault rifle used in the killings. Bowles went across his office and turned off the TV. He locked his office door and opened the briefcase Claymore had given him. Inside, there was a file with a name and date typed on the edge. Bowles opened the file, noticed the CIA seal and looked at the picture of a man named Alex Law. There was a yellow Post-it on the cover. *Give this to Law. Tell him Wyatt is behind it. He'll understand.* Claymore hadn't trusted him to remember.

★   ★   ★

Murial Fipps was a spy. She had spied for her country for over forty years and was quite good at it. She was (thanks to her father, Cecil Conroy) beyond rich and had never done it for the money. She owned Conroy Shipping, which became Conroy International, which now was a holding company of several multinational firms. The Conroy company had gotten so large over the years that Murial couldn't even keep track of it. When friends asked what Conroy International *did*, she said with a wry look that 'they make things,' and left it at that. The fact that Conroy International had been used by the CIA, and the CIA used by Conroy

International, was never brought up in Congress, nor were the $6 billion in government contracts that were given to Conroy over the years to perform services for the nation's multiple and overlapping intelligence services. Conroy and the CIA were as close as Sears and Roebuck.

Murial was sixty-two years old. There was nothing young about her. She had slipped into old age very gracefully indeed, thanks to a host of face lifts and spa appointments, so that now, looking at her across the lavish and glittering dinner table in Georgetown, her guests could see she had that special hallmark of all wealthy dowagers, a perfect mask that was perhaps too tight, but nevertheless respectable in the way it called up the mirage of youth. Large diamonds, Paris couture, and expensive cosmetics had done the rest. It was, in the end, always a little shocking to look at her.

Old or not, Murial was good at her calling, which had been running the parties on embassy row for as long as she could remember. Her house on Division Street in the heart of Georgetown was *the* Washington address. She was a social tigress whose parties were attended by everyone who aspired to play in the Washington bigtime. There were half a dozen foreigners of importance who met with their CIA handlers at Murial's parties because no one at Langley could think of a better place. Murial's code name was HOUSEMOTHER.

There were only eight at the table that night. This particular dinner party, on that beautiful spring evening, would have been similar to hundreds of others — except that it had been called at the last minute. Murial had gotten a call from David Penn, Director of Central Intelligence, asking her if she couldn't round up a few friends. Penn gave her a list of people that he wanted to be invited. Murial had her secretary fax out invitations. Four of the people on the list needed an excuse to be seen together. Penn was one of them, as well as a senator from Texas and two media moguls. The others around the dinner table were extras: a diplomat from Sweden and the owner of the Washington football team and his young wife, who were carefully climbing Washington's social ladder and, therefore, perfect for Housemother's purposes.

★ ★ ★

David Penn, Harvard '57, washed his hands in one of Housemother's beautiful black marble sinks. The bathroom was huge and he

34

felt as if he were in a five-star hotel instead of someone's home. Penn examined himself in the brightly lit mirror. He was impeccably dressed in a dark blue, Saville Row suit with very understated gray pinstripes. He wore tasseled loafers, his hands were manicured and his hair cut just so. He was too well-dressed to look like the CEO of a corporation. The Director of Central Intelligence looked more like a lawyer who was forever trying to impress his clients that he was really worth the enormous fees they paid him. When Penn testified before the Senate Intelligence Committee, he always got good press because he looked and acted like a gentleman in the English mode (that was important to the press because they all read Le Carré and thought that all spooks should somehow be like George Smiley, effete and avuncular). But David Penn wasn't at all the fictional Smiley. He was an American and his people were from Connecticut. His father had been a senator and his grandfather had been one of the early investors in IBM. Penn was quiet, ruthless, determined and devious. He had never actually been an intelligence operative, never carried a gun and never spied on an enemy. He had risen through the ranks of the intelligence bureaucracy because he knew how to get ahead. He looked none of these things now in the sumptuous guest bath of Housemother. He looked, rather, like a quiet, very lean middle-aged man who knew things and wasn't going to tell them.

Penn stared at himself in the mirror. He thought that he looked tired and that disappointed him. He smoothed his silver hair with just touches of black left. He thought to himself, casually, that the President of the United States was not going to survive what they had in mind for him. It was a simple thought and he enjoyed it. He had sold himself to the Mexican drug cartel and didn't feel any remorse at all. He thought he'd feel a little but he didn't. It seemed more like a business deal than a betrayal of his country. He looked in the mirror one last time, patted his hair and thought how much richer he was going to be. Anyway, he reminded himself that he hated the new President. *Sanctimonious blow-hard.* He reached over and ran the water in the beautiful black marble sink. Selling the men who were waiting for him now on the idea had been easy. They all had an agenda — money and power — the basics, as his father used to call them.

Penn went out the door and down the long hallway of the house he knew so well and wasn't surprised to not hear the party noises he'd heard a few moments ago. The guests were all gone, including Housemother. They could be alone now, alone to fine tune their plans to change the face of the country in a few short weeks.

4

Mexico City

The taxi carrying Alex turned quickly onto
La Reforma, then off onto a side street,
bringing them into a neighborhood of narrow
tree-lined streets. Rain-blasted intersections
went by in a film-like blur. Sad little parks
came and went. The din from the rain was
constant and relaxing. On one block a line of
Indian women, pelted by the rain, huddled
like storm-tossed birds in front of the ratty
entrance to a shop. Alex studied the women
as the taxi passed; he'd always been amazed
by the poor and their goings-on. Lately,
because of the rebellion in the south, the
Indians had been the subject of many long
cables from Langley. He knew great plots
were being hatched against them by men that
knew really very little about them. Mexican
politicians were terrified of what they referred
to as 'the Indian gangs.' The women standing
in the rain that morning seemed an odd and
pathetic enemy. Because his assignment was
monitoring Cuban intelligence, he'd been
spared any involvement in 'the Zapatista

problem' and was grateful for it. He wanted no part of that.

Watching the raw-looking wire-and-poles cityscape come and go, Alex recalled an entirely different kind of morning and place; the cozy tree-lined streets of New Haven, and the Yale campus, and that great autumnal moment when he'd been recruited. He'd been told by his CIA recruiter — a well known professor at Yale — that his family's great wealth wasn't going to really *matter*. The recruiter, an imperious sweater-wearing Mandarin in his sixties with ash-stained slacks, told Alex, who had been summoned to the professor's well-rummaged office that morning, that Alex would have to *prove* himself personally in life, that all great men did. The professor, the type so familiar to Alex by then, leaned forward in a studied avuncular way and suggested Alex go on and follow in the Law family tradition. He had simply agreed. He entered the profession without really giving it much thought, other than that he wanted to be like his father, a famous Cold Warrior. He wondered now, as his taxi sped along San Angel's fashionable streets, what he might have been had he said no: a doctor perhaps, a banker like his grandfather? He wondered if his mentors were proud of him, proud of what he'd done with his life. Certainly, he had proven himself. He had, after all, literally toppled governments and changed the course of history during his career.

He wondered, fishing for his cigarettes, if they cared that he'd lost everything in the process: his wife, his family, his humanity. The horrible fact was he loved what he did, and that he could have quit anytime, but never had (even when his career had gone nowhere because of his drinking). Holding his last cigarette, letting the empty pack slip to the floor, he faced the disturbing fact that he loved intelligence work. He loved to manipulate people, and to twist them into his creatures, all along giving them the impression that *they* were the ones in control. Why, exactly, he loved to do this so much, he didn't understand. It was as mysterious to him as the poor he passed in the streets.

He put his fingers through his wet hair and contemplated his strange addiction. Perhaps because his childhood experience had been just the opposite — he'd had no control over *it* at all. He pulled up the cassock and rechecked his pockets for his lighter. His childhood had been a vortex of private schools and little men who hated children and were determined to prove it. He knew the weeks and weeks of hopeless loneliness that only an eight-year-old at boarding school can experience. At that age when a child is meant to bond with the family group, he had been forced to bond with himself instead against buggers and twits and bullies. The process had warped him, he supposed.

He told friends, long after he left Yale, that the private schools he'd attended — starting with the Palo Alto Military Academy — were the perfect training ground for serial killers and intelligence agents because they were based on sadism and secrecy. He'd been one of the boys who had thrived. One of the boys who learned the *ice water smile*. He had organized a smart little Mafia of boys who had ended up running things *their* way behind the backs of their tutors. He had protected himself. He had won. The CIA had only made refinements. He lit the cigarette and his fingers trembled slightly from the booze.

'*Aqui,*' Alex said suddenly. The driver pulled up in front of a group of Catholic schoolgirls, their hair wet from the rain, waiting at the corner. The taxi's front tires sent a wave of gray run-off washing up onto the sidewalk. The girls, all dressed in the same gray pleated skirt and white knee socks, watched the tall, handsome priest climb out of the taxi. Alex's blond hair had turned dark in the rain, his lean figure attractive. The rain pelted him as he paid the driver. Alex took off through the rain at a trot toward the middle of the block.

It stopped raining just as he turned into the gate of the safe house, a huge white two-story colonial mansion. There was a solidity to it that reminded him of his parents' home in the States. Sometimes he would come here just to think or be absolutely alone. Or, sometimes, he'd bring women. There was a great cold aspect to the place that he found oddly soothing. Something about the house reinforced his own loneliness and made it bearable, as if he, like the house, were designed to impress, and be still, and wait for those occasional, intense moments that came without warning in his work.

A cold soulless sunshine broke out as Alex climbed the stairs. He used the heavy, wet painted knocker on the door. He tapped out a code that he'd given to Butch. He had a small tremor of fear for some reason as he tapped. All the intuition that had kept him ahead of the enemy in the past welled up like those messages in the Magic Eight Ball of his childhood — the word *Glad* came up out of the ink.

★   ★   ★

The foyer smelled of Old Spice. 'The kitchen's chock-full,' Butch Nickels said. Butch wore an apron made out of a towel. His friend had taken up residence part-time in the safe house, which Alex had pointedly asked him not to do. But he'd done it anyway. He used it for business whenever he was up from Cuernavaca. 'I'm cooking you lunch. Pork and beans. Only kidding. How about *Huachinango?* I'm practicing for the grand opening of La Casa Nickels.' Alex put his hand out but Butch ignored it and gave him a hug. If Puck had joined the CIA (and not been very good at it), he would have been Butch Nickels. As far as Alex knew, Butch had only two real talents — loyalty (which he'd demonstrated to Alex since the day they'd met) and petty larceny (which Nickels had practiced his entire career at every opportunity at every embassy from Moscow to Mauritania). The conspiracy nuts that warned about CIA side businesses, like Air America or the Burma Triangle, could have used Butch Nickels as a poster boy.

Of all the men whom Alex had met in the agency over the years, only Butch qualified as a real friend. It was only Butch who had penetrated Alex's Brahman aloofness and made friends with that speck of the true Alex that was still alive, always safely guarded, but there. Butch had found it on the first day at the Farm, the CIA's training college. He had helped Alex train for the physical parts, literally pushing and/or pulling him along when need be. Like so many recruits, Butch had been a college football player at Notre Dame. Alex never forgot his kindness during training and his ability to make him laugh at himself at the worst moments. And although he never admitted it to anyone, he always felt a strange kind of relief in Butch's presence, as if Butch could call up the spirit of a childhood he might have had. Butch was the brother he'd never had.

'*Glad* you called,' Alex said, half-kidding. 'Please try and call at a respectable hour in future. We who are still working need our rest.'

'Bullshit,' Butch said. 'You're tired of me calling you and I don't blame you.' Nickels was several years older than Alex. He still dressed the same way he always had, Sears suits and short-sleeved white shirts. He was a Sixties sorority boy at heart who was actually fifty and paunchy, crew-cut and graying. He looked like a junior high science teacher instead of an ex-spook who'd seen most of America's dangerous little wars.

'You were supposed to have come down to Cuernos for your birthday. Don't explain.

But you have to come to the grand opening of La Casa Nickels or *else!*' Butch said. 'We had dinner waiting for your birthday. Patsy polished and dusted all day. The place looks like a Grand Hyatt now.'

'Sorry, old boy. Something came up.'

'Well, the question is, can she cook?'

'No. I had to . . . ' Alex fished for an excuse. He'd wanted to come but had been too drunk to manage the drive that weekend.

'I don't want to hear it.' He shot his hand up in mock anger. 'Will you come down for Christmas, at least? Why not invite Helen down? I can't stand Christmas in Mexico without some pasty-faced Anglos around.'

'You can go home, can't you?' Alex asked. 'You haven't been put on any wanted posters, I hope. And don't think I'll be coming with the old ball and chain. She's asking for a divorce. I got the papers a few weeks ago. All very official,' Alex said. It was the first time he'd acknowledged receiving the papers to anyone. He'd left them in a drawer at his furnished apartment, afraid to look at them. Butch disappeared into the kitchen where he was cooking something. Alex went into the cavernous living room. In loud voices, so they could hear each other, they traded gossip between the two rooms about people they had come up with (most had left the agency

45

and were cutting a wide swath through corporate America).

'Sorry about you and Helen. She's a great gal . . . ' Butch said, coming back in from the kitchen. He'd taken his tie and stuffed it into his shirt so that it wouldn't be stained. They sat across from each other on big yellow couches. Alex watched his friend dry his hands on the towel. Butch had bought a hotel in Cuernavaca with money Alex had loaned him, money that he never expected to see again and money that Butch knew he would never have to pay back. Alex assumed that he wanted more money, as he usually only came up to the capital when he was going to hit Alex up. He enjoyed giving Butch money but had never let on.

'So, how's the hotel coming along?' Alex said, wanting to change the subject away from Helen.

'Wonderfully. Big day is Saturday. The place is by the language schools so we expect to get all the well-heeled students. Dewy-eyed coeds, whole flocks of them, I hope,' Butch said.

'Patsy won't let you near them,' Alex said. 'I'll come down soon. I've been meaning to. Is there any beer in this place? I've been telling them to stock it.' They went to the kitchen. The refrigerator was stocked with beer bottles. Alex took one and glanced at the pots on the stove and shook his head. He remembered that, even in El Salvador, they'd always had a good time because Butch was forever cooking meals in commandeered safe houses and installing gourmet kitchens at the U.S. taxpayers' expense, complete with Wolf ranges and Kolher sinks.

'I saw Glad this morning,' Alex said, unscrewing the bottle top. 'He's in station. He asked if I'd seen you,' he said, sitting down at the little kitchen table. 'Some kind of bullshit about you stepping over the line. You haven't been doing anything naughty, have you? And if you have, I don't want to know. No re-selling of jet fuel to air forces in Abu Dhabi?'

'Alex. I came up here to tell you that something is wrong,' Butch said. The tone of his voice changed. All the normal insouciance was gone. He busied himself with something in a frying pan. Alex realized that Butch hadn't said a word since he'd followed him into the kitchen.

'Wyatt came by Cuernos. Out of the blue. Completely surprised me. We had dinner at the hotel. Just the three of us. I would have called you but thought it would be best if I came up and told you in person. Little ears

47

everywhere . . . ' Butch turned around and looked at him.

'Well, how is the old boy?' Alex said. He couldn't look Butch in the face. They both knew that Wyatt had come between Helen and him.

'Wyatt asked me to put ten million dollars in my account in the States. He said he knew all about your helping me with the hotel. He said I could have a commission, ten percent. But he wanted me to tell *anyone* who came around asking that the money was *yours*,' Butch said.

'Mine?'

'He said that he'd picked you because you had already been giving me money. And some kind of bullshit about you being super rich. That no one would think twice about it because of your family and all. You see, he thinks I'm a rat. Always has thought that. Does he really think I would do something like that? To you?' Butch said angrily. He wadded up the towel as he spoke. 'Obviously, he wants to use you.'

'What did you tell him?'

'I said no. I told him that I was through with all that and didn't want to go back to it. I certainly don't want to launder *his* money. I called you an ungrateful son-of-bitch just so he'd think we weren't getting along. I tried to

48

throw him off. I even told him you'd stopped chipping in on the hotel,' Butch said.

'Did it work?' Alex had put down the beer bottle now and spun it slowly without looking at it. His hangover was lifting finally.

'No. He just stepped up his offer to twenty percent. I thought you should know right away. I think he's trying to set us both up. God knows why,' Butch said.

'Could be. Could be he just knows you are very good at laundering money and that's all there is to it. After all, I would come to you, too, if I wanted a nice quiet retirement fund. Maybe that's all it is. It would be natural to use me as a cutout for that. I *am* giving you money, after all,' Alex smiled and took a sip of beer.

'Alex. Wyatt hates your guts. And he didn't come all the way to Cuernos to eat dinner in a broken-down Mexican hotel with me for the hell of it. If he wanted an off-the-record account, he'd set it up himself and he wouldn't be offering anyone *twenty* percent. And now you say Dr. Doom wants to find out where I am. Wyatt *knows* where I am. If the agency is looking for me, why didn't Wyatt tell Glad where to look? Wyatt is head of Clandestine, for Christ sakes.' Butch got up. 'Unless Glad was fucking with *you*, Alex.' He looked worried, Alex thought. He'd seen his friend look many ways, but 'concerned' wasn't one of them until then. 'Houston — I think we have a problem,' Butch said. 'And one other thing, I got a cryptic message from Richard in Washington saying that you were 'okay.' Richard runs Internal Affairs, last I heard. Why the hell would Richard call me? Obviously, something *isn't* okay, is it?'

'You know if Glad's people are out looking for you, they're going to catch you sooner or later,' Alex said. 'And I can't have that. I don't want to lose my Christmas invitation. We'll have to find you some new digs.'

'Alex, are you *listening* to me? For once in my life, I'm not worried about myself. Okay. Do I have to draw you a map, amigo? There's something going on.'

'Butch, what have you been up to? Why is Glad looking for you?' Alex said. 'The truth now.'

'Nothing. I swear it.'

5

'Are you sure?' Alex said, stubbing out his cigarette in a spotless star-shaped glass ashtray. It was very late now; past one in the morning. His office on the American Embassy's fourth floor smelled of cigarette smoke and disinfectant from the cleaning people who had passed through while he'd been at dinner. The welter of papers on his desk shimmered in the ugly florescent lighting.

'If anything has happened to him, Alex . . . ' Patsy Nickels said to him, 'It's your fault, because he didn't have to go, but he went because it was *you*. Butch went because he wanted to warn you, and he wouldn't use the telephone,' she said. 'Damn you, Alex.' Glad had been in to see Alex after lunch and tried to bully him into giving him Butch's whereabouts, but Alex had lied to him again, insisting he hadn't seen his friend since he'd left the agency the year before. Something had told Alex during his solitary dinner that he should check to make sure Butch had gotten back to Cuernavaca all right.

'Patsy, don't worry. I'll find him,' Alex said. He didn't tell her that Glad was looking for her husband and that he'd tried to rumble him for Butch's whereabouts twice that day.

'Will you? He's all I have, Alex. People like you can't understand that . . . but he's all I have,' Patsy said.

'I swear to you, Patsy, I'll find him. He's probably stopped off somewhere for drinks or to visit . . . '

'He doesn't whore around, Alex! He should have been home by now. It's only a forty-five minute trip back to Cuernavaca,' she said. 'Damn you, Alex. If he's in trouble because of you . . . .' Alex heard her begin to cry and it shocked him. She wasn't the type he associated with crying. She was a tough working class girl who'd set her cap on Butch Nickels and had landed him while she was working at the American Embassy as a secretary in Nairobi. They'd been inseparable ever since. Theirs was the kind of marriage Alex had wished for himself and Helen. It had always struck him funny that Butch could be so nefarious about so many things but never his marriage. When others on their team in El Salvador were up to their eyeballs in whores, Butch would have none of it. Alex had always said Butch was too busy stealing to philander.

'Hold on. Oh God, here come some headlights. It might be him . . . ' Alex heard Patsy drop her phone. He waited what seemed an eternity. He lit a fresh cigarette while he waited and recalled the first time he'd met Patsy years ago in Africa. She was tall, very plain, but with a good figure and earthy manner that made her very sexy. The phone was hung up suddenly, and, for a moment, Alex couldn't believe it. The dial tone turned into a roar in his ear. He realized, listening, that Butch and Patsy Nickels were his closest friends. He put the phone down carefully. Panic gripped him, a panic that he'd managed to suppress while talking to Patsy. He picked up the phone and tried the number again. The line was busy.

* * *

Cuernavaca was warm and it was raining, the way it does there in the summer, so softly that the rain seems, when it falls on you, more like a mist from some distant waterfall than real rain. Dr. Glad and his team yanked Butch roughly out of the embassy car parked in the deserted hotel driveway and led him up the freshly painted stairs of the wide verandah. Patsy had been playing Miles Davis on the stereo in their room and had the door open.

53

Butch could hear the music as they came up the stairs. Patsy ran onto the half-lit verandah and stood staring into the pathetic light as they brought Butch up the steps handcuffed, all the frightful worrying of the last few hours on her unmade-up fifty-year-old face.

'Butch, what's going on?' Patsy said. She was wearing a robe and had her hair tucked up into a gold lamé turban. Most of the hotel's lights were out except those along the top of the verandah. Tinted anti-bug yellow, the spotlights lit the rain and penetrated the darkness, giving the walls a slightly sinister shadow. Butch watched his wife come out of their room. The men holding his arms stood still for a moment. Butch looked at his wife without speaking. They stared at each other helplessly. Seeing his wife, Butch felt fear for the first time since they'd picked him up at the bus station. He struggled to keep the fear off his face. He watched the chiaroscuro shadows that painted the walls as if he were waiting for an idea that would change everything and save them.

'I'm all right, baby. I want you to go into the room. All right? I'll be right there,' he said, not able to look her in the face. It was too much, too enervating. Butch forced himself to give her a weak smile. He was handcuffed from behind. Patsy saw how the men holding her husband looked at her. She saw it and knew instinctively that Butch was frightened for her, too; she'd never seen him look that way before, so ineffectual.

'I will not!' she said. Dr. Glad had been walking toward her in the semi-darkness with his farm boy smile, nodding and deliberately trying to block her view of Butch as they led him away down the verandah. Patsy strained to see where they were taking her husband. Her turban caught the glare of one of the anti-bug lights and glistened. Her eyes fixed on Glad with both terror and hate.

'Patsy, *dear*,' Glad said. 'It's so good to see you again. So good.' Butch felt himself being dragged forward by the men on either side of him. He'd seen too many similar scenes not to know what was coming next. He fell on his knees and tried to pull them down onto the floor. In a panic, he wanted to stop everything the way a child does. He wanted to stop the sound of Glad's voice. He caught a glimpse of his wife. She was trying to get by the doctor and run to him. Glad caught her from behind by the belt on her robe and then by the turban. It was knocked off as he reached to pull her hair, yanking her head back. Butch saw her face jerk up and watched the turban rolling toward him on the floor. Glad wrestled Patsy back inside their room and slammed the door closed between them. The sharp sound of the slammed door reverberated over the cool trumpet music coming from the speaker on the verandah. Butch tried to kick at the men who were punching him. He heard Patsy call his name once hysterically. The music played dreamily in the background beneath Patsy's screams and the thud of punches. The last thing Butch saw was the blurred yellow bug lights before he was knocked unconscious. The three men who'd been beating him picked him up finally and dragged him past the hotel's desk with its view of the swimming pool, lit and looking like a night jewel. He regained consciousness as they hoisted him back on his feet. He didn't hear Alex trying to ring back.

* * *

'There's nothing lonelier than an empty hotel at night, don't you think?' Glad said. 'It's going to be grand, Butch. Very grand.' Butch Nickels was looking at the doctor. The doctor stepped into one of the hotel rooms they'd put Butch into and immediately pulled the door closed. Like most places in Cuernavaca, the hotel *Las Cruces*, a dilapidated Forties' place, had been designed for the town's perpetual summer. *Las Cruces* had an open,

56

wide plantation-style verandah with dark wood shutter-type doors. The rooms were large, with high ceilings and wood-blade ceiling fans, and all the interiors were white, each with a canopied bed, mosquito netting and a private terrace with views of the garden that surrounded the place. The room Butch had been taken to was finished and perfect. Everything was in place for the grand opening. Butch looked around it and realized he'd been a fool for thinking he could keep them away. The idea that it was Dr. Glad who was going to be the one to kill him made him angry.

'Love the fans. Your idea?' Glad asked. 'How do you turn them on? Wonderful. Reminds me of the movie *Casablanca*,' Glad said. The doctor found the dial on the wall that controlled the fans and switched them on. The blades started to turn and move the sultry air. Butch watched them start to spin slowly, then into a blur. He didn't answer the doctor's question. One of his eyes had swollen completely shut so that the doctor and the room behind him took on an odd depthless flat quality as if he were watching it all on some kind of strange TV set.

Dr. Glad dragged a chair over and Butch watched him set it up in front of him. Glad reached over and turned on the light on the nightstand. Butch could see a fractured light through his almost closed left eye.

'Butch, everyone has always said you were stupid. I never bought that. Not stupid like a dog, or a cow, stupid. No, you have what I call gut-brains, don't you, Butch?' Butch shifted his weight. The mattress under him felt weak. It was getting painful to breath. He looked down at his blood-splattered white socks and at the way his body dented the bed. He looked past the doctor to the closed door and tried to think of a way out. He tried to think beyond the pain from the beating and his swollen eye and come up with a plan, but he couldn't hold a thought, nothing would sit, nothing stayed with him long enough. Butch leaned over the side of the bed. As the doctor watched calmly, Butch spit a large glob of blood and mucus onto the floor that splattered Glad's shoe. He felt as if he were falling. Glad had to reach out and steady him.

'You're the type that everyone overlooks because you look like a fire-plug, steal the petty cash, wear cheap suits and eat sandwiches at your desk,' Glad said, his hand on Butch's shoulder. 'Your type always gets away with murder, don't they, Butch? Your type always flies under the radar.' Glad let go and put his long arm on the chair back. 'But you see, I see that as a kind of intelligence, Butch.'

Butch looked at Glad with his one good eye. All his life he had dealt with people like Glad, his betters. All his life he'd figured a way around their superior middle-class reach, ever since he was a kid growing up poor in a New Jersey tenement. The U.S. Government had been one more racket in a life where the lesson had been: if you don't steal, you're stealing from yourself.

'Hey, Glad. *Fuck you*. Let Patsy go. Whatever you want, she doesn't know shit about it,' Butch said. He wiped the blood and mucus from his swollen lips. 'What is it you want?'

'What are you and Alex up to?'

'He helped me with the hotel. That's all.'

Butch's white shirt was torn now and mop-dirty from where they'd dragged him down the entire length of the verandah. They'd removed his tie and belt and shoes and left him in his stocking feet. It was the same thing Butch had done to a hundred men in his time. He knew it was the beginning of the end. He swallowed blood from his injured mouth and asked Glad for a glass of water but was ignored. 'I tell you what. You let me talk to my wife, alone, for ten minutes, and I'll come back here and tell you anything you want, where they buried Jesus or whatever it is you want to know.'

'*Anything?* I expect you to live up to that, my boy,' Glad said. Glad reached over and helped Butch stand up and then went to the louvered door and threw it open. Butch could see the silver mist-rain falling against the yellow-tinted night lit by one of the verandah's ugly spotlights. The music had stopped, the hotel was silent. 'I don't have to tell you what I would do if you fucked with me, Butchy boy,' Glad said from the doorway. He lit a cigarette and offered one to Butch. 'You were with Alex at Cuito Curanavale, weren't you? You see, I remember the old days. It was the pair of you, wasn't it, who ran the old church. You were our Padre Alex's sacristan.'

'Yeah,' Butch said. Butch took the cigarette between his swollen lips and paused for a moment. Glad reached over to light the cigarette for him. The lighter went out twice, but finally Butch managed to get the cigarette into the flame with his shaking hand.

'Our father, who art Alex Law, hallowed be thy name. Thy kingdom is gone, thy will be undone on earth as it is in heaven,' Glad said. Butch walked out of the room limping slightly. 'I've put her in the car, Butch,' Glad said behind him. 'Seemed the best place for her . . . Out of harm's way. Don't want anything to happen to dear Patsy, do we?'

★　★　★

All the way down from Mexico City Alex hadn't allowed himself to think a great deal. He preferred to be numb. It was raining and the pool lights were on. Alex could see steam coming off the surface of the water as he walked toward the body. Patsy, dead, was sitting up in one of the new white plastic chaise lounges by the pool. Alex looked at her wet face staring at him in death. He realized he'd bitten his hand to stop from crying out. Looking at her hurt him physically. Alex stared at the body and at the way the rain made a soggy mess of her robe, it seemed to have melted somehow. He saw the way her hair had come unpinned and bedraggled. In death her legs opened awkwardly. They had shot her in the mouth. The look on her face was startled and blank, all at once, as if she were still trying to communicate something.

Alex walked back out in the dark toward the hotel that was lit up brightly. He unhooked his pistol from its harness and pulled it out. In front of him was the hotel, silent and lit by the strange yellow glow along the verandah. Crossing the grass in the rain, something in him changed: the last bit of sanity he'd clung to was gone. He knew he was crying and he wished to God that he'd find Butch dead, too. He made sure he had the extra clip in the hollow of his back and made sure the safety was unlocked on the pistol.

He walked across the gravel road to the foot of the main stairs that led up to the verandah. He paused at the top of the stairs, then followed the sounds to a corner. He saw Butch looking at him. His face was swollen and he was crying in the darkness.

'Alex, she's dead,' he said. He seemed like a little boy. Alex didn't know what to say. He came up the stairs and knelt next to him in the shadows. The face he saw looking up at him was frightening, not because of the beating but because of the misery in that one good eye that held Alex for a moment. 'She's dead,' Butch said again and he began to rock like a child with the pain of it. 'Why Alex? Why her? Why Patsy?' Alex stood up. He looked at his gun. The one time he wished he could have used it, it was useless. They'd gone.

'I don't know. We have to leave, Butch. You can't stay here.' He stood up and put his gun back into the harness and walked toward the desk that had been fixed with a banner that said *Our first day*. He unfolded his cell phone standing at the desk and dialed a number he hadn't called in years. The number came to him easily along with the picture of his mother and father and a trip they took once to Carmel. He remembered they'd hit a dog in the road and he'd gotten out of the car with his father and looked at the struggling dying animal and felt as if the world was ending. He looked at Butch in the shadows rocking helplessly. *They should have killed him, too.*

Alex heard the phone picked up. 'Hello, it's me, Alex.'

'Alex!' His father's voice was always controlled, but he couldn't hide the surprise.

'I need your help,' Alex said. 'I'm afraid you can't ask me any questions. I want you to send one of the bank's planes to the airport at Cuernavaca, tonight. I have a friend who needs help. I'm going to send him to you.'

'All right. Are you okay?'

'You have to send a plane tonight, without delay,' Alex said again mechanically and hung up. He looked for Butch, but he'd gotten up and was moving slowly through the rain toward Patsy. And, even then, Alex started to think in that cold way he had been taught. *Why did they leave Butch? They had to have a reason.* He thought of stopping him. He wanted to spare him what he was going to see. But he didn't; instead he sat down in one of the wicker chairs and lit a cigarette and waited. He just wanted to be still. And then he was ashamed because he got up and went looking for something to drink.

★ ★ ★

'They want us alive,' Butch said finally on the way to the airport. He hadn't spoken a word until then. 'They want to use us.'

'It looks that way,' Alex said.

'It's funny,' Butch said. 'I remember once in Laos when I just started out at the agency. The head of station had some general's wife killed. I remember her because she was very young and beautiful. I'd met her at the embassy a few weeks before. I'd tried to put the make on her. I didn't think much about it really. I remember the head of station just picked up the phone and he had it done. I drove him to a party afterwards. You know what he told me? He said he would have forgotten the woman by the time they got around to dinner. Were we like that? Were we *that* fucking callous, Alex?'

'I suppose,' Alex said. 'I've forgotten. What difference does it make now?'

'Why Patsy, Alex? Why? She never did

64

anything. She didn't *know* anything. She isn't a general's wife. Alex, I stole gasoline and spare parts and cheated colonels, for Christ sakes. That's all I ever did. I rolled on you, Alex. I told Glad you helped me because that's what he wanted to hear, and they killed her anyway.' Alex wanted him to shut up. He couldn't take it anymore, at least not without another drink. They pulled into the little airport. It would be a few hours before the plane came and he wanted to find a bar.

As they got out of the car, Alex wanted to say that they had known plenty of cases where family members were assassinated for no other reason than to get the target to cooperate, and that Butch had to stop it and start thinking like an intelligence officer again if they were going to survive. But he didn't say any of it.

6

Marbella, Spain

An uncaring Spanish sky met his glance; there was not even a cloud to give it dimension or relief. It went on and on like his life. The glare of it was disturbing, like one of those car alarms that suddenly goes off wildly for no good reason. Alex had been in Marbella, he thought, for two weeks, but wasn't quite sure. Since Patsy's death he'd been through the neck of the bottle. He'd run away from his job and about everything else he could think of running away from.

The sky bothered Alex because it matched his mood, which was tense and exhausted. The weeks of drinking showed — the fermented eyes and shaking hand as he passed the plastic razor under his patrician chin that morning. Even his good looks couldn't paper over the ragged man that faced him in the mirror. He leaned against the wall of the shower as the warm dirty-feeling water poured over him and then listened to the deafening silence when he finally turned it off. He stood there naked and waited for something to wake up — his mind, or his stunned emotions, his ability to care about anything. He would have taken any stirring as a sign of life. An urge finally came as he toweled himself off. *I'll have a drink*, he thought. *I'll have a drink and then I'll feel better about it all.* That had been his mantra since he'd left Butch at the foot of the plane and they had both looked at each other and realized that this time they were damaged and there was no fixing it.

He had made a decision that had frightened him on the plane to Europe two weeks before. He meant to change, return to what he had once been when he'd started out years before: a decent human being. He was going to quit the agency — finally. His career was over. Besides, he'd never needed the money anyway. He felt a dry African wind blow against his face. He leaned against the door and closed his eyes. He realized he was still drunk from the night before. He counted to ten, trying to clear his head.

I have to face what happened to Patsy and get it behind me, he told himself for the hundredth time that morning. He opened his eyes and turned and shut the door on the luxury cottage he'd rented at the Hotel Puente Romano. What had happened to Patsy wasn't his fault. He heard the door click shut. His palms were sweating and he rubbed them on his linen pants as he tried to get hold of himself. He started off down a serpentine garden path bordered by red azaleas toward the lobby of the hotel. His hangover was contained, but just barely. He'd gotten a call that someone claiming to know Richard Claymore wanted to meet him in the restaurant for a drink.

Alex realized suddenly that he had no shirt under his linen jacket. He had dressed in the semi-darkness with a drunk's fear of daylight and overlooked the obvious. He was stunned. It was the first time in all his years of drinking he'd done something so slovenly. *Fuck . . . .*He stopped in mid-stride and fumbled for his door key. *No time for all that. Doesn't matter. No difference. There is no dress code for the rich in Marbella. And besides, Armani matters,* he thought looking down at his pants to make sure he hadn't botched that too. Satisfied with his excuses, he quickened his steps. He held onto the sleeves of his jacket, as if it would help him manage the steps. He made his way down the stairs, sockless in new leather sandals, the emotional scars of twenty years of spying camouflaged by a bold-as-brass smile and by the elegant Armani jacket and sky blue linen pants he'd purchased on Sloane Street in London the day after he left Mexico.

★ ★ ★

The restaurant adjacent to the Hotel Puente Romano is not for camera-toting tourists on budgets. It is exclusive, and the sweating green bottles of Perrier and the white oversized canvas umbrellas on the sunny patio said as much. It was too early for lunch yet. Alex took a table on the patio overlooking the harbor below, where half a dozen multi-million dollar yachts were at anchor (some with their own helicopters), like real super-toys. He ordered a champagne cocktail and swore this would be his last. In his new life, he would stop drinking. Then he heard the voice inside again, the one he'd heard for years, the one that mocked him every time he tried to quit. He lifted the glass and considered his career of twenty years. Then he tried to lose himself in the soundless sparkling sea below.

★ ★ ★

The past had been holding Alex spellbound somewhere between the bobbing yachts and the horizon. Like a child, he'd been wishing he were someone else all together. Someone on the beach perhaps. A tall, broad-shouldered red-faced man in his forties was looking at Alex from behind the maitre d'. The young maitre d' had escorted Bowles out to the table and was already turning back. Alex nodded to the man whom he'd been expecting. Bowles wore jeans and a sport shirt and looked, despite all his attempts at sartorial camouflage, like what he was, a policeman of some sort.

'You said something about Richard Claymore on the phone,' Alex said.

'Yes. Claymore sent me,' Bowles said. Bowles sat down without being asked. They looked at each other for a moment. Each man sought a purchase, some leverage in the face of the other, but there was none. They were too different. Red Bowles was already at a disadvantage because he was completely out of his element in the sybaritic lair of the rich. The restaurant that reeked of money and the foreign *everything* had been exacerbating to Bowles. It only reminded him that he'd grown up poor in East Texas. He'd only been out of America a few times and always found it disorienting. The man he'd come to see was rich, very rich from what he'd read, and he'd always felt strangely defensive with rich people.

'I need your help,' Bowles said. He'd decided that with someone like Alex it was better to get straight to the point.

'Pardon me?' Alex said.

'I said I need your help,' Bowles said. Alex smiled.

'I'm afraid you have me confused with someone else,' Alex said dismissively. He looked for a waiter to help him. He suddenly didn't feel like being chatted up by what he could only imagine was one of Claymore's golfing buddies.

'No, I don't think so,' Bowles said. 'Your name is Alex Law. You're an intelligence agent.' Bowles put Claymore's file down on the table between them. 'I don't have time for a lot of B.S., Mr. Law. I'm trying to save someone's life,' Bowles said. The Texan finally looked around the patio. He seemed to relax a moment but only slightly. He kept his hands on the file as if someone were about to tear it away. There was a clean wash of sweat on Bowles' face.

'Like I said, you have me confused with someone else,' Alex said. 'What you need is the tourist information office, I think . . . '

'Don't screw with me, Law. I'm not in the mood. I've got jet lag, I don't speak Spanish, and the food in this country isn't any good as far as I can tell,' Bowles said. The tall

71

heavyset man sitting in front of Alex looked desperate. He ran his eyes over the Texan's big freckled face. He recognized the face now. He'd seen it somewhere but couldn't place it exactly.

'Claymore gave me your file. He said you were under investigation. He said Glad had been sent to Mexico and was part of the investigation. None of that means much to me, but Claymore said it would to you,' Bowles said, handing him the file. Alex thumbed through it quickly and handed it back without saying a word, just smiling his rich man's smile. 'Richard Claymore. Did you know him?' Bowles asked. He was tired and frustrated, having flown all night and part of the morning to get here. His eyes were watery and looked exhausted, Alex thought.

'Never heard of him,' Alex said, and stood up. 'I think you must have me confused with someone else. Now . . . If you'll excuse me.'

'What about Patsy Nickels?' Bowles said as Alex stood up. 'She was murdered in Mexico. Then you came here to Spain. They've been looking for you all over the world for the last two weeks. They've cabled every embassy looking for you,' Bowles said. 'I don't know what kind of son-of-a-bitch you are . . . But you're going to be *my* son-of-a-bitch.' Alex was standing and looking at him now, unable to move. The hangover and the guilt were working against him.

'Your son is here at the hotel with you. I know that, too,' Bowles said, continuing. 'You're staying in one of the cottages at this hotel — #133. Your son's name is Michael. He's twenty-four and he graduated from Yale fourteen months ago. You paid for his ticket here with your credit card. He arrived two days ago. I'm not just anybody, asshole,' Bowles said finally, 'Now sit the fuck down.'

'You leave my son out of this,' Alex said. He suddenly saw Patsy sitting in the rain with that ghastly mien of terror and wanting-to-speak expression. He remembered it all again as he looked at the Texan's round sweating face. He felt like he would stop breathing. Bowles was speaking to the waiter. He ordered a drink for Alex.

'Another one of these,' Bowles said, holding up the empty for the waiter. Alex looked at them both. 'My guess is you're a burnout,' Bowles said. 'Patsy Nickels was a friend of yours — Butch Nickels' wife. Look at you. You're hanging on by a fucking thread. You forgot to put on a shirt, for Christ sakes,' Bowles said, relishing the irony of a cowboy like him pointing out a sartorial gaff to someone like Alex. And then almost immediately he was sorry. The look that

Alex gave him was too open. He couldn't hide what had happened to him.

'What is it you want?' Alex said. 'Did *they* send you? Is this some kind of absurd test?'

'No. I'm not with them,' Bowles said.

'Why should I help you then?' Alex said.

'Because I think maybe you've had enough. Maybe you want to change things for the better. Maybe you want to live up to your reputation.'

'Who are you anyway?'

'Red Bowles, Texas Ranger.' Bowles put his hand out. For a moment, he wasn't sure whether Alex would shake it or not.

'You're joking,' Alex said. The waiter brought the drinks and set them on the table. It was ice tea for Bowles and champagne for Alex. Alex sat down again, nonplussed by the cowboy.

'No, I'm not,' Bowles said. Alex took his hand and shook it as he stared at Bowles.

'You're a long way from Texas, Mr. Bowles,' Alex said, lifting his drink. 'My son has exhausted me,' Alex said. 'I'm trying to understand him. Do you have children? They can be very difficult. I've arranged a family reunion. Would you like to hear about it?' Alex tipped the drink up.

'No,' Bowles said. 'But I envy you. You have two kids. I read it here.' Bowles nodded towards the file.

'Envying me would be a big mistake,' Alex said.

'What are you going to do?' Bowles asked.

'I'm retiring. They can stop looking for me,' Alex said, wondering how Bowles had managed to learn so much about him since he'd left Mexico.

'I want you to work for us,' Bowles said. 'Claymore told me that someone inside Langley was going to kill someone very important, and I mean to stop them. But I can't do it alone,' Bowles said. 'That's why I'm here,' he said. 'I need someone like you, someone who knows how they work, and I don't have much time.'

'And whom might that be?' Alex asked. Bowles looked at him for a moment. He had planned on telling him later but he decided he had to tell him everything now.

'The President of the United States,' Bowles said quietly.

'You're mad,' Alex said.

★   ★   ★

'*Señor Law. Señor Law, por favor.*' The two men heard Alex's name being paged. The uniformed page alternated between Spanish and English as he moved through the restaurant. Alex ignored him. Bowles looked

75

at Alex, wondering why he didn't signal his presence to the kid. The page switched to French and walked past them.

'Claymore said they were using Corsican Rules. What does that mean?'

'Why don't you ask him?' Alex said.

'I can't. He's dead. Don't you read the papers?'

'No, not lately,' Alex said. 'I've been busy.' He put the empty glass down.

'There was a shooting outside CIA headquarters. They say that Claymore was responsible. The police executed him behind the Library of Congress. They said he was armed, but it's all a lie. I spoke to him just before they killed him,' Bowles said.

'Washington is a dangerous place. I've always said that,' Alex said. They heard the page calling Alex's name again over the lunchtime cacophony. 'Too bad about Richard. I'm afraid I have to answer that,' Alex said. He lifted his hand. The boy came to the table.

'Call, *Señor*. International. You can take it in the lobby if you like,' the page told Alex. The boy was slightly annoyed that Alex hadn't answered right away. Alex produced a coin and gave it to the boy and stood up.

'I'll wait for you,' Bowles said.

Alex went into the lobby of the hotel thinking that it was his father again. He was prepared to tell him once and for all that he had no intention of coming home to work at the family bank. His father had telephoned him twice now, first calling him in London at the family apartment near Brompton Road, where Alex had been hiding out, and said that he'd found a safe place for Butch and that he wanted Alex to come home and run the bank. Alex stopped at the bar and ordered a fresh drink. His father could wait, he thought. He had already forgotten that he'd promised himself to stay out of the bar until after one o'clock.

Alex pulled the door closed to the booth in the lobby. 'Hello,' Alex said.

'This is Johnny,' a voice said. Alex recognized Wyatt Anderson's distinctive voice. Johnny was the code name Wyatt had used for years. Alex finished pulling the door closed. A fan and a light came on. The booth smelled of suntan lotion and the beach.

'Johnny. It's always good to talk to people you dislike. I won't ask how you knew where I was.'

'It wasn't easy,' Wyatt said. 'We've been looking all over hell.'

'Are you still fucking my wife?' Alex said. He was drunk enough to ask it. He waited for an answer, picked up the fresh drink from the wooden ledge in front of him and took a sip.

'I want to talk to you about Helen,' Wyatt said, ignoring him. 'Man to man.' The voice was earnest. Alex recognized the open tone as one Wyatt would use when he wanted something special from an agent of his.

'Man to man?' Alex put the glass down. There wasn't much left of his self, but whatever was left, he knew Helen was at the center of it. All his anger toward Wyatt Anderson was suddenly deflated by the facts. *It was my own bloody fault*. It was the first time he'd ever admitted it to himself and it scared him. *She only did it to get back at me*.

'Listen, everything is forgiven. Everyone understands what happened in Cuernavaca. Glad's off the reservation. It's perfectly all right that you left,' Wyatt said. 'You're forgiven. I want you to work for me now until things are squared away. There's something else I've got to talk to you about.'

'I'll be in London next week. We can talk there if you like. Leave a message at the bank,' Alex said. He didn't have to ask what Wyatt wanted to talk about. He already knew — Helen's divorce papers. Alex hadn't answered her letter yet. 'Is Helen with you now?'

'No, of course not,' Wyatt said. 'Your family's bank?'

'Of course,' he said. 'Nothing has changed. Sixteen offices around the world,' Alex said, rubbing it in. He said it because it was the one thing he knew Wyatt hated about him, had always hated about him — his family's money.

'I'm sorry about what happened,' Wyatt said. 'I want you to know that I didn't have anything to do with Glad.'

Alex hung up and opened the door too quickly so that it made a noise. He knew Wyatt was lying, whatever he said. Wyatt Anderson was the head of the CIA's Clandestine Directorate. People like Wyatt didn't know what the truth was anymore, Alex thought to himself. It was like talking to Scylla.

★ ★ ★

'Business call,' Alex explained to Bowles, full of alcoholic brio.

'I see,' Bowles said.

'Now, what was it you were saying?' Alex was drunk enough now that Bowles was starting to interest him. 'You're some kind of cowboy . . . trying to save . . . who was it? The President of the United States. Shall we circle the wagons . . . or whatever it is you fellows do?'

Bowles watched Alex finish the drink. You don't want to watch a drunk after a certain point, he thought. There was something intensely private about the way Alex was clutching the glass. He was obviously upset by the call he'd gotten. His eyes had darkened and were guarded now. Bowles watched Alex and wondered if he'd made a mistake. Bowles saw his own reflection in Alex's sunglasses, a sweating middle-aged man running out of time. *But I'm better off than he is.* The policeman hoped that he never turned into someone who was half broken, which, Bowles thought, was probably worse than simply breaking and having done with it. *I need him. It takes someone like him. Sane, happy men won't climb into the shit and pull out a ruby.*

'What do Corsican Rules mean?' Bowles asked again.

'It means,' Alex said, leaning forward, 'A shit-treading cowboy like you doesn't stand a chance, *old boy*. That's exactly what it means.' Alex started to laugh. He reached over and slapped Bowles on the shoulder. Alex's lips were wet and glossy, and there was

80

something slightly feminine about his face then, something Bowles didn't like. He'd become completely Janus-faced now. 'It means that when they find you, they're going to tear out your asshole and mail it back to your mother. That's what it means,' Alex said. 'You had better go home and lock yourself in the basement.'

'I think maybe I've made a mistake,' Bowles said. He removed Alex's hand from his shoulder.

'I think I can agree with that,' Alex said, flipping his sunglasses up and smiling ruthlessly at him.

'What about Claymore? He gave his life to get me this file. What about him? Fuck him, too?' Bowles asked. 'And what about Wyatt? I think he meant Wyatt Anderson, the number two man at the agency now,' Bowles said. 'They say you two are old friends. They say that . . . ' Bowles decided he'd better not finish what he was going to say.

'Name rings a bell,' Alex said, turning away and looking out to the sea. He'd gone feminine again. It was like watching a chameleon personality, Bowles thought.

'You're a real Yale shit, aren't you,' Bowles said. He got up and threw a card on the table with his number on it. 'If you think you might find time to give a shit about something other than yourself, give me a call.'

'Wyatt Anderson just called me,' Alex said, still looking out at the harbor. Bowles stopped. 'That was him on the phone. He's up to something. I can tell,' Alex said. His voice had turned deadly serious. Bowles sat down again, surprised by the sudden change of tone in Alex's voice. 'You'll have to do *exactly* what I say. Wyatt is smarter than you are. Start with that. He's had more experience than you have, I know. Do you *understand* that? Even so, there's no guarantee we'll win. I asked you a question, Mr. Bowles.' Bowles nodded. 'Do you understand you are getting into a fight with people who *always* win?' Alex turned to face him. His face once again changed as if a mask had been torn off it. The eyes were bright.

'I'm seeing him in London in a few days. If I find out anything, I'll send you this card to your home address. Then leave a message here.' He motioned for a pen. Bowles handed him one. Alex wrote down a number. 'Find a pay phone somewhere, call and tell me the time and the number, and that's all you give in the message. No cell phones. They can trace those now. Then I'll call you back.' Alex jotted down the number. He handed it to Bowles. 'Corsican Rules mean you don't leave anyone alive,' Alex said.

'Here. Claymore left you a note,' Bowles said, standing up again. 'I thought you should see it.' When Bowles left the table, Alex took out the note Claymore had written.

Alex. I have always admired you. We all did. Wyatt hates you. He hates everyone now. People from the DCI's office had me open an investigation on you that I knew was trumped up. They were claiming you and Butch had stolen money. They're planning some kind of *coup d'etat*, probably starting with the President. They killed Kregan and Ford this morning because they wouldn't cooperate. Now they're going to stop me. I've sent you Bowles. He's clean. Alex, you're the only one who can stop it. I'm sure Wyatt is in it because he called me right after the shootings to see if I was still alive. If you stop Wyatt, maybe you can stop it. I was a fool for staying in it so long. Good luck.

Richard

Alex took the note and lit it on fire with his lighter. He waited until the last possible moment to stand up and let the burning black paper drop over the edge of the balcony and fall toward the beach, golden and perfect and filling with people.

7

'How's the *wahini?*' Alex asked. He had ordered lunch up at the cottage. They'd grouped the umbrellas together so that the afternoon sun was blocked and there was a rich deep shade. You could smell the sun on the canvas, it was blazing hot.

Wahini was the code word they'd made up for Helen when Alex's son was still a boy. Alex had devised a simple code based on tourist Hawaiian while they'd been on a family vacation years ago. He'd been surprised how quickly Michael had taken to using it, practicing with him when they were alone. His son seemed to understand, even at ten, that the code was exclusive and implicitly conspiratorial; that it gave him power over his mother. Michael and he had used the code — innocently enough but against her — as a way of keeping her out. Mother and wife had been relegated to a kind of friendly enemy. Alex brought up the old code deliberately now as a way of reconnecting with Michael, a way of reaffirming the old conspiracy.

'She's fine,' Michael said. 'She's always busy at the paper, or organizing some charity or other. I think it's a nursery for homeless mothers right now. She's bought a second place in town that she's fixing up. I think she plans on giving it to me. But, mostly, she works at the newspaper,' Michael said, watching his father with interest. His son was a handsome kid. He had Alex's blond hair. Michael had come out to the table wearing one of those striped Sixties-style shirts that were in vogue; the colors were raucous and off-putting to someone Alex's age. Michael was tall like his father but without Alex's severe good looks. His were different. On Alex's side of the family the men were scrawny and tall and all looked patrician by the time they were twenty. Helen's side of the family threw Adonises, the glossy, Hollywood kind, robust and athletic. Alex supposed, looking at Michael, his son was one of the Adonises.

Alex leaned back inserting himself into the deepest part of the shade and remembered the small ten-year-old boy under an outdoor beach shower at a Maui hotel fifteen years before, the sand on his feet, his mother washing him. Helen was a sandy beautiful Madonna with sandy child, sun drenched and happy. No one could have predicted the pain that would be coming to them. Hadn't they been the perfect couple, Alex thought, listening to his son — wealthy, beautiful, even powerful because of Alex's family's great wealth. But then, Alex thought looking at his son, fate has plans for everyone, rich and poor alike.

'Does she ever mention me?' Alex asked. He tried to relax as he asked the question but it produced in him a silent tension in his empty stomach. The tension of a love betrayed and lost for no good reason other than his own venery. Alex had changed clothes. He was wearing a pair of seersucker pants, no belt and no shirt, and dark glasses hanging on a black string. There was something terribly un-familial in their mode. It was as if two agents were meeting to exchange information about an imminent subornation, Alex thought; he wanted to infiltrate the Law family and he'd found someone high in that government who could lead him over the wall back to his wife.

'Of course she does. She calls you *Mr. Law*,' Michael said, leaning forward and smiling. His son almost laughed.

'I'm glad you came,' Alex said, trying not to sound foolish or mawkish. 'I really am. There's been so much damn bullshit . . . I'm sorry about that. I mean it . . . You know the truth is, I'd like to come back home. Back to your mother. Back into the bosom of the

86

family,' Alex said. He surprised himself with his honesty. But it was, in plain fact, what he wanted most now. But he understood he would need help. That country couldn't be stormed. 'I miss your mother,' he added wistfully. The smart effete playboy edifice fell away for a moment, and Michael thought he saw a kind of male vulnerability he'd never seen his father show before. He was taken aback.

'I'll put in a good word,' Michael said, slightly embarrassed. 'But you aren't homeless or pregnant, so I wouldn't count on it.'

'Well, I just wanted to say I was sorry for not being *around*,' Alex said. 'And for drinking too much when I was. Even here.'

'That's OK,' Michael said. They couldn't look at each other for a moment. It was too close to real pain.

'I skipped out on the last few years, didn't I?' Alex said, lifting his fork, caught between wanting to be honest and afraid of what he was saying. He toyed with his uneaten lunch. He heard his son laugh but didn't look up.

'Yes,' Michael said. 'You did. But I know why now.' Michael pulled the tab from a second soda he'd ordered. He was eating *his* lunch, a hamburger and potato salad, while Alex drank beer. 'The secret about what it is you *do*. I think I know why you weren't around.' Michael tore the tab off and threw it aside. His son was sun-golden and tan and looked as handsome as any of the wealthy European kids staying at the hotel. Their conversation drifted off in a safer direction, punctuated by splashing in the pool on a terrace below.

Alex knew he couldn't tell his son what he did best, what he'd done for a living, what he'd been awarded medals for; that he'd lied and suborned professionally as a CIA officer for all his adult life. There were times, Alex knew, when a father was supposed to symbolically hand the future over to his son and say: *Here I have gone. You go now.* A time to pass hard-won knowledge on. But what could he pass on — how to circumvent every law known to civilized man? How to assassinate potentates and patriots alike? How to engineer the collapse of whole countries, sit dispassionately in a hotel room while things crumble around you, and then, at the eleventh hour, get up and drive to the airport as if you were a stranger to the terrible events on the streets? (Countries weren't destroyed without blood and suffering after all.) Could he teach his son to be inured to the screams of prisoners in some horrible jail while searching for that one useful face? *I was an intelligence officer; I lied and I cheated for my country. Now you go on. I won the Cold War. See what you can make of it.* Alex decided his silence would be his legacy. His son would be spared any confessions.

'My only secret is: I went completely doggo for the last two weeks,' Alex said, fatuously giving an oblique answer. He was quick to move back into his normal mode, which was lying. Alex picked up the bottle cap from his beer and pressed it into his palm. His son looked at him carefully, judging the answer, then smiling just as carefully. It was the same kind of smile that Alex had used thousands of times when he was hearing a lie. *Is my son running me now? The ultimate spy game — fathers and sons*, Alex thought.

'Grandfather told me. He made me promise not to tell. He was very *Molokaini*.' His son used the old code word for secret or secretive. Alex tried to remember the rules of their code/language through the fog of alcohol. *Something about ini and Hawaiian cities*, he remembered. 'And I know about grandfather too,' Michael said, 'OSS, Wild Bill's right-hand man.'

'Do you?' Alex said. 'I'm afraid I'm a little rusty on our language.'

'Doesn't matter . . . CIA . . . both of you,' Michael said proudly, getting back to what he wanted to talk about. He picked up the remainder of his catsup-smeared hamburger and bit into it, watching his father as carefully as Alex was watching him. 'I know it's true because Grandfather told me things about himself during WWII. He said he couldn't tell me anything about you because he wasn't sure you weren't still in the *game*. Are you still in the *game?*' his son asked. 'Grandfather says no one can be sure. The press stories are probably plants — all that bullshit about you working for the World Bank.'

Alex picked up the beer but didn't drink. He put it next to the sandwich that hadn't been touched. The mayonnaise was starting to seep out and separate because of the heat. It formed a clear little spot on the white china plate with the hotel's logo, a blue dolphin.

'How old are you?' Alex asked.

'What's that got to do with it?'

'I just . . . twenty-four, right?'

'Yes.'

'I was twelve when he told me. I think so, yes, twelve.' Like all professional liars, when Alex told the truth he was almost ceremonial about it.

'You knew about him when you were *twelve?*' Michael said, genuinely surprised.

'Yes.'

'Wasn't that against the rules or something?'

90

'Of course it was,' Alex said. Then he took a drink. All Michael could see was that his father's face was a pleasant stone wall. All traces of vulnerability had vanished.

'You didn't answer my question,' Michael said.

'So then. Now that you've hurdled the old family alma mater, what's next?' Alex said, parrying with another question.

'You aren't going to tell me, are you?' Michael said.

★   ★   ★

Alex had fallen asleep. He woke up and looked at his son. Michael was dripping wet, and the sun was at its worst. Their cottage had its own pool. There was no shade at all except under the lanai and the umbrellas at the table. Michael had gotten out of the pool and picked up one of the scores of American magazines they'd bought in town and sat down next to his father under the lanai, not bothering to dry off.

'It doesn't matter . . . I know everything,' Michael said and disappeared behind a *Time* magazine. For a moment, Alex wanted to tell him the truth about his family, but the desire came and passed. Half asleep he went into the cottage and took a beer from the mini-bar inside the room, twisted it open and stared out over the tiny private pool at the water that was still rocking in waves from Michael's energy in the sunlight. It seemed to be forming up like some kind of nascent diamond.

8

London

If you saw Wyatt Anderson that morning in
Claridge's dining room, you would have
guessed he was one of those successful
corporate gladiators who's pulled his way up
the ladder and managed somehow to keep the
edge it took to get there. No matter how hard
he might try to polish it away, the edge that
propelled him was clearly stamped on his
freckled Scandinavian face, an ex-soldier's
face that was quietly truculent. Physically
commanding, Wyatt never looked quite
comfortable in his expensive suits, and they
were very expensive these days. It was his one
extravagance, the suits and the tailored shirts.
Otherwise, he lived for his work. He had
learned how to dress from Alex. He'd learned
a lot by watching Alex. Wyatt used to study
him the way you would an exotic foreigner.
Alex was, after all, from the land of money.
Alex innately knew things Wyatt couldn't
learn any other way than by just watching
him; like the way Alex entered a room, or the
way Alex had of speaking to people, friendly,

but with that ability to somehow communicate his authority. It was magic. Of course, women noticed it too and found it irresistible. So, he'd studied Alex that first year at Langley's farm and later in Africa, and it had made all the difference with the Harvard and Yale people who ran the agency and looked for pedigree in their men. Without Alex, Wyatt would have stayed with the knuckle-draggers, which is what CIA people call those who go out at night and do the dirty work. But Wyatt had studied diligently, and now *he* was part of the elite; one who ran things. He was second now only to the Director. Who would have thought it? And no one who saw him now in Claridge's would have guessed that he'd grown up in a steel-mill town and never owned a tie until the United States Army issued him one.

In the incredible English tranquillity of Claridge's, Wyatt finished his breakfast and wondered if he hated Alex. If he were honest, he would have to say he felt both love and hate. They had shared things, important things like the Farm at Langley and all the years in Africa. Wyatt realized he didn't feel one way or the other about most people anymore; it was a callousness that had crept over him with middle age. He used people professionally and that also did something to you. It had done something to both of them. Then, of course, there was the question of Helen. Wyatt folded his napkin and got up from the table and started toward the lobby. He'd chosen Claridge's because Helen told him it was a short taxi ride to the apartment Alex's family kept in London near Brompton Road. Wyatt picked up his overcoat in the lobby and put it on. When the taxi turned onto Knightsbridge, Wyatt reminded himself to stop in at his tailor's before he left the city.

★ ★ ★

The block of toney orange-brick apartment buildings was on a small side street off Brompton Road in the heart of Chelsea. The apartment door was already ajar. Wyatt knocked and then pushed it open further. The doorman had called Alex on the house phone. The room was dark and smelled with a reeking fug from cigarette smoke. Wyatt could make out curtains drawn across the entire front of a large living room with high ceilings. A mixture of heavy furniture was outlined in the penumbra. Wyatt moved his hand along the side of the door, looking for a light switch.

'Alex?' He felt himself flush with annoyance that Alex was playing with him. Before he found it, a light clicked on down at the end of the hall, some kind of desk light pointed toward him. It shone brightly in Wyatt's eyes for a moment. Wyatt saw the figure of a man standing at the end of the hallway, the aura of light surrounding him.

'I always thought control of the light was best, didn't you?' the familiar voice said. Wyatt came further into the airless room. The light turned suddenly away from him. Alex was naked, standing in the dimly lit hall. He looked like his own doppelgänger with the sandy blond hair and his lean youthful build. Alex's nakedness somehow seemed perfectly normal. Alex turned the desk light toward the ceiling slowly so that it illuminated the hall, toying with it. Wyatt glanced at the floor. Things he couldn't make out before were illuminated. There had been some kind of party and the party detritus was everywhere. Balloons littered the floor, and emptied fluted glasses and salvers of hardening hors d'oeuvres punctuated the room.

'I wasn't invited,' Wyatt said, looking around.

'No, you weren't. My mistake,' Alex said. A girl came out of the bedroom behind Alex. She was pretty, about thirty, and was wearing only a sheet, obviously still tipsy. She ran into the bathroom, her breasts pressed flat against the sheet. Wyatt could see she'd pierced one of her nipples.

'I would like . . . ' Alex turned around, and the girl was already in the bathroom, ' . . . you to meet Joe Blow,' Alex said, introducing him. 'He's an old friend. We were in a war together,' Alex said, looking at the door. The girl popped her head out. Her hair was dyed Kool-aid red. The idea of war was a total blank on her face. She reached out topless and kissed Alex with paid-for affection and closed the door again.

'Just like old times. I'm hungover and you're ready to shoot somebody. Still practicing Satyagraha, sitting at home spinning cotton, worrying about humanity's future?' Alex asked. He switched off the light. He looked exhausted. The bags under his eyes had taken on a blue stiff look from the non-stop drinking since his crack-up. His arms were thin and he had no pecs. They used to make fun of his body when they were recruits, Wyatt remembered. Wyatt had grown up in a military family, with the cult of the body, and even now, at fifty, lifted weights and was up at six A.M. to run every morning. He could have broken Alex's neck with one hand, he thought looking at him. Somehow that struck him as funny. Alex had never had any interest in his body except as an instrument of pleasure. The strongest muscle in your body is the one between your ears, he'd always said in Africa. Basic training at the Farm had been very hard on him, not the book-learning parts, but the rigorous physical requirements. Alex had willed himself through that part on sheer guts. Wyatt had observed him several times on the verge of collapse, but Alex always stuck it out, drawing on some reserve that nobody had expected him to have. Alex was brilliant at what was real intelligence work — he knew how to use people, Wyatt thought, looking at him. He had always admired the uncanny feel Alex had for people's weaknesses. There had been other bright recruits at the Farm, but Alex had a dark side and an understanding of what really motivated people to turn on their country and, in a sense, turn on themselves.

'She's very pretty,' Wyatt said nodding towards the bathroom.

'Not as pretty as Helen when she was that age. Well, how about a drink? We can celebrate man's inhumanity to earnest young CIA officers.' Wyatt shook his head; it was nine in the morning.

Their eyes met for a moment, then Alex left the hall and came back with a blue silk robe from the bedroom. He flipped on the hall light, then went to the windows in the living room and threw open one of the curtains. Alex came to the red couches in the center of the room and picked up a cigarette box and lighter from the table. His hands shook slightly. The room, lit now, was sumptuous and overdone in black and gold Empire style with a lot of English bric-a-brac.

Alex exhaled cigarette smoke. 'So how's life treating you, old boy? On your way to see my wife? You're really very predictable,' Alex said. He sat down on one of the big couches. 'Nothing ever changes. Three or four times a year, isn't it, that you take vacations together in the South of France — *Cap Ferrat,* I believe. How nice that must be for you both to get away like that.' Alex brought his feet up on the huge Chinese lacquer coffee table.

'Alex . . . '

The girl ran out of the bathroom, not bothering to cover up this time, and Wyatt realized she was a whore. The bathroom door slammed behind her. Wyatt caught a glimpse of a very white rear and then she was gone into a back bedroom.

'I had to convince Helen to send you the papers. She thinks it's bad form to divorce you because you have a drinking problem. You should divorce her,' Wyatt said. 'Why haven't you signed the papers?'

'Is that what I owe this visit to?'

'Yes. I came to ask you face to face. Give her a divorce, Alex.' Alex put down his cigarette. 'I promise I'll marry her,' Wyatt said, 'if that's what you're worried about.'

'Here for favors, are you? I would if you really loved her, but you don't. And, besides, you're a pig. And I won't have her marrying a pig. And then there's the fact that you aren't rich enough,' Alex said, smiling. 'I'm afraid you couldn't possibly afford her.'

'Don't be ridiculous,' Wyatt said. He looked the perfect CIA man, meticulous in his dark suit. *Untouchable*, Alex thought, hating him more now than he ever had. He knew he'd lost her to him, the one they used to call 'the specimen' behind Wyatt's back at the Farm. 'You never loved her at all,' Alex said, almost to himself.

'That's not true.'

'Of course it's true. Don't kid a kidder. No. No, it's quite impossible. I like being married. A man needs a wife after all. Anyway, you don't love her. Never have, really. You do it just to spite me, but she doesn't know that, does she.'

'You don't look well, Alex. Why don't you try a day in the country. Get some air. Clear your head.'

'Oh, there's nothing worse than a cuckold

full of fresh air,' Alex said. They both heard the girl come out of the bedroom. Alex lifted his hand and waved. 'Sorry you have to leave. Thank you so much for the fun. She gives wonderful *massages*, don't you, dear,' Alex said.

'Got to go, Luv,' she said. The girl was dressed all in black, her navel showing. Wyatt put his hand out. The girl took it and then was gone. Alex looked at the door a moment. 'Why don't you sit down or something,' Alex said. 'Do you think two hundred pounds was too much for her?'

'I've had you assigned to the Director's Office while you were AWOL,' Wyatt said, ignoring him. 'I'm your new boss until you decide what it is you want to do. You can go back to the station in Mexico if you want,' Wyatt said. 'Or somewhere else, if you'd rather.'

'Am I supposed to thank you?' Alex said.

'I did it for Helen. She was worried you'd get the stick. I told her you'd disappeared. She made me promise to help find you.'

'Help me by stealing my wife?'

'Alex, stop it. It's your fault and that's why you're so pissed. It had nothing to do with me. If you would have treated her better maybe this wouldn't have happened.'

'You're such a *pal*, helping me out of

difficult situations. I have a terrible headache. Why don't you leave,' Alex said. 'I'm not going to Mexico or anywhere else. I'm quitting. I was waiting to tell you,' Alex said.

'Of course, if that's what you want. But there's something else you should know.' Wyatt sat down across from him. 'Michael has joined up. Did you know? Your father helped him cut some red tape. He told the recruiter that he wanted to be just like his father. Sound familiar?'

'Does Helen know?' Alex said, all the fatuousness suddenly drained out of his voice. He became deathly pale. He smashed the cigarette out. Wyatt saw that he'd finally, after twenty years of trying, gotten to Alex.

'No, I haven't told her. She won't like it, of course. The kid's kept it a secret from her,' Wyatt said.

'And from me. I just saw him. He said something about the state department. I was stupid enough to believe him,' Alex said, sounding confused.

'He graduates from the Farm next month.'

'I want him washed out,' Alex said angrily.

'If that's what you want . . . okay.'

Alex looked up at him. 'That's why you're here. It isn't Helen at all. It's about Michael. You came here to offer him up. Why?' Wyatt smiled, then sat back on the couch. He put the briefcase he carried on the table.

'Because I want to trade you Michael for a favor.'

'What kind of favor?'

'I have a problem in Lisbon,' Wyatt said. 'I was going to send some knuckle-draggers, but I think it should be overseen by someone with experience, someone who can handle it correctly.' Wyatt took a file out of his briefcase and threw it on Alex's lap. 'You want Michael out. I want the money this man stole from his government. It's a lot of money,' Wyatt said. 'This is the deal; Michael will have an accident if I don't have the money by Friday.'

'You'd kill Helen's son?' Alex looked at him.

'I need the money. I can't have Helen without money now, can I? And anyway I know that Michael is safe because I know his father. I'll get the money. And I'll get Helen. All with your help.' He straightened his tie out. 'If you don't get me the money I'll throw Michael out of the helicopter myself. I'll be waiting for your call, Alex.'

'That's less than a week from now.'

'Well, you'd better get on it then, hadn't you?' Wyatt said. 'I suggest you use Butch. He's very good at finding money.'

'And if I get you this money, you'll have Michael washed out without him knowing what happened,' Alex said. Wyatt nodded. 'Without him knowing I had *anything* to do with it?'

'Yes,' Wyatt said.

'Take care of my problem in Lisbon and Michael's out,' Wyatt said. 'I promise. Fuck it up and he's dead.'

'What about Helen?'

'That's different. I told you. I love her,' Wyatt said. 'No deal there. I'll look out after Helen, I promise,' Wyatt said. Alex listened, rubbing his face, and felt sick.

Alex opened the file. 'I heard about what happened to Claymore,' Alex said.

'Psychotic episode,' Wyatt said. 'Who would have ever guessed it? A man like . . . '

'I called Tilly and told her how sorry I was,' Alex said. 'I told her I couldn't believe what I'd heard. She doesn't believe it either. Of course, it sounds incredible that he would kill his two oldest friends,' Alex said, looking up from the file.

'I'm glad you did. I called her too. But it's true, take my word for it,' Wyatt said. 'I suppose if you're leaving, we won't see each other again then,' Wyatt said.

'No. I don't suppose we will,' Alex said. Alex heard the briefcase close. Wyatt stopped at the door. He turned around and they stared at each other for a moment.

9

Lisbon, Portugal

The street in Lisbon where Alex had lived once hadn't changed, nor had the air that smelled of oranges and the sea and whitewash. On the way to the American Embassy, Alex stopped at the house he and Helen had rented when they were living in Lisbon fifteen years before. It was a large and beautiful two-story ancient mansion, with stone walls and a stone floor, painted mustard yellow with big green shutters so it all looked like a painting by Pissarro. It was a capacious and ancient place, full of azulejo murals from the sixteenth century with a backyard big enough to hit golf balls.

Alex got out of the taxi and looked at the house in the warm mid-morning sun. *I could have been happy here,* he thought, digging in his pocket for the taxi fare. He was wearing a sky-blue linen suit and was stone sober. He'd been sober, in fact, since Wyatt walked out of his flat in London.

Alex stood on the hushed street, his sobriety making him sensitive to everything, the light weight of his new suit, the way the breeze came from the harbor behind him. He looked squarely at the house where he could have changed everything once. The house was where his daughter had been conceived and where he had destroyed his marriage, torn it up, the way you do junk mail, just tossed it away. He went to the heavy wooden door, the color of walnut shells, on the garden wall that surrounded the house and the considerable grounds. He knocked, not knowing why he'd come exactly except, like an archeologist, he wanted to sift through the broken pieces of his life and arrange them, catalog his mistakes. He knocked on the door and waited.

He'd heard that the house had been converted into some kind of Catholic school. A young nun asked him if he wanted to come in. He stood for a moment, unsure of himself.

'Sister, good morning. I'm sorry to bother you, but we, my family and I, used to live here. Years ago.' Alex looked beyond the smiling young woman and tried to see the big tulip tree that he remembered so well. It was under that tree that he'd been warned. 'When we lived here, there was a tulip tree in the back courtyard, Sister. Is it still there?' he asked. The nun was a Carmelite, and her face, both deferential and vibrant in all its youth, was sympathetic immediately. She opened the heavy garden door wider and beckoned him in. She took his hand and led him through the gateway. He wasn't sure at first whether she spoke English or not. He tried what was left of his Portuguese. He was afraid of confronting the past, and yet, now, it seemed it was all he had. He would remember, later, the way she'd taken his hand as if he were some kind of pilgrim.

They both looked towards the tree from the patio. Many nights he and Helen had sat under that tree in the summer when it was glorious and full, when it was very warm out, and in the evening they sipped sherry and talked about his leaving the agency. As he walked toward the patio, the nun's sweet voice in his ears, he remembered *that* night. He and Helen were alone together and going over the days' events, most of which he couldn't speak to her about because the American Boys were planning another little war. It was awful not being able to share with her the burdens of his work and all the things he did. He needed absolution for his sins but couldn't bring himself to confess them to her. He understood now, standing here all these years later, that being cut off from people and secretive hollowed you out.

'I saw the doctor. Everything is hunky-dory,' Helen had said. The green light they'd set up under the tree poured into the underside of the canopy, painting it in a soft green verdant tone. Helen's beautiful face was so radiant now that she was pregnant.

'Are you going to find out?' Alex asked. 'If it's a girl or boy?'

'That's a secret,' she said, looking at him. There was that great pause as she looked at him. 'That's *my* secret, isn't it.' There was the pouring of sherry the color of summer, *baby's nectar*, as they called it, into thick Portuguese glasses. He wanted to tell her events they were planning, male things, the way the office was all going to be transferred back to Africa and what he intended to accomplish there. They were going to take the initiative, subvert the Russians, and run them out of the sub-continent, even out of India, if they got half a chance. He would be gone indefinitely, and he couldn't possibly take her and Michael.

'I want you to quit them,' she said. 'I want you to leave them because I am losing you, Alex. And I don't want to lose you. You don't see what they've done to you,' Helen said that night. That sweet, warm night Michael was sleeping above them upstairs, and the nanny they'd hired with the thick black socks and dirty shoes was in the kitchen doing the dishes. The house was lit up around them. He listened and looked into Helen's pregnant face, and he thought of another girl and an act by a river. He thought nothing, absolutely nothing, about what she was saying. He didn't listen in the way any sane person might have. Instead, he watched her, clutching his secrets.

'Don't be silly,' he said.

'You're disappearing in front of me, Alex. Every day it's worse,' she said holding the glass and looking into it, then up at him. 'When you're home with us, you might as well be out doing whatever it is you do. They'll ruin you and they'll ruin us, Alex, if you don't leave them.' He hadn't listened to a word of it.

'I might not be here for the blessed event,' he said, looking at her. 'There's a war brewing.' Helen stared at him a long time in that pregnant woman way, so beautiful and tranquil.

'I know,' she said finally. 'The wives aren't completely without their, what do you call it, channels of information. Is that the jargon? You have so much of it in your business,' she said.

'Patsy told you,' Alex said. He knew that Butch told his wife *everything*.

'Alex, please leave the agency. Leave them *now* while you still can. While I still love you,' she said. 'While I still love you. Do you want me to beg you, Alex? Would that work?'

He hadn't heard her because, by then, he'd gone operational. He'd become a hulking great spymaster, and he *very* much wanted to go to this dirty little war they were planning. Oh yes, he wanted to go. He'd lusted after it. His wife's love had become a devalued coin by then. It purchased only a weak and obscene smile that warm, beautiful, awful night, when he'd traded his humanity for the promise of one more little war.

'They'll ruin you and they'll ruin us,' she had said and she'd been right; she'd taken Michael and left him a few days later. He'd gone to Africa again and won everything but the right to look at himself in the mirror without feeling sick for what he'd done to her.

★　★　★

'We lived here, Sister, my wife and my son and I, in 1980,' Alex said, looking at the house as if he expected Helen and Michael to come out of the kitchen and welcome him

110

back. Instead, he saw an old nun moving slowly down the hall with a student. The young nun turned and looked at him. Her habit, the starched white part, was severe and encroached on all her youth, except for her eyes which were blue and sweet. He supposed she was in love with Jesus. She turned and looked at him with real concern, which surprised him. She paused for a moment. Alex put his fingers through his hair. He wanted to leave but he wanted to be polite. 'I have many problems, sister,' he blurted out. 'I didn't have as many when we lived here. I'm glad you opened the gate. I'm glad I was able to see the old place one last time. I'm here on business and don't know when I'll ever be back again,' his voice trailed off. He was on the verge of telling her that he couldn't risk backing the wrong team, and that he had no confidence in anyone anymore. Certainly not in Bowles. Bowles, he knew, would be cut down sooner or later. He, alone, was nothing against *them*.

'Are you troubled? Is that why you've come here?' the girl asked. She was shading her pretty face to look at him.

'Yes.' He didn't want to say it. He hadn't wanted to say anything, but he seemed to have given in as soon as she touched him at the gate. The physical touch of her hand

— that female energy — had let something loose in him as soon as she'd pulled him into the garden the way she had, as if he were some stray child missing from the school.

'Would you like to come in and have a chat with someone?' she asked.

'A priest, you mean?' and he smiled. He thought of himself dressed in his cassock. He thanked her, taking her hand as she spoke. He wished her well and left across the garden.

★　★　★

A fruit vendor went past in a horse cart. The syncopation to the nag's hoofs on the cobblestones almost made him feel better. Alex went and found himself a good bar and ordered a brandy but didn't drink it. Then he ordered a beer and didn't let himself drink that either. It took a while before he could wipe away the nun's touch, before he could blot out Helen's warning, before he could forget that he was suffering from something that would require mea culpas to remedy. A car pulled up in front of the bar and he went outside.

'Butch,' Alex said, getting into the rented Fiat Butch was driving. 'Thanks for coming. I've got bad news . . . Richard's dead. They killed him.'

Butch quietly took in the news. 'Where is

he, this guy we're after?' Butch said, changing the subject.

'I don't know yet. There will be news waiting for me here at the embassy.'

'What's all this about?'

'I saw Wyatt in London. He's threatening Michael if I don't get the money this Liberian stole from his government and get it to Wyatt, and soon.'

'Michael?'

'Michael's joined the agency,' Alex said. 'Wyatt will wash him out from the Farm in exchange for the money. That's the deal,' Alex said. 'I'll kill him if I have to. To get the money. Whatever it takes,' Alex said.

'If you want me to do it, I'd be glad to,' Butch said, not moving his eyes off the traffic in front of them. Alex looked at his friend. He saw some kind of understanding growing in Butch's eyes, and he realized again how much Butch must have cared about him.

'You know something? Richard always said the job was going to kill him,' Butch said. Then they drove in silence the rest of the way to the embassy.

★ ★ ★

The American Embassy in Lisbon, like so many others around the world, was in the

113

home of a former aristocrat. There was still a large CIA presence in Lisbon, especially for covert operations, because of the former Salazar Government's long-term relationship with the CIA, and because Portugal had always been a springboard for Africa, especially during the Cold War. Alex went down the familiar hallways of the embassy's top floor reserved for CIA use. All the faces were new, the old hands he'd served with were long gone.

There was an intelligence report waiting for Alex in the over-cooled office of John Freemont, the head of the CIA's Lisbon station. Alex thumbed through the pages of the report while Freemont spoke into a phone to his wife in his sugary this-is-your-husband voice.

Freemont shot him a look of the *I-can't-help-it* variety and Alex read on. According to the report, the Liberian he was after was staying in a villa south of the city, alone, except for a mistress. Modipo Mulumbo, a Liberian finance minister, the report stated in cold Langley prose, had looted fifty million dollars of a World Bank loan made to the Government of Liberia three weeks before. There was a handwritten note from Wyatt in the file with the account number and the name of the bank to which he wanted the money transferred. His blood went cold when he saw the name: Western Trust. It was his family's bank. Alex looked up from the file, stunned. There was no doubt now that he was being used, that Michael had been a pawn to get him to do what Wyatt wanted.

Freemont put his phone down. He was short and had a short man's over-aggressive attitude, as if he were still practicing his manly expressions in a mirror. His desk was perfectly clean. There was a picture of his wife and children in a clear plastic frame standing at the entrance to Disneyworld. 'My class read about you at the Farm. We studied your escape from Cuito Cuarnavalle. Classic. I always wanted to meet you,' Freemont said. 'Your man's rented an enormous villa outside of Lisbon in a village called Casa Novo. A lot of retired Brits live there. He arrived just three days ago. Every morning he's off to the square for breakfast with his girlfriend, a French whore from the Ivory Coast. The World Bank people are in a complete panic that the robbery will get into the press.' Freemont was overweight and had a sales-man's spit and polish look. He seemed very young, a post-Cold-War-type, more of a bureaucrat than an intelligence officer, Alex guessed, looking at him. *But they all seemed that way now.* 'Should I send you computer experts? We know he's carrying a computer with him. I suppose it's all in *there*, what he did with the money and so on,' Freemont said, matter-of-factly. He leaned back in his executive's chair and pulled his hands up behind his head as if it were all finished and the money had been found.

'No,' Alex said. And then Alex gave him a look which he thought would say everything. 'It wouldn't do any good. There's only one way now,' Alex said.

'I see,' Freemont said. It was obvious Freemont was bending over backwards to stay out of it. For a moment, it seemed he might ask what Alex intended to do *exactly* to recover the money, but then he seemed to decide against it. His phone rang; he put the caller on the speakerphone. It was Freemont's wife again. She was somewhere in the city and needed more advice on a purchase she was about to make for their house. Freemont put his hand over the receiver. 'Listen, can I do anything else?' Alex shook his head and got up. It was obvious Freemont wanted nothing to do with the case and that Wyatt had given him the word to stay out of it.

'I'll kill him if he doesn't turn over the money,' Alex said, standing up. 'There might be a problem if things go wrong.' Freemont looked up from the phone, startled. He stared at Alex very intently for a moment, as if he'd heard something he shouldn't have. 'Honey, could you hold a minute?' He pushed the hold button.

'What do you mean, *kill* him?'

'I'll need help if things go wrong. Backup. I'll come here to the embassy immediately of course, and then you'll have to arrange things. And I'll need two policemen to come out to the villa with us.'

'No one told me anything about killing anyone,' Freemont said.

'Well, I'm telling you now,' Alex said. He'd purposely decided to test Freemont. If the head of station simply ignored what he was telling him, then there was clearly some kind of plot. If he was clean, Alex knew Freemont would have to stop him and find out what the hell was going on. Even with the CIA, assassination wasn't casual — certainly not spur-of-the-moment — and to be done by an officer himself was clearly illegal nowadays. Alex watched Freemont carefully. There was no way he would let him walk out of the office without calling his superior at Langley — *unless?*

'Fine,' Freemont said finally, staring back at Alex. He pushed the hold button. 'Dear . . . I think we have enough hand-painted tiles,' he said loquaciously, glancing at Alex.

10

'Is there anyone in the house other than the girl?' Alex asked the African calmly. It was dawn, and it was still cold and foggy, and the man in front of them was frightened. They had waited for dawn to break and then the four of them walked down the driveway and knocked on the villa's big front doors. The two Portuguese policemen pushed past the minister as soon as the door opened. 'We don't want any trouble,' Alex said. He stepped into the foyer and looked up the wide staircase in front of him.

'Who the devil are you?' the minister asked. He'd been asleep and was disoriented and groggy. Alex was struck by the African's English accent. The ex-finance minister was standing, red-eyed, in his pajamas. The two detectives brought the girl to the landing above him so Alex could see her. Her blond hair was undone and very long. She was about twenty, tall and strikingly beautiful. The minister said something to her in French.

'We're the people you *don't* want to meet,' Alex said, glancing at the girl, then closing the heavy front door behind him. The minister looked ridiculous in his red silk pajamas, like some kind of stage potentate. Butch had been quiet in the car. Now, he suddenly slapped the African, knocking him back into the center of the foyer. Butch wore a ring and it left a mark on the black man's face, cutting him slightly.

'I don't understand,' the minister said, looking at Butch. 'What have I done?'

'I thought we'd start out on the right foot,' Butch said.

'We're here for the money, my friend,' Alex said. 'There's no point in lying to us. We know all about it and we want to know where you've put it. Otherwise, we'll take you back to Liberia. It's all really very simple,' Alex told him. What had been sleepy-eyed surprise turned to horror on the black man's face. Alex let the threat sink in. Returning to Liberia meant unspeakable torture and the minister knew it. 'We have a plane waiting. Where's the money? If you tell us where the money is, perhaps we can do something for you,' Alex said. He signaled for the policeman to take the girlfriend upstairs. 'We need to know the name of the bank, or banks, where you've put it,' Alex said.

'You can't send me back to Liberia. There's no law in Liberia,' Modipo said. The African had come completely awake now. Alex nodded to Butch.

'No shit,' Butch said.

'Where can we talk?' Alex said. Butch didn't wait for an answer. He grabbed the minister by the shoulder and walked him toward the stairs, partially lifting the smaller man as if he were a rag doll. Alex walked behind them up the stairs, concerned that Butch might be losing control. Alex wondered just how bolted down Butch was now. Butch pushed the African into one of the bedrooms off the hall at the top of the stairs. Alex snapped on the light in the room. The furniture was all brand new. A TV set hadn't been taken from the box yet. Butch pushed him onto one of the new beds with the plastic still on the mattress and stood over him menacingly.

Alex dragged a rattan chair over in front of the African. He smiled. It was part of the game. It had been decided in the car that Alex would play the good cop. He would play the nice American who understood how bankers were really different from everybody else. Butch would be his violent antipode. Alex sent Butch to secure the minister's office, get into his computer and start looking for the money. He heard the door close behind him, and Alex and the African were

120

left alone in the cold bedroom.

'You were educated in England, weren't you?' Alex said after the door closed.

'Yes, the London School,' the minister answered hopefully, as if somehow that would make a difference. 'But what is it you want? Who are you?'

'I suppose you would like to retire there, after this matter is cleared up? I mean London,' Alex said, ignoring the man's question. The minister was very black and his skin was shiny and smooth. His kinky hair had streaks of gray in it. The red silk pajamas seemed to make his skin seem all the blacker. Alex lit a cigarette.

'Yes . . . Or perhaps here. I like Portugal,' the minister said, watching Alex.

'We want the money back. That's all we really care about right now. If you tell us where you put the money, I can make arrangements for you to retire wherever you like.' Alex looked around him for an ashtray. 'There would be no reason for you to be sent back to Liberia. I promise you. If you tell us where the money is and give it back, you won't have to go anywhere,' Alex said. Alex moved for the gun in his pocket.

'St. Regent's Square,' Modipo said. 'I have bought a place on St. Regent's Square. I could go there, I suppose.'

'Fine, but we must have the money you took from the ministry.'

'You won't send me back to Liberia if I tell you?'

'I said I promise,' Alex said. 'You have my word.'

'I want to get dressed. I don't want to be like this, I'm cold,' Modipo told him. He seemed suddenly anxious. Alex ignored him. He was starting to lose his patience.

'Is the money still in one batch?'

'Yes.'

'Where?' Alex said. 'I must know where the money is as soon as possible. Let's get this over with *now*.' Modipo sat back on the bed. His eyes wandered the room for a moment.

'I have something. Something the American government would trade for the money.'

'What could possibly be worth that kind of money?' Alex said. He felt his fingers loosen, and he forced them to clamp down again on the gun in his pocket. 'Call the American Embassy in Lisbon and ask for Mr. Freemont. He knows me. He'll tell you,' the minister said. He glanced at Alex's pocket. Alex's hand was shaking and he tried to steady it. He'd broken out in a sweat.

Alex took the gun out and put it against the minister's forehead. They were both shocked.

The minister started to urinate uncontrollably, as if a switch had been thrown. Alex watched the urine collect on the plastic under him, the puddle growing. It was staining the minister's red robe. Alex could smell it. Alex looked at the indentation of the barrel on the man's skin.

'Oh, God, please don't kill me! Please!' He couldn't stop himself from pissing. Alex backed away from him, horrified.

'Stop it,' Alex said. 'Stop it right now. God damn you, *stop it.*' The gun began to shake so much that he had to steady it by pressing harder against the man's head. The air smelled of piss now.

'You know someone at the American Embassy?'

'Yes. Freemont.'

'And you think the Americans will trade what you have to say for the money you have stolen?' Alex said. The minister didn't answer but nodded carefully as if the gun might go off any moment. 'I think you're lying. I think you're stalling for time, and I don't have time,' Alex said. 'You tell me. I'll be the judge of how important it is.'

He looked up the gun barrel at Alex. Alex heard the door open and heard Butch come back into the room. 'I found what could be bank numbers in his computer.'

'He's pissed on himself,' Alex said, not turning around. 'Open the window.'

'You can go ahead and kill him. We probably don't need him now,' Butch said matter-of-factly and opened a window.

Alex slapped him. The slap was sudden and unexpected. He'd been up all night, and he was suddenly very angry and needed a drink, and it was surprisingly easy to hit him. The cold made his hand sting.

'Tell me what is so damned important that it's worth fifty million or I'll have you on a plane within the hour, so help me God,' Alex said. The minister touched the side of his face where Alex had hit him. There was a knock at the door. One of the policemen asked if he could fix some coffee for the girl.

'Do what you like,' Alex said, angrily.

'They're going to kill someone,' Modipo said finally.

'Who's going to kill someone?'

'They're going to kill someone important, very important.'

'How do you know that?' Alex said.

'I heard it in Monrovia.'

Modipo Mulumbo began to tell his story. He told Alex about the American Embassy in Monrovia and said someone from the embassy called Alex Law had told him he

124

could steal the money. That it didn't matter to them.

'*Alex Law?*' Alex said.

'Yes, an American. He came to my office last year in Monrovia, this Mr. Law. He said he was the new AID attaché at the American Embassy there. He knew all about my activities and how I'd been cheating the government. He had a file with him that documented everything — all my deposits in Europe, every one of them.

'Law asked me where I was getting the money. I told him it was none of his damn business. He said not to get angry, that his office had heard rumors in the capital that there was going to be a leak of my finances. He said I might be arrested and lose the money.

'Law said I could keep things the way they were if I would work with him. I asked him what he wanted. He said he only wanted me to run a few bank accounts under my name. He said that I would get instructions from time to time and I was to carry them out. I agreed. I had no choice. Later, I learned from our intelligence people that Alex Law is a high-ranking CIA officer. That he was famous in Africa. Then I knew that all this was for the CIA.'

'You're sure the man's name was Alex Law,' Alex said.

'Yes, absolutely sure,' the African said. 'And something else . . . I know about someone called Glad,' Modipo said.

'Go on?' Alex said.

'I met him in Monrovia. Law had me set up an account for him at the bank. Three million dollars came from the United States last month, and I was told to keep it on deposit for Glad.'

'You're sure,' Alex said. 'You're sure it was Glad?' He'd fastened on the name. 'Did Law say what the money was *for?*'

'He never said. I put the money in the account at the bank in Monrovia. Glad came and collected it about six weeks ago. He got into trouble in Monrovia with a prostitute. He killed her in his room. I had to go take care of it, and he told me then. He was very drunk and he told me what the money was for. He said he was going to help change America. He was going to help kill the President of the United States, and if I knew what was good for me, I'd get him out of the trouble he was in.'

'And Alex Law — what did he look like?'

'He was a very big, fit man. Always well dressed,' Modipo said. 'He had a rough-sounding voice.'

'What did he look like, this Glad,' Alex said. He stood up.

126

'He was tall and had a pony tail,' Modipo said.

'You're lying,' Alex said. 'You'd say anything to keep the money.'

Alex looked at his watch. It was almost nine in the morning. He had never wanted a drink so badly in his life. He was already supposed to have called Wyatt, who was waiting to hear from him. Alex called for one of the Portuguese policemen to watch the minister. He went and found a bottle of brandy in the living room and had two good swallows, then another longer swallow from the bottle and, finally, he felt something. He sat down on a new white couch, the bottle on his knee. He could hear the girl talking to the policemen who were chatting her up in the kitchen. Butch followed him into the living room.

'I can't find it,' Butch said. There was a long pause. 'Alex, did you hear me?'

'Butch, he just told me *Alex Law* was running him in Liberia,' Alex said. 'He told me *Alex Law* gave him the green light to swindle his government. Now *Alex Law* is going to take his money and deposit it in his family's bank.' Alex turned around and looked at his friend.

'I told you. Wyatt is after us. I told you that in Mexico. I knew it the day he came to see me,' Butch said.

'Well, I have news for you. I think I know why, now. Would you like to hear . . . ? You might want to sit down.' Alex took a swig from the bottle, not bothering with a glass. 'You and I are planning to kill the President of the United States,' Alex said, wiping his face.

'You're joking,' Butch said.

'No, unfortunately, I'm not. I told Freemont that I might have to kill this guy, and you know what he told me? Fine. Never even batted an eye. Richard suspected Wyatt. That's why they killed him. And the shootings out in front of Langley, that was all part of it. They'd asked Ford and Kregan and Claymore to join in some kind of conspiracy to kill Neal White for a drug cartel. Patsy's death is part of it too. I'm sure they intended to kill her from the beginning and blame you, to make you look like a monster later,' Alex said. 'Now you know about as much as I do.' Butch came further into the room. He was stunned. He was carrying the African's laptop. He put it down carefully on the coffee table in front of him. His face was suddenly pale.

'And Wyatt wants you to put this money in your family's bank?'

'Yes. Of course. We have to be paid, don't we?'

'Jesus Christ! What are we going to do?'

'Well, unfortunately, for the time being, I'm going to do exactly what Wyatt wants me to do. So we have to find this money or Wyatt will kill my son. So, please find it,' Alex said.

'It will take too long,' Butch said, looking at the computer and standing up. 'We'll have to do it the old-fashioned way then.' Alex heard the pop of a switchblade. It was a very brutal sound and Alex was glad to hear it. 'If they want a monster, I'll oblige,' Butch said.

* * *

Butch dragged the knife blade across the arm of the chair Modipo was sitting in. Stuffing fell out like guts from a wound.

'You know, you can live without balls,' Butch said. 'I've seen it. I'll have you in Liberia, alive and ball-less.'

'He wouldn't let you do it.' Modipo nodded toward Alex. 'He won't let you.' Butch laughed. 'Oh, I think he will. You know we've done this kind of thing before, he and I. We're old hands at this.'

'I don't give a shit what he does to you,' Alex said.

'I can see what kind of man you are,' Modipo said. The African's eyes were riveted on the knife in Butch's hand.

'Can you? What kind is that?' Alex said.

'Better than that,' Modipo said.

'Well, they're *your* balls. But you're wrong. I'll live with myself if he *fixes* you. I'm giving you one more chance,' Alex said. He leaned against the door. 'What's it going to be?' He held out the cell phone. 'One painless call to the bank, or a rather crude operation?'

'Both of you are *mad*,' Modipo said. 'You're both mad!' There was a long pause. Butch pulled more stuffing out of the chair with the point of the knife. Alex waited by the door, looking into the room. 'I want to get dressed. Then I will show you everything. It's all in the computer,' Modipo said finally. Alex looked at him. The African had a strange look on his face, his black skin shiny in the morning sunlight that had begun to pour into the bedroom. He was in love with the money. Alex had seen the look before.

'Do it,' Alex said. Butch yanked the minister out of the chair and threw him onto the bed.

'All right. All right. It's in Zurich,' Modipo said.

'Good. What's the name of the bank?' Alex slipped the phone out of his pocket and flipped it open.

'Swiss Bank Corp,' Modipo said. 'Please don't take all of it.'

Alex felt oddly better now with the alcohol inside of him, and strangely relaxed. 'Here, they're going to want to talk to *you*,' Alex said, putting the phone to the African's ear. 'Tell them you want fifty million dollars wire-transferred to the Western Trust Bank in San Francisco. I'll give you the account number when they ask for it.'

★   ★   ★

It had taken an hour to transfer the money to Alex's family's bank in San Francisco to the account Wyatt had given him. Alex went to the master bedroom the couple had used. It was large, with all new furniture, like the rest of the house. One of the policemen brought in the girlfriend. The detectives hadn't given her a robe, preferring to keep her half-dressed in just the white bustier that showed off her girlish body and long legs. Butch was leaning against the wall across from the bathroom door and looking at her, his hands shoved in the pockets of his trench coat.

They could all hear the shower going in the bathroom. Alex had given Modipo permission to clean up after the money had been transferred. For a moment, the room was quiet and tight-feeling. The girl's presence added something upsetting and exciting at the same time.

'How long have you been here with him?' Alex asked her. He hadn't bothered to put the brandy bottle down but had carried it into the room with him. The girl looked at Alex as she listened to a translation and then sneered.

'I want to leave,' she said in French.

Alex got up, holding the brandy bottle by the neck, and went to the closet. He found a robe and tossed it to the girl. She threw it on the floor and swore at him. The policemen laughed, thinking it was funny. Everyone in the room realized Alex was high.

★ ★ ★

They had been talking when the door burst open. Alex must have been the first one to see him because no one else moved. Modipo, dripping wet and naked, his nappy hair silver with water, charged into the room with a crazed look in his eye and an automatic in his hand. There was a strange moment, the kind that occurs in combat, when things slow down and you get tunnel vision from the adrenaline. Alex stood there waiting for the African to be shot down.

Modipo's first shot shattered the lamp

beside the girl. She screamed. The second shot hit the top of Butch's thigh. Modipo was firing and talking crazily. Alex watched Butch stagger back, his eyes rolling in pain, clutching for his gun. Butch tried to move forward. Modipo kicked the bathroom door out of his way and fired again. Alex dove toward the hall. One of the Portuguese cops was firing now, hitting the black man once in the gut, but the cop caught the full force of a blast from the African, who had turned on him unafraid. The shot tore through the policeman's groin. The policeman ran out into the hall screaming and holding himself. He tried to make it to the stairs but couldn't and fell, pleading in Portuguese for Alex to help him. Alex reached down for his weapon but remembered he'd unloaded it as a precaution, before the interview; he'd had no intention of shooting the man before he'd found the money.

Alex could hear the minister talking to himself. He looked up from the floor. Modipo had walked back toward the bathroom and grabbed a towel. In shock, he pushed it against the wound in his stomach, then turned around unsteadily, swaying like a drunk, and looked at the girl. He tried to raise the gun one last time to kill her. The pistol wobbled as the blood spread into the white towel he clutched in his bloody hand. The girl begged him not to shoot. Alex stood up and walked between the minister and the girl. He lifted the brandy bottle to his mouth and drank, 'Go ahead, asshole.' The African concentrated on the girl with hate in his dying eyes. He lifted his gun. The tight round circle of the barrel moved unsteadily, trying to find a target in the haze of death. Alex threw the bottle at him but missed, and it exploded against the tile wall of the bathroom behind Modipo, the brown liquid mixing with the blood on the bathroom floor.

'You're dying,' Alex said. He saw the blood dribbling out from the minister's wound and down his black leg. Modipo tried to aim at the girl across the room. Ignoring Alex, he was desperate to take the girl with him for some reason.

He fired once and missed. The bullet shattered the mirror behind her. The minister fell on his knees and lifted the gun to his head. He looked at Alex just before he pulled the trigger. Their eyes met. He said something, then the force of the blast from the automatic knocked his head into the bathroom wall, spraying it with gray matter.

After the shot there was silence, except for Butch groaning on the floor. Everything had gone wrong. Alex could hear the other cop running down the hall. Alex turned around. The girl was sobbing on the floor on her hands and knees, bits of mirror around her naked legs.

11

Camp David

There were six major crises occurring simultaneously in the world, whereas there had been five the morning before. The President of the United States noticed Sierra Leone had been added to the CIA's list of hot spots overnight. President Neal White put the CIA memo down on his desk at Camp David. He took his glasses off and rubbed his eyes. It was late, after eleven, but he'd been up since five that morning. He had one more important meeting before he went to bed. Neal had gotten into the habit of reading in the office at Camp David after everyone else was in bed. He liked to schedule important meetings late at night after a movie or a game of cards with friends. He enjoyed haunting the presidential retreat at night: it was oddly relaxing, and he could think when the place was quiet and he was alone without the constant interruptions.

The stress of the campaign still bothered him. It had been an especially ugly campaign which had left its scars. It had been too close to call right up to the last minute. *The Washington Post* said Neal White was just a lucky country boy from Texas who'd won the election only because the Republicans had picked a candidate who was so old that he'd simply folded in the last days of the campaign. *Thank god*, the President thought, smiling and putting his feet on the desk, feeling comfortable with the victory, finally. He also remembered that the *Post* had said that if he wasn't an outright liberal, he was as close as you could get. His father had been a minister and believed in Christian good. He'd passed that simple-minded goodness on to his son. Most of all, he believed in keeping his promise to the voters that he would get rid of the country's drug problem once and for all. He leaned back in his chair and listened to the nocturnal sounds surrounding Camp David, which were the sounds of silence and crickets and peace. He'd promised the American people change and he'd meant it. Change, real change, inside the Washington beltway, apparently meant making real enemies. There were interests that had no intention of letting him make real change. It had surprised him just how nasty they could be. The President rang for a brandy. The steward came in, a small, delicate-looking Filipino man who was the color of oiled mahogany. The steward had been on the Camp David staff since the Kennedy years.

'Al, get me a drink. In fifteen minutes, I want you to bring Director Penn over to the tennis pavilion. I know he's been waiting.'

'Yes sir, Mr. President, fifteen minutes, sir,' the steward said.

'Tell him to come alone, no staffers.' Al carefully poured his drink. White wondered how many on his staff were on *his* side. From his chair, White studied the smooth mahogany-colored face of the old steward. The old man's hair was still jet black. He had to be seventy if he was a day, White thought. The President's hair had started to turn gray when he was still in law school. He put his hands through his prematurely gray hair and then put his glasses back on.

'Al?'

'Yes sir, Mr. President,' the steward smiled at him affably. The President liked him and he knew it. They were always joking about Manila's beautiful women.

'Al . . . how many spies do the newspapers have up here?' The old man picked up a silver tray and brought him a large brandy, no ice.

'There have always been spies here, sir. We call them tipsters. Sometimes they get paid,' he explained, handing the President the drink and a paper napkin.

'We got any now?'

'Yes sir.'

'How many?'

'Two, sir.'

'You'd be a hell of a good spy, Al, if you wanted to be one.'

'I'm too old for that nonsense, sir.'

'Hell, Al, that's the best kind of spy. Did you ever talk to JFK about the spies up here?' The men's eyes locked on each other. The steward stopped smiling. The old man had idealized Kennedy, and the loss still was painful.

'No, sir . . . Just Mr. Penn then, sir?'

'Yes, Al.'

The President allowed himself ten minutes alone to contemplate his plan. It was audacious, but he was tired of pussy-footing around with these criminals. The moment he'd gotten the word that Berry, his head of DEA, had been assassinated by the cartels, he had decided to strike back. It was a simple plan. He was going to order the assassination of several major drug bosses, and that, as they said, was that, he thought.

The President walked alone to the tennis pavilion. He enjoyed the walk in the fresh, cold night air on the lit gravel path. He descended the stairs into the pavilion. It was pitch black, and he had to walk along the wall to find the switch for the lights. A security patrol of two men went by in a golf cart. The President watched them drive along the path. They were Texas Rangers whom he recognized; one of them held up his hand in a wave. Seeing his fellow Texans made him feel secure. *Screw the Secret Service. Can't trust them anymore*, he thought.

The tennis pavilion was grand and decorated with walnut paneling and big wooden beams. There were pictures of past presidents greeting celebrities and other politicians as they stepped off helicopters at Camp David. The President went to the one he liked the best. It was Jack Kennedy in a pair of shorts, no shirt, greeting his brother, Bobby, and Marilyn Monroe. Monroe was wearing dark glasses. The President heard voices and turned around.

The Director of the Central Intelligence Agency came down the stairs. He was wearing a gray suit and red tie, an elegant briefcase at his side. He walked through the open sliding glass doors. David Penn was sixty years old and hatchet-faced. He was the developer of the Phoenix program, the President reminded himself for some reason. White had been in Vietnam then, just a second lieutenant in the army, and fresh out of Harvard. He'd seen Penn in Saigon getting

140

into a limousine once, surrounded by generals. Now White was President and theoretically Penn's boss. It seemed incredible to him. The CIA man, all smiles, came across the room. The career spook seemed relaxed. It was their first private meeting since the news that the Director of DEA had been found dead in his summer cabin. CNN was reporting that Berry had been taking bribes from the Mexican Juarez drug cartel for months now. Neal put on his good-old-boy smile and they shook hands.

'David. Sit down.'

'Good to see you, Mr. President. Congratulations on the victory.'

'Thanks. Good to see you, David. Care for a drink? I can ring for something,' Neal said. The President was wearing jeans and a T-shirt. He was a lot younger than Penn, and he acutely felt it now.

'No thank you, sir.'

'I thought we should get together and discuss Berry's assassination. I am writing off the DEA. I think they're all compromised,' the President said. 'But before we do that, I want to ask you a question. How bad do you think it is?'

'Pretty bad, sir, but only at the lower levels. Berry *was* dirty though,' Penn said. 'We've confirmed that.'

'I've got a plan,' Neal said. 'It's bold and it might not be legal, but I think we have to get these drug kingpins before they buy the whole damn government out.'

'Yes?'

'I want to, how can I say this, *remove* these gangsters. Take them out. Cut the cartel's head off . . . If you understand my meaning,' Neal said. The President took out the paper he'd written the names on in his own hand. Penn reached over and took the paper and unfolded it. 'That's all the leading dope bosses in Mexico, Colombia and Thailand, as I understand it. I want to *lose* them. Can we do that?' Neal asked.

'We can certainly look into it, sir. It's a very radical idea, Mr. President . . . ' Penn said. He looked tired, Neal thought.

'The *Times* said yesterday that they would probably like to kill me for pressing the drug war. Do you believe it?'

'It's possible, Mr. President. They'd have to get in line though.'

'Very funny,' Neal said. 'We have people who could just go and do it, don't we?'

'Yes, sir. We know people like that,' Penn said.

'Good. This will have to be covered up. Make it look like a big drug war or something. But I'm not going to sit back and watch them buy out the US Government.'

'I think we can arrange that, Mr. President. We might have to bend a few rules though.'

'Won't be the first time, will it? Do you think they're actively trying to get rid of me?' Neal asked again. There had been rumors recently, principally from MI6, that the British had reported directly to the President's National Security Advisor.

'No, sir, I don't. But we'll look into it if you like. That's really not our bailiwick,' Penn said.

He's going to break that stick up his ass if he's not careful, Neal thought. 'I think they are. I'm the one that's turned the heat on. They can't like that, can they?'

'No, I imagine they don't,' Penn said.

'Now about the situation at DEA . . . '

★ ★ ★

When Penn had gone the President got up and stretched. He looked at his watch. They'd been at it for over two hours. Neal picked up the phone that connected him to the White House and was put through to Bowles on a secure line. He'd promised to call his Security Chief as soon as Penn left.

★ ★ ★

143

Red Bowles put down the phone. He wasn't feeling well. It was the stress. He got up and walked across his darkened office in the White House. Neal wasn't just the President of the United States, he was a close personal friend. They'd grown up together.

If I don't tell Neal what I know, I'd better have a damn good reason, he thought to himself. But he was sure others were listening now. The White House was a big sieve, and he couldn't find a place where he was sure it was safe to talk. Even the secured line installed recently was suspect. It had been done by Army Intelligence. If he was right, he would have to keep Neal out of the loop for his own good, but the feeling of dread was growing. It wasn't *if* there would be an attempt, it was *when*, he thought.

12

San Francisco, California

All truly beautiful women have moments when their beauty begins to crack, when it begins to fail them, when they hover between what was perfection and what will be. There was no question that Helen Law was still an extremely beautiful woman — in that stunning Jackie Bisset way that drops your heart into your lap. That morning, she, in an attempt to keep up with fashion, wore a short black skirt, and she pulled it off. In fact, she was drop-dead desirable, but her beauty had cracked. It was a subtle and tiny crack, but it was perceptible now as she heard the surprising words from her editor.

'Paulson is waiting for you on the first floor,' The *Chronicle's* City editor spoke, looking up from a pile of various dailies on his desk. Helen heard the words *first floor* and grimaced slightly. No serious reporter on the *Chronicle's* staff wanted anything to do with the first floor. The first floor stood for raging *Murdocrity* as one wag put it. The first floor had been turned over to the *Chronicle's* new Sunday magazine called *Image*.

In contrast, the City room on the third floor, where Helen worked, was a holdout of older reporters, the serious, bookish types who enjoyed the *Sturm und Drang* of reporting. The City room had forgiven Helen her wealth once they had gotten to know her. Helen had found the other reporters to be intimidating at first, but now, after five years, she'd embraced their culture, their liberal politics, and their skeptical world-weariness, an attitude that, on her, was alluring. Helen had become one of them without realizing it. She had, over the years, ceased being Alex Law's upper-class wife and had become something new.

'Not *Image*, Scott. Not *Breathless*. Please,' Helen said to her boss Scott Merriwether. *Image* was a running joke in the City room. The *Chronicle*'s board of directors had recently hired a new editor from the *Star* to run *Image* with the express purpose of boosting newspaper sales. The new editor, Steven Paulson, had turned the magazine into a cheap newsprint version of *Vanity Fair*, complete with splashy *au courant* photos of stars, lingerie, Lexus ads, and the predictable celebrity-sniffing articles. Of special interest was who was plugging whom in Hollywood. Paulson had even coined a prose style he referred to as 'breathless.' Reporters in the City room had started calling Paulson *Breathless* behind his back.

'Yes,' Merriwether said. 'He's got you for a week and there's nothing I can do about it. So go. And Helen, please don't harass me about this. I have no choice in the matter. He's got the publisher in on it.'

Merriwether looked up from the *Washington Post* he was skimming. He put down the paper and looked at her. He couldn't stand to look at her because he was in love with her as were half of the men at the paper. He was too old for her and he knew it, and it had killed him for years. He had developed a way of looking at her in a glancing fashion that didn't allow for a steady gaze because he found them physically painful. 'Paulson's got an interview with the President scheduled when he's here next week if that will make you feel any better about it. I recommended you. I thought you would be right,' Merriwether said. Nonplussed, Helen walked further into the office. Merriwether was near retirement and Helen knew that retirement would finish him. She was worried about it and had tried to broach the subject a hundred times but hadn't found the courage yet.

'Scott, I thought we should go out to lunch sometime and talk about you . . . '

147

'Helen.' Merriwether looked up at her. He forced himself to look at her face, at the girlish long hair and the chin that was just right and her athletic legs. He knew that she wanted to be friendly in a way no man wants to be with a woman he desires.

He won't last a week, she thought, looking at him. Merriwether had been a real friend during her years on the paper, and she wanted to protect him from something she didn't think he was prepared for. She'd been meaning to talk to him about it, but she was afraid he would take any suggestions the wrong way. Helen looked at him peevishly. The ashtrays on his desk were overflowing. He was thirty pounds overweight, smoked like a fiend and was too old to be there. But she knew he represented something that would be lost forever when he left.

'Will you have lunch with me?'

'Yeah,' Merriwether said. 'We'll have lunch sometime. Now go downstairs and give Pencil-neck his pound of flesh.'

★ ★ ★

Helen glanced at the clock. It was three-fifteen. The conference room on the first floor was thick with the smell of aftershave and recycled air. The hustle and bustle of the City room was absent from the first floor. Here there was a well-ordered corporate tempo where everyone spoke about big ad budgets and stock options. Half a dozen reporters were in the room. Paulson was telling them how the magazine was going into 'Presidential mode'; two weeks worth of coverage on everything from the President's favorite restaurants in the City to his bigtime friends and contributors in Silicon Valley.

The other reporters in the room, most of them pulled in from other Murdock-style tabloids, didn't seem to give a damn one way or the other what Paulson was saying. What *they* really cared about were the free meals that were the *sine qua non* of restaurant pieces. They all looked horribly disappointed that they would be covering the President instead of the usual easy celebrity stories they were used to. Helen stopped listening and opened the file one of the reporters had handed her when she came in. The file had a prepared set of questions and a typed note for her from Paulson.

Welcome aboard. Hope you are as excited as I am about this.

RP

Helen glanced at the list of questions. They were all the tabloid sort: How far did he jog?

What were his favorite movies? Was it true he and his wife weren't getting along? Helen shut the file and decided that she wouldn't do it. She couldn't feature herself asking the most powerful man in the world if he was getting along with his wife.

★ ★ ★

'Merriwether said I could have you for seven days,' Paulson said. Helen looked up at the editor. Like the first floor, his face was orderly and clean and seemed devoid of anything interesting. The rest of the reporters had left the meeting, but Paulson had asked her to stay. Sartorially, Paulson was trying hard for *The Beltway* look: bow tie, tortoiseshell glasses, a loud print on his suspenders, his hair blow-dried to a stiff perfection, and he had a feed-the-public-what-they-want attitude. He fixed her with an intense look, his lips moist, giving him a slightly predatory look. 'Well!' Paulson said. 'Well? What do you think of the questions?'

'No thanks,' she said.

'What?'

'No thanks.'

'I don't understand.'

'I don't know how to do that kind of interview,' Helen said.

150

'What kind?' Paulson's pinned-up smile collapsed back into his forty-something face.

'This kind,' she said, handing him the file.

'Well, I'm afraid no one else will do,' he said. He gave her a queer look. 'Do you know how many stories I've spiked on your family? I spiked one this morning on your *estranged* husband.'

'My husband?'

'Don't you read the papers, dear?'

'What are you talking about?'

'He's in the *New York Times*,' Paulson said. 'Quite a little story on our local boy. I'm sure his father would love to see it in *Image* this Sunday.'

★ ★ ★

Helen opened up a file Paulson had sent up to her desk. It was a clipping from the *Times*; the story had been filed the day before. The caption read World Bank Official Arrested In Lisbon Shooting. The photo, she thought, didn't do Alex justice. He was much better looking in person, but rougher, as if he'd been in harsh climates and weathered many experiences, so that his face showed them all, like some worn paperback book whose cover told you how many hands had been over it. She missed that face, she decided. The

151

photograph stopped her for a moment. She skimmed the article. The *Times* report described an ex-diplomat, Alex Law, from a well-to-do San Francisco family, who had become an embarrassment to the United States Government. There had been a shooting in Lisbon. The article said Alex was staying at the American Embassy while the Portuguese Government made attempts to have him delivered to the local police for questioning. The Law family, the article said, was listed in the five hundred wealthiest families in the US. It briefly outlined Alex's life: the great wealth, Exeter, Yale, a marriage to the daughter of an Annapolis professor, his career with what the writer called 'the diplomatic services before joining the World Bank.' The reporter speculated that the shooting might have something to do with drug dealing. Helen's phone rang before she could finish. It was Paulson.

'I'll do it,' she said. 'The interview. Thank you for not running this. I'm sure it's not true.'

'You should thank Merriwether,' Paulson said. 'He's the one who talked me out of it.'

Helen opened the file again and looked at the photograph. She remembered the day she'd left him in Lisbon. She'd gone to a baby shower given for her by the CIA wives across from the Embassy at the Hilton Hotel.

Helen had chosen a yellow suit with a short jacket that afternoon. She'd been excited for days. The CIA wives were giving her a baby shower at the Embassy. She'd had her hair done that morning at the Hilton. The party was supposed to have conjured up a little bit of America. The tables had place cards, and the women, all in their twenties, were dressed to the nines, all of them fresh-faced CIA wives with new hairdos and pearls and white pumps. There was a girl named Tilly Kregan who was from Texas and was a little older than the other girls. She'd been in Lisbon over a year and knew the ropes. The other girls treated her like a den mother. It was Tilly who met her at the door of the hotel and took her up to the party.

Had they all known it when she arrived? They had gathered around her and Tilly had introduced the women whom Helen hadn't met before. Tilly made jokes in that broad, sweet Texas drawl — but her fingers had been playing nervously with her necklace. They had eaten little sandwiches and told stories about their brave attempts to make a suburban nest in a foreign country with maids who spoke no English. They were all envious of their husbands, who could escape to the pure white haven of the American Embassy, where it really was a little bit of home right down to the hamburgers served in the cafeteria.

Had there been a conscious decision for them to seat her with her back to the terrace? Hadn't all the fresh faces — mascaraed and lipsticked — looked at the waiter a little too intensely when he went and opened the tall French doors so the young women could enjoy the music from the hotel patio? The music was low-slung jazz, played by musicians who'd learned jazz from American records.

Hadn't Tilly engaged her suddenly — now she could see really how sweet she was — with talk about baby names and how would they choose, and she was sure it was going to be a girl. Texans knew, she'd said. And Helen had touched herself where the child was growing and felt happy and full of life, and thought that even Lisbon, with its revolution in the streets, could be beautiful if you had friends, and she supposed the group of young women around the table were hers. She started to tell Tilly that she wanted a girl very badly, and that a name was not a problem because she was going to name her after her mother. Then Helen heard the voice from the terrace as the music died, as if it had been there all along, Alex's voice just below the music. Why hadn't she heard it before? He had shouted something in English, screw something or other. The voice had sent a readable shock across Tilly's face. Some of the other girls looked at Helen for a moment and then went on talking as if they hadn't heard anything. Remembering it all now, years later, Helen saw again how Tilly kept right on talking too, and then Helen heard the voice again, louder and drunk, but it was Alex's voice down there. She'd known it the first time. Helen had gotten up, thinking that she would wave down to him and let him know by the look on her face that she could endure this place if he could. Maybe she'd been wrong to ask him to leave the agency. She'd decided she would ignore his drinking. Tilly looked at her, and perhaps in her big Texan's way might have thought about doing something, anything, but she didn't. She just smiled when Helen said she recognized her husband's voice and that it sounded like he was having a good time. Tilly had taken her hand for a moment, and then Helen had walked across the hotel room and looked down on the terrace below.

'It doesn't mean anything,' Tilly had said. And then Patsy Nickels had come up behind her, too. She'd followed Helen to the open

155

doors. All three women watched as Alex nuzzled some girl they'd never seen before. 'They all do it,' Tilly said. 'They all do it. Maybe it's part of their work.' Helen had left Alex three days later.

13

Dr. Glad punched one of the radio buttons in the brand new rental car. The radio station was just queuing up one of his favorite songs. A showy grin spread across his face. He glanced at Michael Law, who was sitting next to him. *Treat Her Like a Lady*. 'Nineteen Seventy-One, number 8 on the Billboard charts,' the doctor said to the younger man whom he had just picked up. The car was speeding along Hwy. 101 just south of San Francisco by 3Com park. The doctor glanced at the stadium, surrounded by grayish white banners of fog, like some kind of medieval cathedral.

'Do you know my father?' Michael asked, turning toward the doctor. He'd said very little since Glad had picked him up at the airport. He looked incredibly dewy-faced to Glad. It seemed the kid wasn't old enough to drive much less be trained as a CIA officer.

'I've heard of him,' Glad said. 'He's a legend in the agency. One of our stars, you could say. You must be very proud. Very proud indeed.' They'd never met before, and the doctor had been expecting a carbon copy of Alex, but the son was entirely different: naive and quietly gung ho. *Most terribly naive*, Glad thought, smiling at the kid, studying him from behind an ingratiating smile.

'Yes,' Michael answered after thinking about it. 'I *am* very proud.' Michael Law, full of himself, looked at the doctor. He'd been told he had to go through just one last battery of tests before graduating. There had been so many tests in the CIA's recruitment and training that Michael hadn't thought too much about it. He'd simply done as he was told, which was to meet a Dr. Glad at SFO three days before he was to visit his mother.

'Well, you'll be right up there with him, I'm sure,' Glad said, turning off the highway. 'Right up there with the old man.' They rode a long time again without speaking. As they turned off the highway Glad slapped him on the knee suddenly, startling Michael.

'You know what's wrong with young people today?' Glad said. 'I'll tell you, Michael. I can call you Michael, can't I?' He went on without waiting for an answer. 'They don't have enough fun. They work too hard. Take everything too seriously. All that worrying about safe sex,' Glad said, slapping Michael's knee again. They finally pulled into the driveway of a beautifully maintained house on the Presidio just behind Crissy Field. Glad turned off the engine. 'The tests are going to be somewhat involved,' Glad said. The doctor modulated his voice so that it all sounded reasonable and necessary. 'Shall we get on with it then? Or should we do a couple lines of coke first? Just kidding! See what I mean? You're so serious. Stop it, Michael. You're going to love this. Trust me,' Glad said.

The two of them went into the house. US Army Officers' quarters once, the house had been remodeled and was freshly painted. Glad led him through the living room to the back. There was a young man Michael's age sitting in the kitchen reading a magazine. They nodded to each other. Glad ignored the young man and kept talking to Michael in the same reassuring tone, saying how this would only take a day or two and then Michael could be off to his mother's. Michael dropped his backpack on the kitchen floor and followed Glad into the back of the house. The doctor stopped suddenly in the hallway in front of a closed door and turned to him.

'Now, are you ready?' he said.

'Ready,' Michael said. Glad nodded approvingly and opened the door to the room.

'A lot of people get frightened right away by all this equipment,' Glad said behind him.

'I bet you're not.' Michael eyed the new medical equipment. He could tell that the setup was impromptu. The paint on the walls was too bright; the equipment was too badly arranged, as if it had just been put in an hour ago.

Glad adjusted the glow on his salesman's smile, turning it up several watts, as he walked by Michael, who was still eyeing the equipment. 'Ninety-nine percent of all candidates walk through this, *absolutely walk through it*,' Glad said reassuringly as he studied Michael's face. Glad hurried on, 'What we're going to do is simulate a bout of psychological warfare conducted by one of our enemies to see how you stand up. What you're made of, so to speak. We want to see if you have the glands for intelligence work.' The doctor slapped him on the back. 'Your father went through this, *everyone does*,' Glad said. Glad moved to one of the narrow laboratory porcelain-topped tables and fooled with what looked like a tape recorder, turning it on. He whirled around and faced Michael. Glad seemed to be sucking some kind of power from the room, speeding up slightly and wanting to get on with it. 'Can't be one of us unless you get by me, though,' he added.

★ ★ ★

'What the hell is that?' Michael asked. He nodded toward a cylindrical white tank in the center of the room. Glad turned around and reached for the white lab coat that he'd laid over a chair. He slipped it on. Waiting for an answer, Michael watched Glad's tobacco-stained fingers move over the coat buttons.

'You mean the tank? Sensory deprivation. You've never seen one before?' Glad said, looking at it like you might some old bit of decor. 'Just like a bathtub with a few bells and whistles is all. Well?' Glad said, finishing with the buttons on the lab coat. He pulled at his sleeves once. 'I'm afraid you'll have to strip naked, my friend,' Glad said, finally looking up. Michael caught a whiff of alcohol on Glad's breath.

★   ★   ★

'Your father has . . . ' Glad said casually as he was taking Michael's blood pressure. Michael was naked now, just a towel draped over his thighs. ' . . . quite a record,' Glad said. 'I'm sure he's very proud of you.' Michael didn't answer him.

Michael climbed into the tank. The water was heated and not uncomfortable. 'How long will I be in here?' he asked. His voice was tentative now. He'd lost the resolve he'd

161

brought with him into the room. He'd caught another whiff of alcohol on Glad's breath while Glad was taping the sensors to his chest. The idea that Glad, a doctor, might be drunk had surprised him. It violated his childish trust in white coats and starchy medical authority.

'Oh, that depends,' Glad said, reaching for the control to the lid. The young man Michael had seen in the living room came through the door of the room. Both were looking down on him now. The young man gave Michael the thumbs up. Michael tried to smile as he heard the motor start to draw the tank lid down over him. He realized suddenly that he'd never even questioned what it was *exactly* they were going to do to him. *Everyone has gone through this he says. If I question it, they might wash me out.* He clung to his goal. He wanted to be a CIA officer, part of that famous fraternity. He leaned back into the water and watched the lid retract over him, finally clapping him into total darkness. With great relief, and unexpectedly, he heard the sound of the motor again and the top retracted. Michael wondered if it was over already and was relieved to see Glad's face staring down at him again. *Maybe they were just testing my nerve,* he thought.

'Sorry,' Glad said. 'Almost forgot the shot. Stupid of me.' He was holding a hypodermic syringe. He squeezed the plunger, and Michael watched as a clear liquid dribbled over the tip of the needle, then Glad's big hand took his wet arm. It was then that he felt his heart start to pound with real fear.

★　★　★

The sensory stimulation, Glad imagined, was a shock after three days in the tank. The lid of the tank open now, Michael Law was floating in the water, naked, face up and semiconscious. Glad removed the special goggles and earphones from the kid's head. He put rubber blocks under the body at the hips and shoulders, careful not to pull at the wires that monitored heart rate and body temperature, or the cable that brought in the sound and pictures used to tear at the psyche.

The phone rang. Glad left the tank and went across the room and answered. He could tell from the background noise that it was a car phone connection.

'How's it going?' Wyatt asked.

'Fine. He'll be ready in time.'

'Good,' Wyatt said. 'Don't push him too far. If anything happens to him, I'll kill you myself.'

'He's fine,' Glad said absently. 'You could say he'll be half-baked.'

'I want him to be able to function; his mother is expecting him,' Wyatt said and hung up. Glad put the phone down and lit a cigarette. *Fuck you*, he thought to himself.

The doctor lowered the water level in the tank so that Michael's body settled onto the rubber blocks. Almost immediately, the characteristic sweat began to form on Michael's chest. Glad toweled off his torso carefully. In a few moments, the greasy-looking sweat covered him again. The doctor ran his hand over it. This was the critical stage and any number of things could go wrong.

A moan filled the room, then the gentle sound, a one-sided conversation, and then the howl Glad had heard so many times before. The kid's stomach muscles tightened suddenly, and the sweat and water beaded on Michael's abdomen as if he were being squeezed. The doctor lifted the syringe and tapped it carefully. *I don't want any mistakes. I have to be careful.* He sank the needle into the muscle of the upper arm, which was marked from scores of other shots.

Before Glad closed the lid to the tank, he repositioned the special glasses and earphones and then shifted the rubber blocks out from under the body carefully. He was smoking, and an ash fell from his cigarette into the water. Michael's chest sank back into the tank. Then there was the sound of the motor closing the lid for the last time. Glad went to the equipment at a side table. He turned up the music in the earphones: Nirvana, Smashing Pumpkins, Led Zeppelin, Aerosmith. He checked the screen on the television monitor and saw images passing on the screen in a blur, the same images the kid was seeing in his goggles. Glad spoke into a headset.

'We want you to be someone. We want you to be someone *important*.' Glad leaned forward and pushed the small control in his hand, speaking into the microphone of his headset. The monitor in front of Glad was running with video pictures of extreme sports. The music was Led Zeppelin. Glad watched on the monitor as the image of a snowboarder faded into the eruption of a volcano shot at close range, the flows of lava, miles of burning orange ground, and superimposed over that, a race car cartwheeling into destruction and breaking apart in slow-motion. The sound effects were in full quadraphonic amplification. Glad moved the volume knob up two clicks and heard Led Zeppelin's *Babe I'm Gonna Leave You* and prayed nothing would go wrong. He prayed that he'd gotten the LSD levels just right. His face was sweaty from the heat in the room and the tension.

'Listen to me,' Glad's voice came in through the earphones, excited and demanding. 'You know who you want to kill, don't you?' A picture of the President of the United States came on the screen, and then a gunshot tore through a pumpkin at close range in slow motion, followed by a sickening burst of halo-making matter. 'He's the Enemy,' Glad said.

In the warm floating nightmare, the music was overwhelming and Michael Law felt the force of it destroying him. He'd been literally holding himself together. He'd wrapped his arms around himself. The self, the core of him that he'd clung to for days, was washing away, braking off, cracking open and being smashed, overwhelmed by the hallucinogens and the three days of darkness. The part of his self that remained watched the lava field, orange and black, rolling toward him, burning everything in front if it, an unstoppable force of nature. He started to scream as the lava came at him. He began to claw at the lid and sides of the tank in a desperate attempt to get out of the way of the lava.

'MOM! MOM! OH GOD! MOTHER HELP ME!' Michael felt for the side of the tank and started to pound on it. The blows were useless. 'MOTHER HELP ME! MOTHER!!!'

'This ain't your momma,' Glad said, looking down into the monitor. *This ain't your mother's brainwashing machine.* He laughed at his own joke and hit the CD select button and got Led Zeppelin's *Babe I'm Gonna Leave You* on the CD player and hit replay. Glad turned off the lava just as the flow seemed to engulf the screen. He put a picture of himself on the monitor. *Oh babe, babe, babe, babe, I can hear it calling me back home!* Michael began to sing along with the music. It stopped suddenly.

'Michael, do you hear me?' Glad said. 'When you hear my voice, you're going to do what I say. From now on. All right?'

'Yes. I hear you,' Michael said over the music. 'I'll do what you say. Yes.'

They brought him out that evening to the living room. Michael's eyes were dilated and his skin was a yellowish color from all the drugs. He looked, the young man thought, like a hopeless junkie in the last stages of addiction. 'Well, you can pull him off the bar-be because I think he's done,' Glad said, helping to hold him up.

14

A yellow cab took Alex through the streets of his childhood. They raced through a wide San Francisco intersection only a few miles from the ocean. A stained marble sea god emerged half naked from a fountain. They passed it and entered a quieter neighborhood with wide beautifully landscaped streets. The very large houses of the rich peered from behind walls and gates and fences, when you could see them at all. The streets echoed the special silence of the very rich. A veil of misty wet fog clung to unseen rooftops and hedges. A morning fog was changing moment by moment: diaphanous and shimmering on one street, and, then, like an impenetrable concrete wall by the next.

'Turn here,' Alex said. The cab turned into the driveway of 110 Park Street. A wide ivy-covered gate barred the entrance. They sat for a moment. There was a code box with a phone. The driver asked Alex if he knew the code or if he wanted to get out there. Alex didn't answer. He stared at the heavy-looking ivy-covered gate. The digital numbers on the taxi's meter rolled quickly on as if they were counting down something important. The ivy-covered gate was one of his earliest childhood memories. *The gate to the Law's kingdom,* his grandfather had called it once. It marked the beginnings and endings of so many parts of his life.

★   ★   ★

The cab driver turned and asked again what he should do, and Alex said nothing, pinned down by his memories. A loud honk startled him. Alex turned to see that a new red BMW convertible had pulled up behind them. The gate started to shudder and then retract. The cabby made way for the car behind them as it pulled up alongside. A silver baseball cap pulled down over her long auburn hair, Helen stared at Alex for a moment, then sped on through the gate leaving it open behind her.

'*I got a woman way over town,*' Alex sang.

'What?' the cabby said.

'Ray Charles. Where are you from anyway? Go on, *follow that car.*'

★   ★   ★

They drove down a neat gravel driveway which veered to the right. The narrow road, like a verdant lumen, followed a hedge of rhododendrons towering and dropping over them on their left; in full bloom, the hedge's white blooms were startlingly beautiful, like snow in June. Alex realized now, seeing it all again after being away, what a cloister the place was. The compound had been in the Law family since the eighteen-nineties. There was an other-worldliness about it. The high walls made the separation from the outside world complete, socially and physically hermetic. Perfect, Alex thought. *'I got a woman way over town. She's good to me,'* Alex sang, taking it all in again, watching it all come back. He could smell the June honeysuckle's scent, redolent and sweet, hanging on the cool air as they passed. As they turned the corner, the estate was revealed, spread out like a jewel box that has been kicked over.

★　★　★

Sprawling lawns separated two huge brick Tudor-style houses, side by side. The cab driver whistled. The taxi stopped, finally, a few feet from the BMW, which had pulled up to the front of one of the houses. Alex watched Helen get out of her car. The lines of the Ray Charles song playing in his head, he was hoping he wasn't too late, but knew that

170

he might be. He watched her for a moment as she stood by the car looking into the taxi. She had a look of complete bafflement on her pretty face.

'Alex? *Good god!*' Helen said. He rolled down his window. She slung her gym bag over her shoulder as she spoke and leaned in so she could see him. Alex watched the muscle of her thin arm and the sweaty underarm that had darkened her leotard to a deep gray. There was a flash of a smile. She wore a tight white body suit under her leotard. She had one of those long bodies — all waist and legs. The cabby ogled her furtively.

'Been to the gym? You *are* the trophy wife. They should put you in a magazine,' Alex said from his window. The cabby got out and removed Alex's suitcase from the trunk and sat it on the gravel drive. 'He doesn't know who Ray Charles is,' Alex said, getting out. Helen tried a second smile, this one less girlish and tighter, a kind of warning that she didn't want to be chatted up. Then her expression set as she studied him.

'You look terrible,' she said. He hadn't shaved. Alex paid the driver, fumbling with the change. He picked up his worn Louis Vuitton suitcase. The cab started down the long driveway and disappeared, and they were

171

alone. Helen fought a strange urge to run up the stairs and lock him out.

'Imagine someone who doesn't know who Ray Charles is,' was all he could think of to say.

He was wearing an expensive herringbone overcoat that suited him, buttoned up over a white *Hard Rock Café* T-shirt, a pair of blue jeans, and dirty running shoes. He'd lost weight since she'd seen him last — what was it, two years ago, she thought, for an hour at their son's graduation from Yale.

'You look like Mick Jagger's advance man,' Helen said, deciding that a joke might carry her through. She stopped toying with her car keys. They had built the house behind her right after they were married. Alex hadn't been inside in years. She wondered what had possessed him to come home. Alex turned around and looked across the lawn at the imposing older house he'd grown up in.

'Is *he* here?' Alex asked, his back to her for a moment.

'Yes, of course.'

'How is the old boy?' Alex said, turning back toward her.

'Wonderful,' she said. 'Absolutely wonderful.' His wife, Alex knew, loved his father dearly. It was almost as if he were the son-in-law and she the daughter.

'Good,' he said. 'Glad to hear it. He's a healthy sod.'

'He worries about you. He keeps your car up. Has it washed once a week . . . pays your dues at Cypress. Did you know that? He talks about you like you're away for the weekend. Never a bad word about his boy Alex,' she said.

'Really?'

'Yes. You had better come in, then,' she said suddenly. Helen went up the stairs ahead of him. She was shaking slightly and Alex pretended he didn't notice. She pushed the door open. 'I suppose I should say welcome home,' she said, holding the door for him. The tone of her voice was resigned, the color quickly leaving it. Alex drew himself up and followed her inside. Looking at him, she was suddenly glad he was back after so long, if only because she had to end it, and she decided, seeing him now, that it was better to end it face-to-face, *mano a mano*. Alex's blue eyes shone youthful as he sat the suitcase down on the floor of the foyer.

'No place like home,' he said. 'I'd like to stay, if I could, for a few days, till I find digs. Do you mind?'

'Yes, of course. I'll have a room made up,' she said with a smile that was intended to put him at ease. She put her gym bag down on the marble entry table and tried to keep up with her emotions that were in riot. 'Where have you been? I've lost track.' She strained to put the color back into her voice. She told herself that he deserved something from her because they were friends. But she wasn't sure what it was.

'Listen, Alex, I . . . '

'I was hoping to cohabitate,' Alex said, interrupting her quickly. He'd decided to interrupt her anytime she might speak of divorce. He smiled. 'Still cold in the old foyer.' He took a drink from a flask and then slipped it back into his overcoat. 'You know, like the French Government is cohabitating. We could have great fun. Like the old days. We can go for walks on the beach and maybe I'll go to the gym with you.' Helen broke out into a smile. The thought of Alex in gym clothes was funny. He did a few steps as if he were in Jazzercize class.

'I'm afraid not,' she said, answering his question. 'What happened in Lisbon?'

'Just got back,' Alex said. 'Taking some time off. Think I still have a job, but I'm not really sure.' He avoided her question, which she was used to.

'I read about Lisbon,' she said.

'That? Complete fabrication. Don't let it bother you.'

All the dirt of the *New York Times* article she'd read came back to her. She was ashamed for him suddenly, looking at him, disheveled and still working as a field agent when she remembered what he had been and what he could have been: the youngest station chief in the CIA's history. There had once even been talk about his someday running the agency. He had the pedigree. Agency people had said he had everything it took — the brains, and more importantly, the connections.

The maid appeared and took Alex's suitcase. They stood for a moment and made small talk, standing on the big black and white marble squares of the foyer.

'Do you want to call your father or should I? To let him know you're here.' There was a Marin watercolor on the wall that he remembered buying in San Francisco with Helen right after the wedding. He went up to it and looked at it carefully. The house smelled just the way he remembered: flowers and furniture polish, smells he associated with his mother and that seemed to be part of all Law houses wherever they were. He stole a glance at the big living room and wished for a moment that his mother were alive. Then he turned back toward Helen and smiled an honest smile, not the lying kind he could deliver on cue that was as enthusiastic as it was empty.

'You call him,' Alex said. 'I came home because I'm still in love with you,' he said. The words spilled out of him unexpectedly. She had moved to the mirror and was picking up the phone. She put it down.

'Alex, I sent you the divorce papers. Did you get them?'

'No, I never got them I'm afraid,' he lied. 'Sorry. Big mistake though. Divorce is so permanent. I advise against it. Bad move, divorce.'

'Alex, we haven't lived together in *years*.'

'Till death do us part. That's what I heard. No mention of divorce, was there?' Alex said. Helen picked up the phone again with no intention of using it. She thought if she did, it would give her a moment to compose herself, to get a leg up. It was too sudden seeing him like this. He was pathetic and she hadn't been prepared for that. She'd been prepared for everything, but not his pathos.

'Michael's coming in this afternoon for a visit. I'm supposed to pick him up at the airport at one. Would you like to come with me?' She cradled the phone against her ear.

'Here? You're kidding,' Alex crossed the space between them and reached for her from behind. She smelled his breath and felt the heavy coat press against her. It was awkward and he was too high to make it a smooth pass. She squirmed and turned to face him. She moved her hand up on his chest but didn't try to stop him for some reason. But she didn't kiss back. The whole physical movement died as suddenly as it had started. He could smell her and he could feel her breasts through the leotard. He kept thinking that she would warm to him. He moved to kiss her neck before he realized that she wasn't responding *at all* and that he was being a complete fool and stopped it. They both heard the buzzing in the phone caught between them.

'Sorry. Can't blame a husband for trying. Was that a 'no' to cohabitation then?' he said, moving away.

'You mean you've come home to claim rights, Alex?' The maid went up the stairs and pretended not to hear.

'I still love you. Why don't you try *that* on while I clean up. It feels good to be back at the old homestead,' he said, turning toward the stairs.

She was surprised herself that he wanted her in that way. 'Everything where it was, I bet. The old room. I hope you haven't changed it all. I loved the old stuff . . . continuity,' he said. The rollicking insouciance of his Irish mother was back in his voice now, but there was something fragile about it, she realized. Alex went toward the stairs, embarrassed about the rejected kiss but hiding it.

'Alex?' He turned around three stairs up, hands shoved in his pockets, like a teenager that had been denied the family car. 'Alex, do you want to go to the airport and pick Michael up with me?'

'All right. Why not?' he said. 'I'll take you both to lunch.' He thought of telling her what Wyatt had told him about Michael, but when he looked at her, he didn't have the heart. He knew it was going to kill her and that she would blame him and he would lose her for good.

★ ★ ★

When he'd gone upstairs, Helen picked up the phone and called Alex's father. 'He's here. Alex. He just arrived.' She wasn't sure why she was calling Alex's father first thing, but it made her feel better. Malcolm Law was like a father to her. They had lived close to each other since she'd come back pregnant without Alex years before. Malcolm Law had in many ways filled in for his son. He'd been her children's ersatz father and her confidant.

178

He knew about her affairs and had actually encouraged them. But she knew he'd never given up on her and Alex patching things up.

'Good,' Malcolm said. 'Why don't the three of you come for dinner tonight. Let's say seven o'clock. Is he sober?'

'I think so, more or less. Of course, we'd love to,' she said, and hung up the phone with both hands. Helen picked up her purse and gym bag. She looked up at the stairs where he'd been standing. She decided to sleep with him, as a way of saying good-by. She set her mind to it the way women can when they are evening up the cosmic order. *One last time,* she thought, going up the stairs.

★ ★ ★

He was still attractive, she thought, looking at him. Helen was sitting up in the bed when he came out of the shower. Alex had a drink in his hand. He was naked except for a big white towel around his narrow waist. She looked at his body while he rubbed his hair with another towel. She couldn't remember the last time they'd slept together. He didn't notice her at first, the room was huge and she hadn't made a sound. She had her knees up in the bed. He stopped moving the towel over his hair when he saw her. 'If you say anything, it will spoil it,' she said. Alex put the drink down on the end of a huge Biedermeier dresser and came across the room. He was still wet when he climbed into bed. Helen could feel the length of his wet body. He kissed her and, this time, she kissed him back.

★　★　★

'Trouble is, I'm still in love with you,' Alex said as he threw the curtains open. It was bright outside. The sun ripped apart the last of the fog.

'No you're not,' she said. 'You wanted to sleep with me, that's all.'

'And you took one look at me and couldn't resist.' Alex looked across the room down at her body. He couldn't help comparing it to the girls he'd been screwing in London. Helen was prettier and bigger, more womanly. She hadn't really changed, nor had her lovemaking. She had always been passionate and had appetites that seemed to belong to someone else because she was so undemanding outside of the bedroom. She pulled the pillow up behind her. Her exercise regimen showed in her straight shoulders and the cup of her breasts.

'Alex, I want a divorce. I haven't changed my mind.'

'You don't love Wyatt,' he said. He pulled the window open. *No more drinking today*, he said to himself.

'How do you know that?'

'I just know,' he said. 'Part of my training.' They were quiet for a moment. He felt the cold burning air rush his face. He crossed the room and sat on the edge of the bed.

'This has nothing to do with Wyatt. I want this for myself. If you love me, you'll do this, Alex. I know you care about me. I know we care about each other. But I can't *do* this anymore. I don't want to, not *this*,' she laughed. 'You know what I mean.'

'I would like to give up drinking,' Alex said. He got up from the bed again and went back to the open window. He looked down on the garden and the heart-shaped box hedge they'd put in when they'd built the place. Inside the heart the gardeners had planted white and yellow freesias, the last colors of a dying spring. 'Do you think I can?' It was as if he hadn't heard anything she'd said.

'Of course you can, if you really want to.' He turned around and looked at her with a sadness tinged by something she didn't understand. It was more than the divorce. It was something else, something worse, that he was nursing.

'I'd like to change. I thought you might

181

want to help me. I think you are the only person who can,' he said. He picked the towel off the floor and slipped it around his waist. He had used a tone of voice she'd never heard before, and it surprised her; a beaten tone. It was the tone of a man who had lost his way in the world. She remembered the maze at Hampton Court when they were on their honeymoon and how they'd laughed at everyone who couldn't find their way out.

'I can't help you anymore,' she said. She was sorry the moment she said it.

'What if I ask you to? What if I *need* you?' he said. 'You're the only person who knows me, really knows me. I need you right now.'

'I think it might be too late for that, my dear.' Helen threw the covers off the bed and slid out. 'Will you give me a divorce? Please, Alex.' He wanted so much to tell her about the danger the family was in, what they'd done to Butch and Patsy in Mexico and that he was frightened and up against it, but of course he couldn't. He was disgusted with himself and sorry for what he *hadn't* done in his life. He thought that if he could confess the really bad things to her, he might be able to put them behind him and go on somehow.

'You see, it's strange because you're one of us. I mean because your father was in the *game*, because you grew up with my kind,

182

and because you're my wife. I can trust you. Don't you see? I can't talk to *outsiders*,' he said, facing the window. 'Outsiders can't understand my kind.' She was putting on her robe. He'd finished the drink, but she could see he was cold sober now. All the affectation in his voice was gone. He was like a man who'd gone to his bank manager and been turned down for a loan, surprised that his credit was exhausted.

'What are you saying, Alex?'

'Can we still be *friends* at least?' he said. 'I need a friend right now.'

'Yes, of course.' She put on a black silk robe as she spoke. 'I can help you stop drinking. If you tell me how, I'll try. I promise, but I want the divorce. You can stay here as long as you like, but I want a divorce.'

'All right,' he said. He knew when he said it that the only chance he had for redemption had vanished. She hadn't understood how close he was to falling apart. *Love was part of it*. He wanted her to love him the way they had loved before, that was part of the cure. He closed his eyes for a moment and realized that he would never love anyone again, that what had been had died. There was no going back now. He was officially lost. He would be Alex the bastard CIA man, Alex the professional liar, Alex the foppish drunk for

183

the rest of his life. He was drowning right in front of the lifeguard. 'Did you ever get those cabbage roses I sent once from Kew Gardens?' he said, looking out at the garden. He heard the door close to the bathroom. She hadn't heard him. He had the strangest desire to cry but couldn't. He tried to remember the last time he'd cried. It had been that first night at military school when he was only eight and they had turned off the lights, leaving him completely alone. 'Can you imagine anyone not knowing who Ray Charles is?' he said into the empty room instead.

15

In his youth, Alex's father, Malcolm Law, had been compared to Gary Cooper. He had the same open all-American face. It was a dangerous face to give to such a rich man. Malcolm was on the cusp of old age and hated it, because he had things he wanted to do before he died and because he missed the adulation and his former prowess. He had been accustomed to defeating his enemies. This enemy, time, the Great Destroyer as the Hindus called it, he knew would beat him. He got up from the remains of his lunch and went to the back of the dining room to look out the window. The maid had told him *sotto voce* that Alex had come to get his car. Malcolm wanted to see his son and Helen together. He'd wanted to see that for years now. The black Jaguar he'd kept like new all these years pulled out from the garage, Alex behind the wheel. The elegant car, an XKE, rolled into mid-driveway and stopped. Helen came out of their house and got in. Malcolm watched them drive off to pick up his grandson. The dining room he stood in seemed especially empty once the car had gone. He went back to the head of the long table and thumbed through the *Barron's* he'd been reading. He picked it up and tucked it under his arm, unsure of how to manage his son. He wanted to see him settled before he died but doubted he would.

He ran his finger around a corner of the table with every intention of leaving the room and going upstairs. But he didn't. He stroked the corner again. The smooth textures of wax and wood were a kind of connection with his past.

The table brought back memories of Alex's mother. She had bought the table in the Fifties. Malcolm moved back and tried to remember the style. 'French Empire,' was it? He couldn't remember. He only remembered that it had cost a small fortune and they'd had a tiff about it. Maria would have known the provenance of the table, but she was dead, and a lot of the details of their life together had died with her.

Maria had been the perfect society wife. High style had been expected of them because he was the President of Western Trust Company, and that high style had been important for a spy as well. Maria — an O'Halahan before he'd married her in Guatemala City in 1947 — had known about such things instinctively. He really had been no good at idle small talk and the bonhomie essential for entertaining, beyond entering the living room dressed to the nines and mixing the drinks while Maria commanded the battery of servants and produced a dinner party. At just the right moment, his wife would appear in the living room as if by magic, thin, tall, red-haired, dressed beautifully, always ready for anything, including hard-boiled dowagers and their crusty, very rich husbands who might be persuaded to deposit large amounts of money in her husband's bank. Maria had known all about his being a spy. She had always been proud of him because of what she knew he'd done for his country and against Fidel Castro.

Why was he remembering all those little things about Maria now? Pins she had worn in her hair. The way she would hold Alex by his pudgy wrist when he was a little boy. The white gloves she wore that were in style when they were married. The rooms where they had made love. The little gulps of air she would take. Malcolm held his cup of lukewarm coffee in front of him.

Maria's people were rich. They owned half of Guatemala after having once been poor in Ireland. She was a doctor's daughter. Malcolm had needed a woman with social graces and that special energy required in society to make a dinner party *flow*, as she used to say. She was an alchemist at seating. Never a mistake — dowager here, Lieutenant Colonel there, foreigner (if not too foreign) next to the English banker so that the English banker could drum something into the poor foreigner's head. The English were forever trying to drum something into one and call it pleasant conversation. Once, he remembered, how a banker went on and on about the Suez, and about Nasser being a 'Nancy boy' in secret. Malcolm could still hear the man spouting off in that high Tory voice about 'the importance of English continuity.' Maria placed wives so they could make eye contact with their husbands because she said that eye contact was necessary for *flow*.

Malcolm shook his head and ran his long fingers again over the waxy table. *Women are different*, he said to himself out loud. *They have more brains*. He'd never told her he'd been a CIA officer. She'd worked it out for herself. She'd asked him point blank once in the kitchen of their flat in London after one of his many trips to West Germany.

'Are you some kind of spy, Malcolm?' Point blank. And he had lied, but so obviously she never had to ask him again.

★　★　★

At seven o'clock, Alex and his son, wearing dark suits, and Helen, in a lime green evening dress, trooped across the lawn that separated the two houses. As they walked, Alex put his arm around his son's shoulder. Twice now, he'd tried to use their old code as a way of checking in on him, but Michael hadn't responded. He seemed distant and preoccupied. Alex knew then that there was something wrong. He decided it was probably the stress of being at the Farm. The expression on his son's face was odd and vacant, so different from when they'd met in Spain only a few weeks before.

Helen broke in between them and put her arms around both of them. She'd been happy all afternoon, like in the old days. Alex had them stop in front of the fountain in the middle of the garden. It was a beautiful evening, the air redolent with honeysuckle.

'I remember when your grandmother bought this,' Alex said, looking at the fountain. He looked at them both. Helen looked beautiful, and he fantasized for a moment that they were a real family and not what they'd become, a collection of intimate strangers.

'She bought it in Venice, didn't she?' Helen said.

'Yes, she had it shipped over. I remember my father asked her who was going to pay for it. It was a standing joke between the two of them.' Michael bent down and turned on the water, remembering where the valve was. They watched the water flow down the white marble.

'Ah . . . he knows the secret places,' Alex said. They watched the water pour out of the mouth of a Florentine angel with dark spots on its marble body. Alex stole a glance at his son. There was something wrong with him but he couldn't say what. He tried smiling at him. An automatic smile appeared on Michael's face and then disappeared as he turned to look at the fountain. They'd gotten their hooks into him and changed him already, Alex thought.

'Well, I think we should go,' Helen said, taking them both up again.

'Yes, of course, we don't want to be late for the reunion,' Alex said. They walked the rest of the way in silence.

★   ★   ★

'Of course, if you'd rather relax a few weeks, go ahead,' Malcolm said. The subject being discussed was Alex's taking charge of the bank. The four of them were all in the dining room having coffee. The French doors had been opened and they could see the fountain in the moonlight and hear the play of the water.

Alex got up and left the room for a moment. He went out to the living room and poured himself another brandy. He wanted to be alone. He walked into the familiar living room and up to a Sargent painting of Florence and stood for a moment, contemplating the strange expression on his son's face.

'I don't think I'm cut out for it,' Alex said, returning to the table and interrupting their conversation. 'All that money to worry about — depositors, old ladies in at five percent. I suppose I'd have to give away things: is it coffee mugs or coffee makers? Or is it toasters, now? Anyway, I'm not to be trusted. A man who drinks his weight in Armagnac once a week. I hardly think I'm the type you would want at the shareholders' meetings.' The conversation moved on after a moment of silence. They were all pretending not to notice that he'd crossed the line with his drinking. Their conspiracy made him angry.

'And foreign service training, is it rough?' Alex asked, interrupting when it seemed Michael's lies had gotten as thick as they could get about his days spent learning foreign etiquette. Father and son looked at each other across the table. Michael's hair was very short. A military brush cut had replaced the long blond hair he'd worn in

Spain. It was another signature of the CIA's academy. They looked at each other, not like father and son, but like strangers. Michael was appraising him, weighing the question for its meaning.

'Nothing I can't handle,' Michael said dryly.

★　★　★

After Helen and Michael had gone home, Alex entered his father's library. 'How about a drink?' Alex said.

'It's late, Alex,' Malcolm looked up from the book he was reading at his desk, surprised to see his son was still there.

'Is it?' Alex said. 'I thought we had time for a nightcap.' There was an anger in his voice that he tried to control. The light of a brass desk lamp colored his father's face, making it look waxy and old, like one of Reuben's rich old burghers. There were business papers and spreadsheets from the bank on a massive cherrywood desk. 'Your damn desk is as big as Suharto's,' Alex said.

'What's wrong?' Malcolm said.

'Nothing. I thought we'd have a chat, that's all . . . Now that I'm back home,' Alex said. He looked around the room he remembered so well. It hadn't changed in twenty-five years. It had that sense of sanctum sanctorum and authority that had so impressed him as a boy. This room was the masculine center of the house, all the other rooms mere adjuncts to this headquarters. Alex looked at the red English library couch where he'd sat as a boy and received his 'talking-tos.' It was where he'd been told he was being sent off to military school.

His father offered him a cigar and he took it. Alex studied the wall where there was a gallery of family photographs going back to his grandfather's time, hung in a kind of linear family history. He moved from photograph to photograph, stopping in front of his own wedding picture. There was a photograph of his father and mother and Helen and himself in the garden, taken the day they were married in June, the men dressed in morning suits, the flowers in riot behind them. 'Do you remember the wedding?' Alex said, turning and clipping the end of the cigar with the cutter his father had pushed across the desk.

'Of course I do. Everyone said you two were the most beautiful couple in San Francisco. I think they were right.' Alex contemplated the photograph. He had forgotten how beautiful they'd been once.

'Helen was so damn young! Do you think

she had any idea about us?'

'I doubt it,' Malcolm said.

'I don't even think she really knew how rich we were. Not at first. I don't think she cared,' Alex said, lighting up.

'No, I suppose not,' Malcolm said. Alex heard the sound a clipper makes, like scissors.

'People go to clubs to smoke cigars now. It's become very fashionable. The middle classes want to be like us,' Alex said, dropping onto the couch.

'I'm afraid it takes more than a cigar,' his father said. Alex smiled at his father's joke. There was a big old-fashioned black onyx lighter on the desk that Alex remembered from when he was a kid. He picked it up and lit his father's cigar for him. He walked over to a wall of books, mostly on finance. His father had one of the country's premier business book collections. It was a front, like a lot of his father's life. In fact, Alex knew his father understood very little about banking. It had always been a cover for his real interest, which had been spying. If the bank had prospered, it was because Alex's grandfather had hired good people to run it. Most of them had been pensioned off now, and he knew Malcolm was worried about the future.

'You don't give a shit about banking, do you,' Alex said. His father looked at him carefully. He knew he had been drinking, but he also knew that Alex, drunk or sober, was someone you didn't want to underestimate or patronize. It was always best to answer the question.

'That's not true. I do care. Especially since I took over. It's true I had a lot to learn, but I've done the best I could. Sometimes it seems to run itself,' he said. Alex returned to the leather couch under the family photos. 'What you cared about was the agency,' Alex said.

'Alex, what's *wrong* for god sakes?'

'Why was it so important to you that I go into the CIA?' Alex put the cigar into his mouth.

'Because I thought you'd be good at it,' Malcolm said.

'Did you?'

'Of course. And you were even better at it than I was. I knew that early on. You understand people,' his father said. 'That's a talent.'

'It ruined my life, you know,' Alex said. 'I had to do things that I'm not very proud of. Things that don't stand the light of day.'

'Alex, you helped win the Cold War, for God's sake. Don't you realize that? We both did.'

'But *how* did we win it? With the Nazis you

brought back here to build atom bombs?'

'That was in the coldest of the cold days of the war. The hydrogen bomb cost a few moral dollars. That's exactly my point: we used monsters to fight monsters. And we were right to do it. I'd do it again tomorrow. But I was blind not to see that things were changing.' His father leaned back in his chair. 'I regret now that I pushed you into it,' his father said. He put the cigar down and leaned forward in his desk chair. 'I admit there were too many dictators we foisted on people, especially later during your watch.'

'It's a little late now, isn't it?' Alex said. 'I mean for the people who had to live with Papa Doc and the like. What do we tell them?'

'Tell them we kept them out of a gulag. I'm sorry. The fight was dirty, but some are.' His son looked at him. Age was softening everything about his father except his politics.

'Did you know about Michael? And don't dare lie to me,' Alex said. His father put down the cigar and got up. He'd been waiting for the question since Alex arrived.

'How did you know?'

'I just know that's all.'

'I tried to stop him, but he begged me. He sat right there where you're sitting now and he begged me, Alex! I didn't know what to do. I tried to reason with him, but he begged me to make calls for him. They weren't going to take him because of . . . '

'Because of me.'

'Yes, because of you. I relented. I made the calls for him.'

'Did you?'

'Yes. I'm sorry. I should have spoken to you first. I regret it now. But, Alex, if you would have heard him. He'd wanted, he said, his whole life to follow our example. To be what his father and grandfather had been. What was I *supposed* to say to him?'

'No, of course.'

'As soon as I'd done it, I knew it had been the wrong thing to do,' Malcolm said.

'I want him out before he graduates. If we wait it'll be harder. They don't have to explain to a recruit why he's washed out. That way he'll never know we're responsible. You won't have to take the blame. No one will. It will be our secret,' Alex said.

'All right. I'll make the necessary call in the morning,' Malcolm said. He picked the cigar up from the smokeless ashtray and sat down again. 'Alex, I want to start over. Can we do that? You and I, fresh and clean.'

'That's a beautiful thought,' Alex said, getting up. There was a ship's decanter on a tray with sherry and port bottles on a butler's table. 'All right, why not, let's try,' Alex said. He poured his father a drink. 'Michael probably thinks it's like a bloody Clancy novel,' Alex said. 'Thinks he's going to be like Harrison Ford.' Alex handed his father a drink. 'Well, I thought I was going to be like James Bond — serves me right. Thanks for sending the plane for Butch,' Alex said.

'Are you going to tell me what's going on?' Malcolm said.

'Not now . . . ' Alex looked at his father very deliberately. 'There's an account at the bank. I want you to find out whose name it's under.' Alex leaned over and wrote a number down and slid it across his father's desk.

16

Alex climbed out of the pool into the cold morning air feeling slightly sick to his stomach. It was foggy and cold, but he didn't feel it. He'd decided he would confront Michael, and that had gotten him started. He'd brought a bottle of vodka down to the pool with him first thing in the morning, which had shocked one of the gardeners who'd known him since he was a boy. The man had stood on the other side of the gate and watched him disapprovingly.

Or do I just need an excuse, Alex wondered, grabbing a towel from the chair he'd dropped it on. The water running off him stained the pink concrete surrounding the pool. *Why am I afraid to confront him*, he wondered, *and why do I need a drink to do it?* There was an old-fashioned tennis court across from the pool and cabana. Alex dried himself off and looked out across the hedge and path at the green-painted asphalt deck and white lines of the tennis court. He waved to the gardener and gave him a thumbs up.

There was a forlorn sadness to the scene, a feeling of abandonment. Alex stared at the empty tennis court and remembered the way it had been once. The net looked ancient and sagged in the center. No one played anymore, so there was no reason for new equipment. He turned and walked into the cabana.

Inside the cabana, nothing had changed — the red tiled floor, the watercolors from Haiti he'd sent his parents years before, the old-fashioned bathing trunks hung up on pegs. The room was a snapshot of his family's past. The Sixties, he decided, was the era when the cabana and the tennis court had been in full swing. Alex took the cell phone he'd brought down with him and dialed the house.

'I'm sorry, sir, but your son said that he was having breakfast with his mother,' the maid said. Alex had gone into Michael's room first thing that morning and asked Michael to meet him in the cabana for breakfast. Michael, half asleep, had agreed. Alex had planned on telling him the truth: that he was going to have him washed out of the Farm.

'I see,' Alex said. Alex finished his drink and sat it down on one of the wicker tables. 'Is he there now?'

'He's with Mrs. Law, sir. They're having breakfast right now.' The maid asked Alex if he still wanted breakfast sent down to the cabana; he hung up on her. Anger spread over him like some kind of sickness. He'd been stood up. The two drinks he'd downed were just enough so that he was high and energetic.

He dressed in the cabana and then went up to his father's house where he took a pistol from the gun case they kept in the library. He crossed the lawn between the two houses, not sure what he intended to do exactly. He tucked the pistol in his belt and entered Helen's house. He could hear their cheerful voices in the breakfast room where they were having fun. Helen's voice was sparkling. He'd been excluded from their love and he resented it. He'd kill their good time as soon as he stepped into the room, he thought.

At one point, he heard Helen laugh. *They certainly don't want to talk to* me, he thought.

The breakfast room was one of the prettiest rooms in the house. Comfortable and well lit by a bank of windows that overlooked the rose garden, the wallpaper a canary yellow, it was intimate and homey in a way the other rooms weren't. Haggard and defeated, Alex leaned against the door, out of place and unnoticed at first because they were doing the crossword together. Michael and Helen stopped and both looked up at him. Helen had her arm around her son's shoulder. They looked, he thought oddly, like lovers. He was jealous of them and their intimacy shouted at him. Their plates had been cleared away, and there was just coffee and a sterling toast rack and little silver pots of jam left on the table. Michael was dressed in a T-shirt and hadn't shaved off his nascent blond beard.

'Alex? I wondered where you'd gone off to. Gloria said she saw you in the *pool*,' Helen said. His son's eyes changed when he saw him. The warmth went out of them, and they were suddenly cold.

'You're drunk,' Michael said. His mother looked at Michael and then at Alex. Neither one of them had noticed the pistol yet.

'Michael . . . don't talk like that,' Helen said as she reached over and touched his hand. She saw the gun in Alex's hand, finally, and froze.

'He's drunk and it's ten in the morning,' Michael said.

'No one has asked me to sit down,' Alex said. He pushed himself off the door and came to the table and sat down heavily across from them. The wrought iron chair made a loud sound as he dragged it. He brought the pistol out and laid it on the table. Everyone took on a frozen quality then, as if they'd all been blasted with cold water. Helen looked at him.

'Sorry to break up the party. And I don't want to be a wet blanket, but I thought it was time for a family discussion. You know, like other families have, sitting around the old kitchen table . . . ' He hit the table with his open palm. The toast fell from the silver rack and the cups rattled. 'Well, this is my kitchen table, isn't it? Let's have a family pow-wow.'

'Alex, put the gun away,' Helen said. Michael reached over and grabbed for the pistol. Alex backhanded him and sent him into his chair. The loud powerful slap caught Michael in the nose. Michael, his nose beginning to bleed, looked at his father, stunned.

'Now, let's get something straight, you and I,' Alex said. 'You have made a mistake — a very big mistake. And I'm here to tell you why,' he said. Alex put the pistol in his lap so it couldn't be grabbed.

'You're mad!' Helen said. 'Michael, call the police. *Jesus, Alex.*'

'Tell your mother what you've done. Go ahead and tell her the fucking truth. Or don't you want your mother to know what it is you plan to do with that fancy education we bought you.'

'I don't know what you're talking about,' Michael said.

'You don't? I think you do. Go ahead and tell her. I think she would like to hear it from you. Go ahead and tell your mother the truth for once.'

Michael picked up a napkin and pressed his nose where his father had slapped him and sniffed. Blood was trickling onto his white T-shirt.

'I've joined the CIA,' Michael said.

'Is that true, Michael?' Helen asked.

'Yes, it's true,' he said.

'You see, our son has seen Harrison Ford on the big screen and he wants to help old dictators cross the street at night. He wants to save women and children from those terrible terrorists in the hills,' Alex said.

'Alex, shut up for god sakes . . . ' Helen turned to Michael. 'It's not right for you, my love. Look what it's done to *him*.'

'He's crazy and I'm not,' Michael said, nodding toward his father.

'Oh. I *am* crazy. That's the first thing you've said that makes any sense,' Alex said. 'I'll have a cup of coffee, Helen.' Alex took the pistol and placed it on the table again. He watched their faces.

'Alex, give me the gun,' she said as she reached for the pistol. Alex shook his head.

'I'll have a cup of coffee.' He poured a cup of coffee from the porcelain pot into his wife's cup and dragged it over in front of him. 'And what is it you think you are going to accomplish?' Alex said. 'Why don't you tell your old mom and dad that?'

'Mom, it's a family tradition. You know that,' Michael said. He turned to her. 'I didn't want to upset you.'

'He doesn't give a *damn* about how you feel . . . ' Alex said. 'He wants to be Harrison Ford. Do you think Mr. Ford ever pushed a woman out of a helicopter because she wouldn't talk to him?' His son looked at him for the first time, eye to eye. Michael's nose was bleeding through the napkin. '*Do you?* They left that part out of the movie. Left it on the cutting room floor, didn't they. Oh, she begged me not to, but, you see, she was the enemy. Think you're up to *that*, old boy? Will you come home and brag to your mother how you witnessed someone's testicles shoved into their mouth on orders from men who will have forgotten it by lunchtime?'

'*Stop it, Alex. Stop it!*' Helen said.

'Well, I just want to know what parts he plans on dressing up for?! The close up, when someone begs you not to leave them in jail and you know something unspeakable might happen to them? Or the shot, when you leave your hotel room with a beautiful girl on your arm — but she happens to be a ten-dollar whore. I want to know how you see the ending? Do you feature medals pinned on your chest by the President? I think that's how they do it in the movies — medals and yellow ribbons when you've put the world right as rain. The music wells up. Everyone goes home. You don't have a fucking clue what you've gotten yourself into. You're just a kid with a hot need to use one of these. That's what you want, isn't it. You want to shoot someone, carouse with Navy seals, go on midnight operations . . . a little bitch to sing you the *La Vie En Rose* when you get back all bloody and victorious.'

'Alex, you're drunk. Give me the gun,' Helen said. Alex stood up abruptly, turning over his coffee, and pointed the pistol at Michael, both hands on it, his eyes wide, spittle in the corners of his mouth. He heard Helen screaming.

'You want this one? I think he should see it down the barrel the way they will. Guns don't come with rule books or a copy of the Geneva Convention. You won't find human rights scribbled on the barrel. Do you notice anything written on it? Do you!? NO! It only says Smith and Wesson. And they don't give a *damn* what you do,' Alex said. 'You see, the bad guys aren't going to turn out to be actors. They'll be ordinary men and women who hate you for dropping out of the fucking sky and turning their country into a bloody psycho ward.'

'He's crazy!' Michael said. 'Look at him!'

'Am I?' Alex was sneering at him now, contemptuous and unafraid. 'I was your age when I started. No, younger, I think.' Alex pointed the pistol down, leaning on the barrel, both hands still wrapped around it. 'Do you remember, Helen?' Helen shook her head, on the verge of hysteria. 'Yes, I was twenty-three, I think. I was stupid like you. I thought I was going to save the world for democracy. What do they tell you now? I'd like to know. What is it they fill your head with?' Alex said. He took one hand and wiped his mouth.

'Alex, this isn't fair. You're scaring us. This is your *son!*'

'Not fair? Imagine how other people are going to be scared of him when he flies into, let's say, pick a place, go ahead: Haiti, Mexico, the Congo. Don't you think they will be frightened of the young American who seems to have the say over life and death? But then, *you* never came with me to the prisons, dear. You were always at the bridge games and around the pools. I'm afraid that's not quite the same. Perhaps if you'd seen someone in their cell, shitting in their pants, with the doctors and the torturers getting their toys out, maybe then you'd understand,' Alex said. 'You haven't said what they tell you at that school, Michael?! What do Professors Smith and Wesson say now to justify it all?'

'They tell you that America is the leader of the free world. And we want to keep it that way,' Michael said. 'Now I'm going to get up and I'm going to call the police, mother. He isn't going to shoot me. He's drunk, that's all,' Michael said.

'You see? He's already showing initiative. They'll like that.' Alex reached over the table and hit him again. This time he fell out of the chair onto the floor. Alex pointed the gun at him. He pulled the hammer back and put it against his son's cheek. He heard Helen scream. He saw the pot of coffee turn over and the black liquid soak into the white blood-spotted tablecloth. He heard Helen scream again as he felt his finger on the trigger and looked down at his son's face, the blood squirting out of his nose now. He saw the look of fear in Michael's eyes that Alex had seen a hundred times in a hundred young men.

'Sit down or I'll shoot you, so help me God, I will,' Alex said. The boy stood up, pulling at he tablecloth to wipe his nose.

'*God. Please, Alex. Put down the gun!*' Helen begged.

'How many people have you killed at close range, boy? I've killed — not counting all the people I've thrown out of helicopters — four at close range. One was a kid who was about fourteen. I've lost the feel for things. I don't let myself hesitate. I just pull the trigger,' Alex said.

'Sit down, Michael,' Helen said. '*Oh God, Michael, do what he says.*'

'Mother, he isn't going to shoot . . . '

'I said sit down! For god's sake, can't you see he's mad? Is this about *me*, Alex? Is that what this is about?' she said. 'God, it *is*, isn't it! This is about us. You're the classic asshole father who's going to kill us because we won't do what he wants,' she said. 'Your morality is bullshit. This isn't about him. This is about *me*, isn't it? Shoot *me*, then. I'm the one who's leaving you, not the boy, for Christ's sake.'

Alex blinked. He had the forty-five out hovering over the coffee pot. 'Just a family discussion around the old kitchen table,' Alex said, catching his breath and focusing on his son. He held the gun out in front of him. Sweat fell into his eyes and stained his shirt under the arms.

'Alex, give me the gun,' Malcolm said. His father walked toward him wearing a gray robe. The maid had caught him in the driveway. He held his hand out. His father was not at all frightened by him. Alex put the gun to his head and pulled the trigger. The hammer fell and nothing happened. The sound of the trigger made Helen scream.

'Empty. You see, it was only what we used to call dry-fire training,' Alex said. He started to laugh. Malcolm lifted the gun out of his hand and slipped it into his pocket. 'Just in time. The original gangster,' Alex said. In a beaten tone of voice, Alex asked for cream for his coffee as if nothing had happened; then he blacked out.

★   ★   ★

That afternoon the maid said Helen was in the sun room. Alex remembered, on his way down the hall, that the sun room had been in *Architectural Digest* once, right after he and Helen had been married. The magazine had referred to Helen as the wife of a very successful banker, a beautiful lie. They had been pictured (Helen in a simple tennis dress that showed off her good legs) sitting relaxed with their arms around one another, a handsome young couple who, in a week,

210

would be off for an 'adventure in Europe,' the magazine reported in extravagant prose.

Alex walked into the bright sun-lit room. He felt guilty about what had happened and was unsure if Helen would even speak to him now. It was a beautiful afternoon and it seemed somehow that she would. He was relieved to see she was alone, a view of the acre of garden behind her through big windows at her back. She'd called in sick and was wearing the white silk robe she'd worn in the morning when he'd made a fool of himself. Alex knocked on the door-jamb, afraid and, oddly, not afraid. He suddenly felt like asking her to marry him again, as if by doing so he could wipe away everything that had happened. It was as if the violent drunken interlude had cleared his head and now he could see things the way they should be. *That's what I came back for*, he thought, *to get her back*. It was all perfectly clear to him now, watching her with her afternoon paper spread out in front of her. A bowl of orange-colored primroses sat on the table, still-life perfect. His father had told him Michael had gone back to Washington and that she would be alone and he should 'patch things up,' as he'd put it. Alex couldn't remember much of what he'd done, only bits of it. He remembered the slap. He remembered the pistol's snapping emptily in his hand. He only knew for sure what his father had told him, and it had sounded stupid and juvenile, but he wasn't sorry. *It had to be done. I'm only sorry for the way I did it.*

'I should be mad at you. I should hate you,' Helen said looking up. 'But why is it I feel you did it for me?' she said. 'Sit down, Alex, and stop looking at me like that. You look awful. I knew you were coming. Malcolm called and begged me to listen to you.' Alex knew, sitting down, that she understood something about him no one else did, some important, key thing. Sometimes when he was drunk, he thought he knew what it was, but in the morning it was always gone. He looked at her for a moment in the sunlight and realized for the first time that they meant something to each other that had nothing to do with their children or their marriage or even sex. It was the deepest possible man-woman exchange. He poured coffee for himself, walking on egg shells. The afternoon sun began to work over the room in earnest. 'How about I promise to never point a gun at anyone in my family again,' he said finally.

She smiled and shook her head. 'You're impossible, you know that.' He knew her well enough to know she had forgiven him for his ridiculous scene with the pistol.

'I was going to mail this to you.' She handed him a large envelope. Alex took it. He surmised from the size of the package that they were another set of divorce papers. He put them down in front of him. They began to talk. Helen, he thought, finally seemed relaxed around him. They talked about Michael at first. They agreed that Helen was going to have to accept that he was grown now. The more they talked, the more Alex forgot everything that had happened in the last two days. They talked about the old days, easily, and laughed once or twice about the way they'd been when they'd first met. All the time he was thinking about the power she had over him. *I love you,* he thought.

'Alex, I want to be friends. Can we be? I don't think I have many,' she said, looking up at him. He knew the moment she gave him the envelope that she was right to do it, and that it was over. After all those years, it was going to end now.

'Of course we can.' He took the gold lighter out of his pocket and lit a cigarette, relieved the end had finally come. He'd been dreading this moment for so long. 'Is it Wyatt? Are you going to marry him?' Alex asked, putting the lighter down carefully.

'*Heavens,* no . . . ' she said. He felt

suddenly better. 'You knew about Wyatt, did you?' she asked. Alex nodded.

'Then, by all means, let's get a divorce,' he said. They broke out laughing. Alex got up and kissed her on the cheek. He felt sad that it had all gone wrong back then, but there was nothing anyone could do about it now.

'Alex, did you mean it, about being friends? Can we be?'

'Yes. I meant it. And I'm sorry about yesterday. The way I went about it was all wrong,' he said, looking at her. Then he looked around the room that he had always liked so well and wanted to tell her again that he was sorry for all his unkindness in the past. He felt suddenly very sad that whatever she knew about him would never be articulated. 'Got to go.' He picked up the divorce papers and tried to smile. 'Why did we cheat on each other? I don't even remember now,' he said. 'I don't even remember her name . . . or care. It was all so very stupid.'

'We did it to get back at each other. We were young. Young people do stupid things. Where are you going?' she said, smiling at him. He was surprised she cared enough to ask.

'That's a secret,' he said. Helen smiled again because she thought he was joking, and because it was so in keeping with their relationship.

'I'm leaving you an envelope, too. If something goes wrong . . . If you need to get hold of me, it tells you how,' he said cryptically, pushing his chair back under the table.

'What are you talking about, Alex?' She moved the hair out of her eyes.

'I thought we were friends now,' he said. 'Just humor me.'

'Where are you *going*, Alex? What's going on?'

'It's out on the piano,' Alex said. He turned around at the door. 'You know I still love you. I always have. I just want you to know that,' he said.

17

Langley, Virginia

Alex had taken his father's Gulf Stream jet to Washington. He called Bowles on his cell phone while they taxied in at one of Washington's smaller executive airports. They made arrangements to meet in Georgetown later that evening. On his way out of the plane, Alex told his father's pilot that he might not be coming back and that he might not want to wait. The pilot, an old friend of the family and a former Langley man himself, said he would wait for him, no matter what happened.

★ ★ ★

Alex knocked on the door of Tilly Kregan's suburban Virginia house. Tilly opened the door and stared at him for a moment, not believing it could be him. When she realized it really was Alex, she threw her arms around his neck and cried without saying hello or even saying his name, just crying and hanging onto him until he walked her into the house

216

and closed the door behind them.

Alex didn't say anything at first, he just walked Tilly down the long hallway. She stopped in the hall and hugged him again. Wider in the hips and twenty years older, Tilly was still a pretty woman, in a pair of jeans and a sweat shirt. She reached out to a photograph on the wall and brought him to it. Tilly wiped the tears from her face and grabbed Alex by the arm. There was a photograph of the four of them in front of a temple in Thailand in 1979 — Paul, Tilly, Helen and Alex. They stood in front of it for a moment.

'Do you remember that day in Thailand?' she asked in her warm southern lilt that he'd always loved.

'Yes, I remember,' Alex said finally.

'Well, darlin', come into the living room and let me fix up some of those wicked martinis we used to like,' she said. They went and sat in the living room. There were deep shadows from the tall pine trees in the backyard. Tilly went to a wet bar and began fixing the drinks.

'Paul knew, of course, later, about you and me. Did Paul ever confront you, punch you or anything?' After Helen left him, he'd reached out for Tilly and she'd fallen in love with him. He was sorry he'd done it now. It

217

hadn't been fair to her.

'No,' Alex said.

'Helen didn't know about us?' Tilly asked, bringing him his drink.

'No,' Alex said. 'Never.' Tilly sat down next to him.

'She wrote a few years ago, but I never answered. I didn't want Paul to be reminded of it anymore. We were selfish,' Tilly said. 'I hated you for a long time. I wanted you to divorce Helen and marry *me*. How is Helen? She was always so beautiful. We were all so envious of her . . . ' Tilly saw that he was shaken and reached over and touched his lips, still in love with him. 'We loved them, didn't we. We loved them and we hurt them.' Alex didn't say anything for a moment.

'We're getting a divorce. Got the papers this morning,' Alex said. All the way to Washington in the plane he'd just felt numb, but now, for some reason, the pain was coming and he stopped it, choked it off, because he didn't feel he had the right. Not after what he'd done to Helen.

'I was never ashamed of what happened between us. Maybe because I fell in love with you. Paul liked you . . . admired you . . . all of them did. They kept track of you.' She reached for a picture frame with two heart-shaped photographs on the coffee table.

'I have a grandchild . . . look.' Tilly turned around. 'Last year. Can you believe it?' Alex took the frame and saw a young, black lieutenant with a girl he guessed was Tilly's daughter in a military wedding pose and, next to it, a photograph of Tilly's new grandchild.

'Alex, why are you here? Is it because of Paul?' Alex put down the frame he'd picked up. 'There's something terribly wrong, isn't there? That's why they lied about Paul's death. But they always lie, don't they. That's what Paul always told me. He said they've lied so much they don't even remember the truth anymore. They killed Paul, I know they did. He was afraid that morning — I could see it. He was shaking when he left the house. He didn't sleep the night before. Alex, he knew . . . He knew they were going to kill him.' Tilly reached for his hand and held it. She put her drink down and didn't say anything for a moment. 'If you expect me to cry or something, I can't. I don't know why . . . ' Tilly looked at him. He saw now how she'd aged, the lines in her forehead and around her eyes.

'I want you to fix us some coffee and then come back and tell me everything that happened. All right?'

Tilly nodded her head. She got up and

went to the kitchen and came back with coffee on a tray.

'The night before he died, we had planned a bridge party here at the house,' she said, pouring the coffee. 'Paul never missed one of those parties; never. He came home and told me he was going out after dinner and that I would have to scare up somebody to take his place. I knew something was wrong then. He'd seemed preoccupied at dinner. I asked him where he had to go. He gave me one of his looks that meant it was company business. But there was something else. Richard Claymore came and picked him up. I recognized the car. I think there was someone else with them. It might have been Ford, but I don't know for sure. They're all dead now. Richard Claymore was killed the same day they killed Paul. It's preposterous to think that Richard killed Paul. They were good friends. He would have been the last one to shoot Paul.'

'I know,' Alex said.

'Paul didn't get home until after our guests had gone home. It was very late. He was upset. He hadn't been feeling well. He was supposed to have a stress test for his heart that week. I'd been worried about him. That night, he was very upset, pale. He didn't sleep well that night. He got up about four in the

220

morning and went downstairs and never came back to bed. I followed him downstairs. He was sitting right there where you are, just sitting there in his pajamas, staring into space.

'I asked him what was wrong. He told me that there was something they wanted him to do and he couldn't do it. I'd never seen him like that. I told him to tell me, that I wanted to help him, that I loved him and he was scaring me. He told me things sometimes that he wasn't supposed to, but we'd been married so long. I knew the work he did. He told me it would only make things worse if I knew. Then he looked at me, Alex, and said they were going to do something *very* bad. He said the drug cartels were probably behind it, that they'd finally gotten through to the director. He said there was a plan already in place and they needed him, Claymore, and Ford to act when they got the order. He said they'd offered him a monstrous amount of money at a meeting that night to go along with it, whatever *it* was.'

'Did Paul know what they were planning?'

'I don't know. He wouldn't tell me. I asked and he said it was too dangerous for me to know anything about it.'

'Where was Paul working?'

'He was working under Wyatt on the third

floor. He oversaw all the company's disinformation campaigns.'

'So he was liaison to all our stringers?'

'Yes. He told me once there were hundreds of journalists here in this country who took money from the agency in exchange for planting stories under their names. Most of them were at the newspapers, but some were TV people, too. He told me that some were famous journalists who no one would ever suspect of working with the CIA.'

'Tell me about that morning.'

Tilly clenched her fist and brought it down on her thigh. 'He told me that they wouldn't like it that they hadn't signed on right then and there. Maybe, he thought, Ford would. But he was sure Richard wouldn't. He could tell, he said. He said that Richard was souring on the agency now. Richard was only staying on because he was so close to retirement. They usually drove in together in the morning, Richard and Paul. We were having breakfast when Richard called and said that he had decided to take his car in to have the tires changed. Paul told me as soon as he put down the phone that Richard wasn't going to go along with it.'

'And what about Paul?' Alex asked.

'He was scared . . . I don't know. Maybe he would have. They never gave him the chance.

They must have decided that night that he couldn't be trusted.'

'You're sure Paul didn't know anything about it . . . before that night?'

'I don't think so.'

'Tilly, did they offer you a job in the building?'

'Yes, how did you know?'

'They usually do when an officer is lost in the line of duty. Did you take it?'

'Yes. I had to, there wasn't going to be enough money. We have two boys still in college.'

'Good. Where is the job?'

'They took me in at Paul's section on the third floor. I'm there doing clerical work. They really don't ask me to do much. It's kind of a joke, really.'

'I need to get into Paul's computer. Is there a replacement for him yet? Is someone using his office?'

'No. Paul's office is still there — his computer, records, everything. They let me go in last week and take out his personal belongings. His secretary said they hadn't gotten around to closing his files up.'

'Can you get me onto the third floor? It's dangerous for you if they catch me. If I'm caught, it won't take them long to put us together.'

'Why are you doing this, Alex?'

'I want to pay them back and stop them if I can,' Alex said. He put his coffee down. He wanted to tell her more, but he knew that he couldn't. If she were caught they would make her talk.

'They'll kill you, too. Anyway, you can't stop them,' she said.

'If you give me a chance, I might be able to. I'll need to get into Paul's files, Tilly . . . '

'All right.'

'You're sure?'

'Yes, I owe it to him.'

'How can I get by security to the third floor?' She smiled and he didn't understand. Tilly toyed with her coffee cup and then put it on the table in front of them.

'The Company, the divine Company, is going to get you in. You're going to walk onto the third floor with me.'

'I don't understand.' She smiled at him and went over and poured herself another martini. The pain in her eyes had been translated into something on her face — anger or hate or both — Alex thought, watching her.

'They've given Kitty Ford a job, too. You remember Kitty, don't you? Kitty Ford. Always talked too much?'

'Where?'

'Security. She prints out badges. There's something else I didn't tell you, Alex.' Tilly got up and crossed the room to a closet. 'I haven't even told my daughter. I've been afraid to tell anyone. That morning, Paul left his briefcase at home. They came to look for it, but I said he'd taken it to the office. I have it. I went through it. There's a notebook with all his computer codes. I wasn't going to give it to those bastards. He wasn't supposed to write them down.'

They heard a key turn in the lock, and Alex felt for the gun he was carrying. The front door opened and a young woman pushed a baby stroller through the front door. 'Mom?' Alex moved his fingers away from the pistol under his coat.

'Honey, I want you to meet an old, old friend of your father's . . . '

18

Kitty Ford was sixty years old. She looked like any rich suburban grandmother when she climbed into the back seat of Tilly's battered Volvo and described in detail the nature of the security checks inside CIA headquarters. She reminded Alex that all visitors would be stopped at the elevators and questioned directly, without exception. Employment status at Langley made no difference. All visitors would have to have a legitimate work-related reason for being on the third floor whether or not they were CIA employees. Ford, her face heavy with makeup and the stress, described as best she could, what to expect and how to answer the guard's questions. She told them that she had been unable to get Alex anything but the lowest level security badge, which all temporary, outside visitors received and that allowed access to about fifty percent of the building, but only a small area on the third and fourth floors. When she was finished describing the procedures, Ford reached over the seat of Tilly's car and touched Alex on the shoulder.

'I . . . I want to thank you for trying,' Kitty

told him. Then she got out of the car and disappeared into the crowd of employees entering the building.

★　★　★

Alex and Tilly entered the main entrance of CIA headquarters at eight-thirty in the morning. As in all office buildings at that time of day, the human traffic was all one way. Employees by the hundreds left the parking lots, coming in to start the workday. The pair took the elevator up to the crowded halls on the second floor. Alex's visitor's badge hung from his coat pocket. Alex glanced at Tilly as they rode the elevator up from the main lobby. If Tilly was scared, he couldn't tell. Alex noticed that some of the employees in the elevator glanced at Tilly with a look of recognition and respect: *The wife of one of the fallen heroes.* Her husband's name had been added to the list on the wall of the main lobby of CIA headquarters with other officers killed in the line of duty. He hoped no one would recognize him.

Their crowded elevator stopped on the second floor. They stepped out and queued up at a cordoned area where all badges were presented before employees could proceed to a second bank of elevators that took you up to the restricted third floor. Alex fingered the badge Kitty Ford had given him in the parking lot; its plastic cover was slick. He pinched it and tried to relax. Ford had advised him the badge would get him through two checkpoints. He would have to pass both to get inside her husband's office on the third floor.

When his turn came, Alex smiled at the black woman guard in the white shirt and side-arm who checked badges. The guard glanced at the badge and nodded. Alex, just one of the herd, stepped to the left to the bank of elevators. Tilly had told Alex that the check on the first floor would be only cursory. The second one would be more difficult. On getting out on the third floor, Alex knew he would have to face Langley's Internal Security officers, who had been trained at the Farm, not mere rent-a-cops.

* * *

The guards waiting for each load of employees from the elevators were just what Alex expected, intimidating, active-duty Green Berets. The one who pulled him aside was huge, with red hair and blue eyes. The trick, Alex remembered from his own training days, was for the guard to intimidate any potential spy or terrorist so that he would give tell-tale signs; just the wrong nuance, and they would take him downstairs for further questioning. Unlike the first checkpoint, the two men seemed impervious to the long line of visitors impatient to get on with their work day. Alex watched them question a woman carefully. The redhead had gotten close to her, asking questions quickly. He made her unclip her badge and hand it to him. *They want me to shake*, Alex thought. *Don't shake when you hand them the badge. They're watching for involuntary nervous system reactions*. Alex remembered his instructor's description of what made people give themselves away to the trained eye. Alex watched the big man take the woman's badge and examine it, noting something on a pad. In a moment it was Alex's turn. He unclipped the visitor's badge as he stepped forward putting on his best smile.

'Mr . . . '

'Norton,' Alex said. He held the badge out as it was pulled from his fingers.

'What floors are you visiting today, Mr. Norton?'

'Third.'

'What's your business here, Mr. Norton?' The young man's eyes were sharp, looking first at his face then at the badge, really looking at it this time. Alex stared directly into the redhead's eyes, meeting the man's stare evenly. *Make eye contact. I'm as phony as a two-dollar bill*, he said to himself.

'Office of Management and Budget, study of employee medical costs.' Alex gave the story that Tilly said was plausible. She'd been working on the project herself, a routine government review of medical benefits. OMB had sent several different auditors to her department to work on the study.

'Mr. Norton, I'd like your office telephone number at OMB.' Alex smiled and turned around for a moment, the chatter behind him had begun to change slightly, the snafu in the line was beginning to irritate people. He glanced at Tilly behind him, then gave a number. The redhead made a note of it.

'Oh come on, can't we get on with it! I'm going to be late,' Tilly said, feigning exasperation. The guard waved Alex on, handing him back his badge. The redhead stopped Tilly for a moment and reminded her of the rules. The other guard interrupted the redhead with a knowing look, reminding him that she was one of *them*. Alex saw the words *Kregan's wife* on the man's lips. The redhead nodded and let her go without any questioning.

* ★ ★

Alex looked at Tilly's hands gripping the strap of her handbag, her shoulders shaking slightly. She put the purse down at her desk. She called Alex *Mr. Norton*, going through the routine they had designed to keep the other employees from focusing on him. But her speech pattern had turned wooden. She spoke in an officious tone, saying that she would get the files he needed but hoped he wouldn't have to bother her the way his colleagues had. Alex assured her that he wouldn't. A bleached-blonde turned around, one of the twenty or so women in the clerical bull pen, and looked at him as she was starting her computer. She turned back around, satisfied that he was nothing out of the ordinary. A younger woman came up and asked Tilly if she was going to buy the lottery tickets for the club, or if she wanted her to. Tilly looked at her blankly a moment and then quickly opened her purse. Tilly took the lottery money from her purse and handed it to the girl. 'Hi,' the small black girl said casually to Alex. 'Mutt and Jeff are a drag, huh? Every morning it's the same damn thing.' Alex smiled and nodded. Tilly waited for the girl to leave.

'God, they *will* call that number . . . ' she

231

whispered. Alex touched her hand. He could see she was on the verge of panicking. 'They'll run it on the computer and know it's no good.'

'Yes, but not until things slow down out there. We still have time. More than you think.' He looked her in the eye. 'Too late to turn back now, anyway.' Alex looked out toward the elevators. The two guards were still at their post. Alex waited for Tilly to get hold of herself. She walked to the wall where there were long file cabinets. She switched on the electrically-controlled carousel and jogged through one of the cabinet's drawers. She grabbed several files from the medical section and came back and handed them to Alex.

'You'll have to find an empty desk,' she said. Alex nodded. 'We're out of work space here.' She nodded to him. *Okay, now,* the nod said.

'Thank you, Miss,' Alex answered. Tilly pointed down the hall toward her husband's office.

Alex took the files from her and walked out of the bullpen and down the busy hall. He went straight to the door with Kregan's name still on it and tried to turn the knob. It was locked. There was an electronic keypad. Alex stopped for a moment and felt his own heart starting to speed up so that he could hear it beating in his ears. He *had* to get in. *Anyone watching?* He stepped back, put the files under his right arm and turned around, deliberately, as if there were something irritating him. Why hadn't she said it would be locked? Alex looked back down toward the bullpen. Tilly was sitting at her desk. She glanced up at him then turned away. *I've come this far* . . . .Alex felt himself start to sweat. He noticed the two Green Berets were looking at him. He raised his hand; the huge one who had questioned him earlier came down the hall.

'Mr. Norton, you look lost, anything wrong?'

'The door seems to be locked.' The redhead looked at him, not blinking. 'One of the ladies over there said the office was empty and I might be able to use it this morning. The bullpen's a little noisy for government work,' Alex said. The joke seemed to work. The redhead fished in his pocket, watching him carefully. Alex noticed the Special Forces pin on the man's jacket lapel.

'How's General Conner?' Alex had read in one of the news weeklies that Conner had been given command of the Berets. He'd known Conner in Africa.

'You know the general?'

'I served with him in Africa. Does he still

sound like he's got a diesel truck parked in his throat?'

'Sure does . . . ' The redhead reached over and punched in a number and unlocked the door. 'Were you in the Force?'

'I was a warrant officer. Listen, thanks a lot . . . ' Alex said.

'What did you do?'

'I tried to stay out of General Conner's way,' Alex said. The redhead smiled knowingly and walked back down the hall. Alex stepped through the doorway and closed the door behind him. He leaned against the door for a moment and let his heart slow down until the pounding stopped in his ears. He walked through the outer office into a much larger inner office. The computer terminal was there. Alex got out the sheet of codes Tilly had saved from her husband's papers and booted up the computer. The screen lit up and asked him for the current password. He typed in the one Ford had noted at the top of his notes: STEELXRAY. Kregan had been unable to remember the half-dozen or so passwords required for him to use the computer, Tilly had said. He had broken one of the agency's commandments and written down the alternating passwords, with notes on their use, in his Day Runner. Alex knew it was the worst kind of security breech Kregan could have made. Had Kregan been caught, he would have been prosecuted and lost his pension.

The computer screen went blank, began to shift, then gave Alex a confirmation. He was suddenly looking at a choice of menus displayed over the CIA's symbol. He glanced at Kregan's notes. Each menu on the screen had been noted in the book with its corresponding security code. Alex chose the menu marked *Print Media*. The program prompted him for a code. Alex double-checked the code in the book, then typed in the password: *PULP*. In a moment, Paul's files, date-stamped on the day before he was killed three weeks before, came up on the electronic desk top. Alex clicked on *Print Journalists* and the screen started to move, shifting long columns of names and news organizations. He clicked on the most recent date. *SF Chronicle* popped up with a code name FASTHOLD. FASTHOLD RECEIVES TOP RATED CLEARANCE FOR SECURE COMMUNICATION DIRECT TO DCI. Alex hit the print button and the printer began to print the entry. The page came out blank. The computer screen froze suddenly. Then it was asking him for a confirmation of his original password. He re-typed *STEEL-XRAY*. The screen dissolved and was replaced with a flashing *UNAUTHORIZED*. Alex desperately typed *STEELXRAY* a second time, hoping it would somehow bring back the screen.

UNAUTHORIZED COMPUTER ACCESS ON THE THIRD FLOOR. UNAUTHORIZED COMPUTER ACCESS ON THE THIRD FLOOR. SECTION H TERMINAL. CHECK TERMINALS SEVENTEEN THROUGH SIXTY.

A woman's computer-generated voice came over the PA system in every office on the third floor. Alex heard the cold, recorded voice come through a small speaker in the ceiling. The phone next to him began to ring on the desk. He turned off the computer terminal and picked up Tilly's files. Debating with himself, he picked up the phone.

'What did you do?' It was Tilly's voice.

'Something went wrong.' Alex could hear the recorded announcement on her phone.

'You'd better leave. Wait, I'll be right there.' The phone clicked off. Alex got up and went to the outer office. The security system warning continued to drone on, repeating itself. He heard a knock at the office door and went to open it. Tilly stepped into the room.

'They're checking all the offices. You'd better go. Don't try to leave the floor until the alarm stops. There's a cafeteria at the end of the hall. They won't bother with that.' Alex looked at Tilly. 'I'll make a scene here. A very loud one,' she said. 'I don't care. I hate them. Find out who killed Paul. That's all I ask. I'll wait here. They'll think I used the computer . . . Go on.'

'They won't believe you. Come with me. There's a chance.'

'No!' she said. Alex held her hand for a moment and then slipped out of the office into the confusion in the hallway.

19

Wyatt nodded to the guard at the door of the elegant-looking safe house in Langley. It had been four hours since Tilly had been discovered in her husband's office. A tall CIA security man opened the front door. There were less than forty-eight hours to zero hour, and Wyatt could see the tension in the officer's eyes. If they failed, he thought, they'd all be in federal prison in a few days. Wyatt walked past the guard. There was a TV playing in the background. Two more CIA officers in casual clothes were sitting at the kitchen table across the hall. Wyatt asked the man who had opened the door where Tilly was. The guard told him she was in the living room watching TV.

Tilly Kregan was sitting on a couch watching *Wheel of Fortune*. A guard was sitting across from her. Tilly looked up at Wyatt, then back at the television screen. Wyatt went to the TV set and turned it off. It got very quiet in the room.

'Tilly . . . It's been quite a while.' Tilly put her knees together and didn't answer. She kept her eyes on the blank TV screen, the fingers of her left hand twisting her wedding ring. 'I was very sorry to hear about Paul . . .' Wyatt said. She sniffed but wouldn't look at him. 'Tilly, there's no point in playing games. We're old friends, aren't we? We started out together, Paul, you and I . . . Alex, the rest of them. Helen.' Wyatt watched Tilly's lips quiver with anger.

'I thought they'd bring you. Paul always said they'd bring in the people you know first. I want to watch television,' she said.

'Maybe later,' Wyatt said. Wyatt motioned for the guard to get up and leave them.

Tilly smiled weakly. 'Did you kill Paul?'

'You know Richard killed Paul,' Wyatt said.

'Stop it! I'm not an outsider, remember. For twenty-five years, Paul told lies for you people. I know all about you and I know how the lies work.'

'Do you, Tilly?' Her eyes met his, then turned away. 'Have you been with Alex, Tilly? Did you take him into Paul's office? I checked on you. You failed our computer test when they brought you on. You can't even turn a computer on,' he said.

'Why would I see Alex?'

'You tell us, Tilly. You were lovers after all. But we're your family now, not *Alex*. Alex left the family, Tilly. He's not our friend anymore.

239

Was it Alex, Tilly? Has he gotten you into trouble *again?*'

'Don't give me any of that family crap. I don't believe it. What good did it do Paul? You murdered him.' Wyatt noticed the matter-of-fact way she was talking. He knew she was trying to keep herself from sounding as scared as she must be.

'That's not true, Tilly. I've told you . . . Tilly, how long have you known me?'

'Too long.'

'I was at your wedding when you and Paul were married. Do you remember?' She didn't answer him. 'Tilly, we're friends from the old days. I care about you.' Wyatt saw a smirk cross the woman's face. 'I understand how you feel about Alex. We all liked Alex. But this is bigger than Alex, Tilly. This is about our country. About changes we have to make to keep it great. It's bigger than you, or me, or anyone, including Alex, Tilly. Do you understand that?' Wyatt had sat down across from her and was touching her knee while he spoke; his voice was low.

'I remember when you were just a knuckle-dragger. Do you remember that, Wyatt? You used to be jealous of Alex. I used to watch you watching him at our dinner parties, studying him, his clothes, his manners, everything about him. You wanted

240

to be like him, didn't you? That's why you went after Helen, wasn't it? Just to find out what made Alex tick. And it was you who said he was a drunk, wasn't it? You told the grayheads back at the office that Alex was a drunk when it was a lie . . . When you were in bed with his wife.' Tilly had come halfway off the couch, animated with hate. Wyatt saw how much she hated him and was surprised by it.

'We all liked Alex in the old days, Tilly. But you have to help me now.' Wyatt reached over and held her chin. She turned away from him and he slapped her twice, turning her face each time, the second time harder than the first. The agents in the kitchen heard the slaps and turned to look.

'Tilly, knowing me isn't going to stop this, do you understand me? There's only one thing that will stop this.' Wyatt punched her once in the stomach, grabbed her by the throat and brought her close to his face, lifting her off the couch. She was choking, her face red from the blows, her glottis jammed expertly by his thumb. There was a knack to it. Too much pressure and she would asphyxiate, just enough thumb to keep the windpipe closed off as she tried to cough from the punch in the stomach. When you know the technique, it was so easy, Wyatt thought.

He felt the air struggle to get past his thumb. He felt the way her throat tried to widen itself and saw Tilly's eyes roll to the back of her head. Then he let up, just enough to let her suck air, enough to keep her alive. Then he tightened down again and punched her stomach again, knocking the last of her breath out past his thumb. She panicked and clawed at his hands. Wyatt knew she was dying. He loosened again, this time letting the esophagus open all the way, and felt the air rush through it past his thumb. He pushed her back into the couch and watched her hack, her face an ugly blue color.

★ ★ ★

'Now, Tilly, are you okay?' Wyatt had gone to the kitchen and gotten her a glass of water. The agents had gotten quiet while they watched him run the tap. The sound of the woman's anguish was hard for them to take. They were younger every day, Wyatt thought. They hadn't seen anything and didn't know that what he'd done to her was nothing compared to what he would do if he had to.

'Drink, it will make you feel better. Cold water will stop the throat from swelling too much.' He handed her the glass. Wyatt knew the effects of the choking passed quickly. No pain, really. Just the hacking cough, then the swelling. She took the glass of water from him. Her hands were shaking, the blue color leaving her face. 'Listen, dear, you're in control of this. You were from the very beginning. Now, I want to know what you told Alex, and what Alex was doing in Paul's office.'

'Go to hell . . . ' she said, her voice thick-sounding. She gripped the clean glass with both hands. 'Pig.' She coughed a little, the water spilling over the rim of the glass. Wyatt took the glass from her carefully and put it on the table next to her.

'I want to show you something . . . ' He reached out and held her hands, felt her tremble. 'I want you to look carefully because time now is so important, Tilly. Do you understand?' Wyatt let go of her hand and slid the video he'd brought with him into the VCR under the TV set.

'You'll see something interesting. Look, I want you to see, Tilly.' The TV screen came alive. In a moment, her daughter and her grandchild were on the screen. The baby was on the carpet and crying. The camera panned the room, stopping when it found her daughter's face. Tilly screamed. Her grand-daughter was trying to touch her mother's head. The camera pulled away. Tilly's daughter and son-in-law were both on the carpet face down, guns at their heads. The husband was trying to talk to his daughter. There was no sound as the young black lieutenant lifted his head and tried to speak first to his daughter and then to the camera, his face distorted from a horrible beating.

'Oh, my God. Oh, my God,' Tilly was sobbing. Wyatt hit the pause button on the machine, and the black man's face stood frozen, the ugliness of the beating clear for Tilly to see. She kept screaming so that the agents in the kitchen came out to see what he could be doing to her. She would talk now, Wyatt thought to himself, watching her.

* * *

When Tilly was finished answering his questions, Wyatt stood up. Alex still didn't know much more than he had before he'd gone to Langley, he decided. Their plans were still safe. There were only forty-eight hours to go before it would be too late for anyone to stop them. Wyatt lied to Tilly and said that she would be free to go in a day or two.

'You promise they will be all right. I've told you everything,' Tilly said. She was ashamed of herself for telling him about Alex.

'You're sure you don't know where he's staying.'

'He never said.'

Wyatt nodded. 'Tilly, I want you to know you did the right thing.' She looked at him a moment, then went to the television and stood in front of the empty screen.

20

The taxi stopped under the streetlight on the quiet residential street. Alex paid the cabby. They'd driven around Georgetown for half an hour before he gave him Murial Fipp's address. Alex crossed the street and went up the stairs of the familiar house.

'Mrs. Fipps,' Alex said. The butler looked at him a moment then stepped aside. There was a small three-piece jazz band playing in the dining room. The party consisted of a collection of Southern congressmen with their wives who were being lobbied by Conroy International as part of a funding bill the CIA wanted passed.

'Alex, is that you? Good Lord! Have you joined a rock and roll band?' He'd changed his clothes at a Salvation Army store. He'd gotten rid of the suit he'd worn into Langley and bought some jeans and a Pendleton shirt and baseball cap. The clothing was used and made him seem like any other of the capital's hundreds of street people. A few of the partygoers stole a curious glance at him.

'Auntie Murial . . . ' Alex threw his arms around the old dowager.

'Good god, boy.' She put her arms around him. Alex had known Murial Fipps since he was a little boy. The love affair that she'd had with his father was the first secret he'd shared with his father. It was their affair that taught him how men lie. He'd learned to lie by watching his father. His parents were living in Washington at the time. Murial insisted then that he call her *Auntie*.

The weekends he spent at Auntie Murial's horse farm in Virginia, Alex remembered, were almost perfect. The fact that his mother never accompanied them didn't seem strange to him then. It was true that sometimes he would wonder why his mother hadn't been invited. He'd asked his mother once why she never went to Auntie Murial's. She'd only said she didn't like the countryside. It was her first lie to him and he'd caught it.

'I had to see you,' Alex said. 'I need some help.' He didn't bother to explain. Murial Fipps looked at him and shook her head. 'I thought if I could go out to your place and lie low . . . I didn't know where else to go. Until I can explain . . . ' he said. They were talking at the foot of the stairs. The old woman looked at her guests for a moment and nodded.

'Of course I'll help you, dear,' she said. 'An hour, dear, give me an hour.' Murial gave

Alex a kiss on the forehead and then she grabbed someone by the elbow and was again working the crowd of congressmen and business executives. In a moment, the butler was at Alex's side saying that Mrs. Fipps thought it best if he waited upstairs in the library.

★   ★   ★

Murial's big gray Mercedes rolled through the dark streets of Washington and onto the Beltway. Although Alex knew they were looking for him, he finally felt safe because she had the one car that they wouldn't stop.

'I really loved your father. Did you know that?' Murial said from the darkness. Alex looked out on the summer night. 'He was so different from all the men I'd ever known. He was so complete somehow, so tall and commanding. He riveted people when he came into a room.' She looked at Alex with the tight-stretched face that seemed pinned behind her ears, and Alex tried to imagine her forty years ago but couldn't. Instead, he asked her if her place in Virginia was still as he remembered, with the horses and the fields, and the big barn with the horse shower and heaters, where the stable boys wore white jackets. She told him it was all much quieter now. She still had a few horses, but she didn't ride to hounds anymore. While she spoke, Alex realized there was something wrong. They had turned off the freeway too soon. He looked at her. She was asking him to tell her how his father was.

'You know, you're like a son to me, Alex. I haven't forgotten those glorious days you spent with me and your father.' Alex watched the road in front of them and knew then she was trying to distract him. They'd turned off the highway onto a two-lane road. He saw headlights come up fast behind them.

'You tipped them off, didn't you!' The headlights were closing in. 'But you see, I expected that.' He reached across and put his gun against Fipps' ribs. 'You know what Dad used to call you? The spider.' Alex laughed under his breath and told her exactly what to do. 'Pull over,' he said. He had her get out of the car and stand on the side of the road. He watched her move her arms, signaling the car behind them. He waited a moment as the car moved slowly onto the shoulder. Then he climbed behind the wheel, put the car in reverse and floored it. He saw the old bitch's face looking at him as he swerved around her and backed into the oncoming car full throttle. He got out of the car. The men were pinned behind their air bags. As he shot into the car, the air bags were cut with holes from his automatic. He turned around and saw Fipps was sprawled out on the dirt shoulder of the road looking at him, that horrible mask-of-a-face caught in the headlights.

'I should kill you,' he said. He dropped the empty clip on the ground and slammed home a fresh one.

★ ★ ★

Alex had Fipps park down from the main house. She slammed the car door as they got out. The sound bounced against the outbuildings behind them. The evening was cool and the full moon gave the farm buildings a yellowish glow. The main house, on their right, across the white gravel road, was huge and in the Palladian style. To Alex, it had always seemed more like a hotel than anything else. Three big spotlights bathed it in white light. No lights were on inside the mansion from what Alex could see. It was eleven at night — the staff, he hoped, would be asleep by now.

Alex pointed to the barn and told Fipps to start walking. He could see from her face in the moonlight that she was reviewing her options. She would maybe scream on the chance that someone would hear. He lifted his gun and pointed it at her chest. For a moment there was a standoff; she paused, then turned around and began to walk. Twice she turned to look at him over her shoulder. She began talking, saying that Tilly was dead. 'Wyatt did it himself, right in the safe house,' she said. She assured him that they would kill him, too. He told her to shut up.

'You'll be dead in an hour,' she said, turning around in the moonlight. 'I'll watch them kill you.' Then she sunk her hands in the deep pockets of her long black coat and smiled at him, sure of herself, confident that she would be rescued.

'Shut up,' he said again. He pushed her forward up the hill toward the outline of the huge white barn.

Alex rolled the big barn door open. He heard the soft sound of lubricated rollers. He pushed Fipps into the barn and told her to switch on the lights. He watched her open a metal box on the wall. Six halogen lights on the ceiling forty feet above their heads began to crackle and pop, the light growing in intensity until the entire barn was lit as brightly as a hospital operating room. Everything inside the barn was exactly as he remembered it — the walls of oiled pine, the fixtures polished and shiny, and the bridles and saddles hung on long metal racks. A palace for horses, his father had once called it. The horses began to whinny as he shoved the big door closed behind them.

'You won't stop it, Alex. We aren't going to let you,' she said. Alex pushed her further into the barn toward the big horse shower.

'I want you to call Penn. You have to get him to come here, alone.' Fipps stared at him, the harsh halogen light shining on her over-operated-on face, the skin unnaturally tight around her mouth. Several of the horses had come and hung their beautiful heads over their stall doors. Fipps was showing her *real* face now, and it was hate-filled and contemptuous of him. The hate seemed to pull her face even tighter.

'Go screw yourself,' she said.

Alex walked to one of the stalls and looked at the big thoroughbred that had come and stuck its muzzle out. He rubbed the stallion's chin with the barrel of his automatic.

'Call him or I'll kill you.'

Murial smiled at him with party-girl teeth. 'No,' she told him. Alex kept massaging the chin of the animal, heard its soft whinny and its hoof stamping.

'They'll kill Helen, and they'll kill you, Alex. I promise you.' Fipps looked quickly at the barn door, then back at him. Alex walked up to her and held the automatic against the tight skin of her cheek. He felt the automatic's pimply grip tight against his palm.

'I have nothing to lose,' Alex said.

'You won't shoot me.' Her mascara-caked wide-open eyes focused on his. He cocked the automatic and moved it from her cheek and fired. The shot pounded her eardrum. She screamed and tried to run toward the door. It was easy to catch her. She broke down sobbing; her tough-lady front was broken. She fell to her hands and knees and begged him not to hurt her again. He almost felt sorry for her. He told her to get up and call Penn.

★ ★ ★

Alex waited by the gate a quarter mile below the big house. He knew that Penn wouldn't come alone, of course. At nearly midnight, he saw the lights on the road. He waited for the limousine at the gate that blocked the way into the farm. The car's headlights painted the gate's metal bars. The driver rolled down his window to speak into the security phone. Alex stepped out of the shadows and fired at the driver, hitting him in the side of the head. Another security man, riding shotgun, tried to escape out the passenger side of the car, but Alex shot him in the back through the open window as he fought to get his door open. Then all was quiet. He reached over and punched in the numbered code on the gate's keypad and watched the heavy gate slide open. Finally, he opened the limousine's back door. The Director of the Central Intelligence Agency was looking at him. He ordered Penn behind the wheel of the car and they drove on through.

★　★　★

Penn saw Murial sitting on the floor. Alex had tied her wrist to the saddle rack with a bridle. Murial looked at Penn and said she'd had to do it. Her makeup had run. She looked ancient now, a hag with diamond earrings.

'They won't be long, you know. They always know where I'm going.' Penn turned to look at Alex. He looked completely relaxed.

'I know that,' Alex said. The dapper little man got closer to him, seemingly unafraid of Alex's gun.

'They'll catch you, too. I'm afraid your friend gave you up, and now she's dead. And we'll get Bowles too. He wasn't the only one who was listening in.' Alex hit Penn in the

254

mouth with the butt of the pistol, knocking him to the ground. The barn filled with the noise of frightened horses. For a moment, Penn looked at him in disbelief, then spit out the teeth that Alex had knocked back into his throat. The blood came out of Penn's mouth in little greasy-looking strings. *They had never believed it was all so real,* Alex thought to himself. People like them had always been spared the violence that had surrounded them for years. *It had never touched them, until now,* he thought.

'Like you said, we don't have much time,' Alex said. 'I want to know when and where you're going to kill the President.'

Penn got up off the ground slowly. He reached into his pocket and pulled out a handkerchief and put it against his bleeding mouth. 'I'm afraid I can't help you. We don't talk to renegades. But I tell you what, it's still not too late for you to come back into the fold. You're really one of us, aren't you, Alex? You miss the action, don't you. We've let you have your larks; we've taken care of you. This could be *your* chance, too.' Penn talked from behind the bloody handkerchief. 'There's a new order coming and it will be different. We'll call the shots. You'd like that, wouldn't you?'

'I'll only say this one more time. If you tell

me, I'll let her go,' Alex said. 'I want to know when and where.'

'Listen, old boy, we're both gentlemen. I don't think there's any reason to hurt Murial . . . '

'Well that's where you're wrong. I'm not a gentleman, haven't been for quite a while.'

Alex walked back to one of the stall doors and swung it open. 'Where and when?' Alex fired the automatic. The animal reared and kicked at the side of the stall, terrified. Penn dropped his hand away from his mouth.

'God, David, tell him. Please tell him. He's crazy, look at him.' Alex went to the rack, grabbed Fipps by the hand and untied her.

'Well, Penn, what's it going to be? This is your friend here. You wouldn't want anything to happen to her, would you?'

'I don't have friends. I have interests. Go on, get in if that's what he wants.' Penn walked up to Fipps and pushed her through the open door himself. Alex closed the stall door behind her. Fipps fell down in the straw. The big animal moved, snorting nervously behind her. Its ears were pointed straight back.

'Tell him, David. Tell him, *please!* Alex, they're going to kill the President in San Francisco this coming weekend, but they didn't want me to know everything.' She called Penn an ugly name. 'Please don't do this, please.'

'You know what I want,' Alex said looking at Penn now. Penn stepped back, dabbing at his face and shaking his head *no*. 'I need to know *exactly* where and *exactly* when.' Fipps was looking at Alex, frightened. The horse bumped her shoulder. She stood up and moved further back into the stall. The stallion circled her, snorting, its big head bobbing, ears back, exhibiting the electric reflexes of a big frightened animal.

Alex lowered his gun. 'I'm going to count to five, David. Then I'm going to fire this gun and we know what's going to happen to her if I do. When and where are you planning to hit President White?'

'David, please, for God's sake, tell him! Tell him, David.' Alex watched Penn dab at his bleeding mouth.

'Alex, listen to me. I'll tell you . . . ' Penn suddenly lunged for Alex and caught his wrist, trying to fire the gun. A shot tore through Penn's chest. The noise sent the horses into a kind of collective panic. The big stallion reared. Alex saw Fipps try to avoid the hoofs. He tried to step into the stall to pull her out, but the horse was between them and reared again. Then there was screaming and it was too late.

The crowded bar was across from George-town University. The brass-and-mirrors-style bar was filled with a late night crowd of lawyer and dentist types, four deep at the bar. T-Bone Walker was playing on the sound system. *This,* Alex realized, taking it in, was a bad place to meet. It would be impossible to tell if *they* came in. Alex pushed his way past the young men and women and walked to the end of the bar. Red Bowles was sitting at the very end, looking tired and very out-of-place in the thirty-something crowd. Alex squeezed in next to Bowles, keeping his eyes on the entrance.

'Well, you took your sweet-ass time.' Alex had called him from Murial Fipp's barn and told Bowles they had to meet immediately.

'Sorry, but I had to be sure I wasn't followed,' Alex said. 'They're going to strike in San Francisco next weekend sometime. I don't know exactly when or where.'

'How did you find out?' Bowles said, stunned.

'My father knew a woman named Murial Fipps. Have you heard of her?' Alex asked.

'I was at her house a week ago with the President. Penn was there. They're very chummy,' Bowles said.

'Not any more. She's dead. So is Penn
. . . I just left them,' Alex said.

'Jesus Christ,' Bowles said incredulously.
'The President is on his way to San Francisco
first thing in the morning . . . then Tokyo.
He's asked me to come with him. We're
leaving from Dulles in a few hours. You have
to find out where and when.'

'You can't go as planned. They know all
about us. And if we're not careful, we'll be
dead men. You'd better come back to San
Francisco with me.'

'I'll have to call the President and make
some kind of excuse. How are we going to get
out of Washington? They'll be all over . . . '

'Don't worry,' Alex said. 'I have a plane
and pilot waiting for us in Alexandria. One
other thing. Just to keep you interested. I just
got a call from my father. Wyatt had fifty
million dollars deposited in my son's account
at our bank. And I helped him do it. I'll tell
you all about it on the plane.'

'Sounds like you're doing a mighty fine
job,' Bowles said smiling.

21

'This story will make your career,' Paulson said. He was wearing his signature bow tie with little dollar signs on it. He'd come up to the City room to speak to Helen himself. He told her that the publisher had decided to move her to the magazine on a permanent basis.

Paulson explained that the magazine had arranged for her to start the coverage of the President's visit with a series of articles describing the visit from inside Neal White's entourage on an hour-to-hour basis. 'Twenty-four hours with the President,' Paulson told her. 'That's the title for the piece — you start the coverage tomorrow at the news conference. The President is meeting with some editors at noon. You're going to spend the next twenty-some hours with the President of the United States . . . but not looking like that,' Paulson said.

'Who thought this stunt up?'

'I did — pretty good, huh? You get the whole magazine for the story, with photos. We're going to blow *The Examiner* out of the water,' Paulson said. He gave her the

President's schedule for the next two days and sent her home to get ready, telling her that her private interview was now scheduled the following morning at the President's hotel.

★ ★ ★

The door to Merriwether's office was open. He barely looked up at Helen when she came in. 'I've been moved permanently to the magazine as of today,' Helen said.

'I know. I was going to tell you,' Merriwether said.

'I don't seem to have any choice in the matter,' Helen said. Merriwether nodded.

'You'll get over it. Anyway, I'm sure you're heading for TV,' Merriwether said. 'That's every journalist's goal these days, isn't it? Everyone wants to anchor the six o'clock news.' He looked up from his computer and studied her.

'I'm not ready for presidents and all that. I don't even know what to call him.'

'Try *Mr. President*,' Merriwether retorted.

'I just got his schedule. Look.' Helen held up the schedule Paulson had given her. 'I have an interview with him tomorrow morning. Can you imagine . . . I get a free baseball game out of it tomorrow night.' She scanned the itinerary. 'How's this for an intro — 'President White and I shelled peanuts and talked world affairs . . . .''

'Helen, you're a good journalist. You deserve this. I expect to see you at *The Times* or *Post* some day. We're all being moved around a bit while the President is here. The publisher gave Paulson managing editor status. Paulson's coordinating all the presidential coverage,' Merriwether said. Helen was surprised to hear it but didn't say anything.

★   ★   ★

'Now, gentlemen, I want you to know that this wasn't my idea. As soon as the President gets back on the . . . whatever they call it . . . '

'Air Force One,' Merriwether said.

'Yes. As soon as he's on the way to Tokyo, I will disappear back to the first floor.'

Merriwether was watching Paulson the way you would someone who has broken into your house in the middle of the night. The *Chronicle's* executive editor and city editor were also watching him. They were younger and seemed to accept what Merriwether couldn't: a tabloid man was now running *The San Francisco Chronicle*. And even if it was only for twenty-four hours, he would still be running it.

Paulson's eyes found Merriwether's face, then looked away as the details of the coordinated effort between all sections of the newspaper were hammered out. The majority of the coverage was dedicated to the human interest side of the President's visit. When Paulson was finished with the other editors, he asked Merriwether to follow him down to his office on the first floor. The Sunday Magazine's office seemed unnaturally quiet compared to the newsroom. Even the furniture and carpet seemed more like they belonged in a lawyer's office. Merriwether followed Paulson into his office. Paulson closed the door, a little too dramatically.

'Eureka!' Paulson said when he got to his desk. Merriwether looked at the man for a moment and didn't understand what the hell he was talking about. He'd always had his doubts about Paulson.

'You're the most experienced newspaper man on the staff. Thirty-nine years . . . I am assigning you to the hardest job I could find. Eureka, I want you to go up there and cover the President's visit. Here's the schedule.' Paulson handed Merriwether an official White House schedule of the two-hour visit Neal White planned to the lumber town. Merriwether looked down and read through the itinerary. Day after next, the President was going to Eureka via helicopter to meet with lumber company executives to discuss environmental issues.

'You're kidding,' Merriwether said.

'I never kid about the news,' Paulson said.

★　★　★

The Lineup, kitty corner from the Hall of Justice on Brannan Street, had been a cops' bar since the Sixties. Merriwether had probably spent more time in The Lineup than he ever had in his one-bedroom apartment in Pacific Heights.

Helen came into the bar and waited by the door, letting her eyes adjust to the place's dim yellowish lights. She spotted Merriwether at the bar and went over to him. 'You wanted to see me?' she said. She noticed he was a little drunk. Merriwether ordered her a beer without her having asked for it. 'It's ten in the morning, Scott. I don't think I need a beer. I have to be at the Fairmont in twenty-five minutes.' She was nervous. Merriwether shook his head.

'There's something screwy going on,' he said, his elbows on the bar.

'What do you mean?' Helen had heard from one of the photographers at the paper that morning that Paulson was sending

Merriwether to Eureka. It was ridiculous, but she was surprised that he'd called her and told her to meet him here. She was sure it was to complain about the assignment.

'I heard. It's crazy. I don't know what to say. He could have sent anyone to Eureka . . . I guess he just doesn't like you.'

Merriwether shook his head again and snuffed out his cigarette. 'No, I don't mean him sending me to the sticks. I mean there's something up with Paulson.' Helen looked at her watch. She had exactly twenty minutes to cross town and make the interview with the President of the United States before he gave a news conference that was going to be broadcast live. She was sure now that Merriwether was drunk.

'Look, Scott . . . I'm sorry about . . . '

'Helen, *listen*. When did Paulson first mention the President going to 3Com Park to you?'

'Yesterday, when he came up to see me. Why? It was on the schedule.' Merriwether looked her in the face. She'd never seen him look like this. He picked up the pack of cigarettes on the bar and shook out a fresh one.

'The police didn't know about White's going until an *hour* ago. It was a last minute change to his schedule. Lieutenant Guasco

265

just told me. He's the man in charge of SFPD's security team. And SFPD didn't know a damn thing about it until this morning.'

'What do you mean?'

'I mean, how did Paulson know the President's schedule before the cops knew it?'

'Maybe the publisher told him. He's going to be with White today. Maybe the President's people mentioned it to the publisher and he told Paulson.'

'Maybe.'

'Scott, what are you trying to say?' Helen looked at her watch. She was disappointed that Merriwether had called her there just to tell her that Paulson had some kind of privileged information. She glanced toward the door and then at her watch.

'Helen, I'm telling you I think there is something wrong here.' He lit the end of a fresh cigarette. 'Haven't you asked yourself why Paulson might suddenly be calling the shots at the paper? Now, especially? Doesn't it strike you as strange?'

'I know why. The owner likes him because he has increased circulation. I guess that's hard to take . . . I mean that it took a TV guy to sell more newspapers. I don't like him, but, well, look at it from the publisher's point of view,' she said. 'I've got to go.'

'Yeah . . . okay.' Merriwether turned around. He stopped looking at her. She could see he was hurt. She chalked it up to a battered ego and the fact that he'd been demoted after so many years at the top.

'Scott, I really have to go now. I'm sorry about all this,' Helen said. Merriwether dragged on his cigarette and waved her off.

22

'I don't have much time,' the President said. He'd been talking with Helen for twenty minutes. The head of the California State Democratic Party committee had called and asked as a personal favor if he would allow the *San Francisco Chronicle* to do a twenty-four-hours-type story while he was in San Francisco. Neal White was glad he'd agreed. The reporter was beautiful and charming and he enjoyed the break. There was nothing more energizing than talking to a woman with long legs — especially when they wore short skirts and hung onto his every word.

'But I can assure you that it's been a pleasure . . . By the way, I know your father-in-law, Malcolm Law. Met him once or twice,' the President told her. Helen was surprised. White explained he had asked staff for some background on her after he'd agreed to her publisher's idea.

'Had to make sure you weren't a George Will type . . . ' the President joked. 'No heavy policy stuff in your background.' There'd been several interruptions, but for the last ten minutes or so they'd been left alone in the enormous hotel suite. Helen decided she liked Neal White. She was surprised by his affability and his lack of pretense. He'd had coffee brought in and they'd talked casually. He flirted with her the tiniest bit and it somehow put her at ease.

'I promise not to get in the way,' she said self-consciously.

'Not to worry. Charming women are always welcome,' he said. An aide came in and made it clear that the interview was over. There was to be a briefing with staff before a news conference in the lobby of the hotel. Neal stood up, they shook hands warmly, and he told Helen that he would make sure to call on her at the news conference.

★ ★ ★

Helen had now been seen by 20 million people on CNN. The President, good to his word, had called on her at the back of the room to the surprise of the mainline heavy-duty journalists at the front of the press conference. The cameras had all turned around when she stood up and asked her question. The producer back at CNN headquarters in Atlanta had demanded to know who in the hell she was. A production assistant quickly typed 'local press' under her face as she spoke and displayed it just before they cut away to President White for his answer.

A few journalists looked at her as she walked through the lobby of the Fairmont Hotel now. She felt excited and had to admit she was glad the publisher had chosen her to do the story. Her life was changing. She hadn't thought once about Alex all day, she thought, catching one of the famous journalists she'd seen on TV looking at her. He nodded to her and she nodded back.

She hadn't eaten anything all morning and decided to go to Mason's and have lunch. She found a table on the California Street side and ordered a sandwich and a coke. Several more journalists acknowledged her as they passed her table. She could get used to this, she thought — national television, CNN. After all, what was so bad with hanging out with presidents and being on TV? Maybe her mother had seen her.

Her cellular phone rang. Helen took it out of her purse and clicked it on, thinking that it was someone who had seen her on TV and was calling to congratulate her.

'Helen?' She glanced out at the traffic on California Street. 'It's me, Scott. I want you to tell the President's security people what I told you. Please. I think someone should know.'

'Scott. I thought we went through this already?'

'Helen. I'm asking you a personal favor now. Please. Tell someone.'

'All right. I'll tell someone, but I'm going to be a laughing-stock.'

'Never mind that, just tell them the San Francisco Police didn't even know about the President going to the baseball game tonight until this morning.'

★   ★   ★

She decided to report Merriwether's concern to the Secret Service. Helen went up to the President's floor, found one of the assistant press secretaries she'd met that morning and whispered to her that she wanted to speak to the Secret Service. The young woman, harried, looked at her for a moment and then asked her why. Helen said that she'd overheard something she thought she should report to the right people. She tried not to sound as ridiculous as she felt. The press secretary looked at her, then went back into one of the hotel rooms. When the door opened, Helen caught a glimpse of the President in a warm-up suit sitting with

271

several other men around a large conference table. The door closed. Helen turned around, not sure she'd done the right thing now and afraid the press secretary thought she was some kind of nut. The comfortable atmosphere in the hallway made the threat seem ridiculous to her. *Damn Scott*. She had a career to think about, and he, her *mentor*, was ironically screwing up the assignment of a lifetime.

'Yes?' A large clean-cut man in his forties had stepped out of the President's conference room and was standing in front of her. Helen noticed the Secret Service trademark earpiece communicator clipped to the lapel of his suit coat.

'Are you with . . . ?' It sounded foolish but she asked anyway. 'You know, the Secret Service?'

'Yes. Is there something wrong, Miss?' the man asked. He took her by the arm and moved her away from the door of the suite. The door opened and the men Helen had seen with the President came out, followed by the press secretary, then the President himself. Neal stopped for a moment and asked Helen where she'd been, joking that she was supposed to cover the whole twenty-four hour visit. She smiled and said she'd had lunch. Neal said he was going out for a jog in Golden Gate Park and assumed she planned on writing about that, bragging that he did three miles a day. She told him she hadn't brought her running shoes. Clearly disappointed, he said it was a pity and then left, his security team leading the way to the waiting elevators.

'Please follow me,' the agent said.

'I just wanted to report something.'

'I think it's best if we discuss this in private,' the Secret Service man explained.

Helen nodded and followed him down the hall.

★   ★   ★

The Secret Service agent had taken Helen to an empty hotel room at the end of the hall. He closed the door behind them and asked her what it was she'd overheard. Helen explained, saying that someone had called her on her cellular phone and said that the San Francisco Police had just found out about the change to the President's schedule. She'd decided to report this because she thought it was the right thing to do, not because *she* was taking it seriously. The agent asked her if she could identify the caller. Helen said she could.

'You did the right thing, Mrs. Law. We take

any and all tips seriously. Could you wait here a moment? I want my boss to hear what you just told me,' he said.

'Of course . . . It won't take long, will it? I'm supposed to be with the President right now,' Helen said. The man stopped by the door. 'Routine really. Shouldn't take long at all. I'll be right back.' But he hadn't come right back. Helen waited half an hour. She started to get angry. She was expected to leave with the President for a speech at the Commonwealth Club at two o'clock. Missing the jogging foray was one thing, but she couldn't miss the speech. She checked the President's itinerary in her purse. He would be getting back to the hotel in less than ten minutes. She went to the television and flipped through the channels, stopping on a local news show. The anchor was explaining that the President was about to return to his hotel. They cut to a reporter out in front of the Fairmont. Helen stood up. Behind the reporter, she saw Paulson and the Secret Service agent who had just questioned her in a heated conversation. They were standing on the steps to the hotel. *Paulson looks agitated . . . ?* She watched the Secret Service agent who had left her. He moved a cellular phone to his ear. The station cut away for a break suddenly. The phone in the room began to ring. Helen reached over and picked it up.

'Hello. Mrs. Law.'

'Yes?'

'Sorry it's taken so long. I'm with my boss right now. I'll be back with you in a moment. Please stay put. It's very important that we question you further on this.' Helen put the phone down. *Why was he lying?* She left the room as quickly as she could without looking like she was running. She took the elevator down to the lobby. The elevator door opened and Paulson was standing in front of her. The elevator bell rang as he stood there.

'I think we have a problem, Helen. You'd better come with me.' Paulson reached over and grabbed her wrist, hard. She saw the Secret Service man behind Paulson start toward her. Helen hit Paulson as hard as she could in the chest, the way she'd been taught by her brothers. He fell backwards coughing, grabbing his throat. She pulled out the mace she always kept in her purse and blasted the two of them. She ran through the crowded lobby and jumped into the first cab she saw.

23

Red Bowles closed the door behind him and
snapped on the room light. The Edwards
hotel, where Alex and he were hiding out, was
one of the worst dumps he'd ever seen. There
was only one window in the room, and he'd
kept the paper curtain drawn since they'd
arrived the day before. They'd gone out to
breakfast together but Bowles had no
appetite, too anxious to eat now. He'd gone
instead and bought a morning paper and a
deck of cards from a liquor store across the
street. Even at ten in the morning, the streets
around the hotel were full of low-life street
people. The Texas Ranger looked at his watch
for the hundredth time that morning. Alex
had said he would be back in less than an
hour. *Then what?* he wondered. More than
once that morning, he'd thought of going up
to the Fairmont to be near the President after
seeing the news conference on CNN. Bowles
knew from the call he'd made to a friend on
the President's staff that the last of the Texas
Rangers had been pulled off the President's
security detail the day before as they were
boarding Air Force One.

The gas heater on the wall next to him kicked in, and he felt a sudden flush of warm air and another wave of anxiety. Rock and roll music started up again in the adjoining room. Whoever was in there was playing the same acid rock songs over and over. Led Zeppelin's *Baby I'm Gonna Leave You* began to play again. Bowles listened as the mind-numbing music flooded the room. He felt like banging on the wall — he'd complained to the desk clerk twice but nothing had been done about it.

The room heater kicked off. Bowles began tossing playing cards into his cowboy hat in the corner. The music coming from next door had stopped. Now there were loud voices. A man's voice said something about a bag of weed. He heard a woman's voice. A door opened out in the hall and then it slammed shut. Bowles looked at the card in his hand, the queen of spades, smiled to himself and tossed it at the hat. It glanced off the brim and landed on the dirty carpet. The music started up suddenly, and Bowles wondered how much longer he could take this pressure.

In his mind, he went over the details of Neal's itinerary for his last day in San Francisco, hour by hour. He should be in Golden Gate Park right now, taking his customary three-mile jog. He'd be back at the

Fairmont in . . . Bowles looked at his watch . . . exactly thirty-seven minutes. He put down the deck of cards and picked up the morning paper he'd bought. There were two front page articles on Neal's visit to the city. He started one, a color piece on the President's visit. Bowles got down two-thirds of the way into the article and suddenly stopped.

'*The President will be the honored guest at the city's annual Fourth of July celebration at 3Com Park, to be followed by a Giants vs. Dodger's game. The President is . . .* ' Bowles reread the paragraph out loud. '*The President is scheduled to throw out the first ball at eight o'clock.*' There was no mistake. He remembered telling Neal's chief of staff not to do the Fourth of July celebrations at 3Com. He'd taken it off the President's schedule himself, saying it was too risky.

God damn them. He strode to the opposite corner of the room. The walls seemed to be closing in on him. *I have to wait for Alex.* But now he at least knew where they had to go. Someone had put 3Com Park back on the schedule. He looked at his watch. *What is taking Alex so long?* He reread the article; the event was a little more than six hours away. *Don't panic. There will be enough time.* Bowles picked up the deck of cards and

278

started throwing them at his cowboy hat, but his fingers were shaking slightly now.

* * *

Alex had left Helen a note saying that if she needed a safe place while he was gone, she should go to an address she'd never heard of and wait for him. At the time, she thought it sounded ridiculous. Why would she need a safe place? *She* wasn't in any trouble. When she got into the taxi at the Fairmont, she was glad she had a place to go. She gave the driver the address and name of the hotel, and sat back, her heart beating out of control. *Had Alex known she would be in trouble?* The taxi slid down California Street heading for Van Ness, then turned left on Leavenworth and left again on Turk. She wasn't exactly sure where the Edwards Hotel was and asked the driver. He looked in the rear view mirror and said that it was on Turk just above Market Street. He grinned at her in a way that she didn't understand.

The Edwards wasn't what she'd expected. The people on the street looked vicious. She hurriedly paid the driver and disappeared into the hotel's seedy lobby. She went to the clerk behind a ridiculous cage. She began to understand the driver's look. She said she wanted the key to Room 455, 'Mr. Law's room,' she said. The clerk, a pasty-skinned white man in his twenties, gave her a key.

Helen climbed the dark stairway, still frightened by what had happened. She told herself that she would be safe here, at least until she could sort it all out. She had to find out what Paulson had been doing talking to the Secret Service and why he'd grabbed her. Why had the agent lied to her? None of it made any sense. Two young women passed her on the stairs. The girls looked at Helen and burst out laughing.

'Lost your golf clubs, babe?' one asked. Helen hurried to the top of the stairs and heard the girls still laughing at her. She found number 455 and used the key she'd been given.

★ ★ ★

'I'm a friend of Alex,' Helen said. The man sitting on the end of the bed was pointing a gun at her. She didn't know what else to say. He motioned her into the room. 'Alex told me to come here if I needed a place to go.' She thought if she kept talking, he would put the gun down. The man stood up and told her to close the door. She did as he said.

'Now, turn around, drop the purse and

kick it away from you, and put your hands on the door. If you turn around, I'll kill you. Do you understand?' Helen nodded, dropped her purse, then kicked it away from her. She heard the bed creak and the man step up behind her. She felt his hand start to touch her, first around her chest, then under her arms, pulling her skirt up to feel around her rear and the small of her back, then between her thighs. She bit her tongue, hoping that it wasn't going to be what she thought. When he was finished touching her, he told her she could put her hands down and turn around. Rock and roll music started up suddenly next door, very loud.

'I hope you like whatever the hell that is,' the man said. 'That's the only thing they seem to play.' Helen turned around. The man had a reddish complexion and was smiling at her. 'Red Bowles, glad to meet you.' He was looking at her driver's license.

'Are you a friend of Alex?' Helen said.

'I guess so. Why don't you tell me just what you're doing here,' he said.

'Alex said I should come here if . . . well, if something went wrong. I think something's wrong. Are you working with Alex?' Bowles looked at the woman. She was very pretty, and so different from the women he'd seen for the past two days.

'You're his wife, the reporter?' She nodded. 'He mentioned you. What's wrong?'

'I'm not sure. I have something I have to tell Alex. How can I reach him?'

'He'll be here any moment.' Bowles thought she looked relieved. 'I didn't mean to scare you. Sorry.' He tucked the gun into his belt. 'Have to be careful.' He could tell he'd scared her badly. He realized just how tense he'd been. He'd just put a gun to the woman's head and groped her private parts. 'I wasn't expecting anyone to come through the door, and people keep guns in funny places.' Bowles got her a chair and put it by the window. He rolled up the yellow shade that had kept the room in darkness. The sudden light was a strain on both their eyes. The midday sun shone off the red brick wall on the other side of the courtyard.

'I know you . . . You work for the President. I saw your picture somewhere; *Newsweek*, I think,' Helen said.

'That's right,' Bowles said. He picked his cowboy hat off the rug and emptied the tossed playing cards onto the greasy-looking dresser top.

'Now, what's wrong? You said something was wrong.' Bowles fixed his eyes on her again. 'You wrote something in the morning paper, didn't you, about President White?

You're covering him.' He remembered seeing her byline.

'Yes, I am.'

'Why aren't you with him now?'

'I got a phone call from someone at work. They told me that the police hadn't been told until the last minute that the President's schedule had been changed. They asked me to tell the Secret Service, which I did. They put me in a room and, the next thing I know, on TV, I see my boss at the paper is talking with the Secret Service man. It seemed very strange. It didn't make any sense at all. I started to leave the hotel and my boss and the Secret Service man tried to stop me. Something very strange is going on. I know that.' Helen stopped for a moment and looked at the white lines between the bricks on the wall outside. She was confused. A few moments ago she was running away from her assignment and she wasn't exactly sure why, and now she was standing here talking to a man who should be with the President and, instead, he was sitting here in some fleabag hotel waiting for Alex. She decided it had to be a nightmare and she would wake up and everything would be all right.

The music was suddenly turned up louder next door — the *ANNN ANNNN ANNNNNN ANNNN ANNNNN ANNN* of the guitar. *OH OH OH OH OH OH OH — all night long*. Bowles moved closer to her. 'I'm going to call Alex. Do you have a phone? I don't want to use the hotel phone.' Helen handed him her cell phone, barely able to hear him over the music.

'Alex, it's me, Bowles. Where the fuck are you? I got your wife here with me . . . They're going to do it tonight at the baseball game. They've changed his damn schedule.' Alex had felt his phone vibrate as he waited for the light to change across from the hotel. He opened it and heard Bowles's panicky voice.

'I'll be right there. I just want to make sure it's safe.'

24

'Is Michael with you?' Wyatt said over the phone.

'No. I'm on my way to the safehouse now,' Glad said.

'You have to make a detour, there's a problem, Alex has killed Penn. He's with the President's security chief at a hotel downtown. Room 455 on Turk Street, the Edwards Hotel. We've been listening to his wife's cell phone. They have to be stopped,' Wyatt said.

'Fine.'

'Go down there and have the kid take care of the problem.' Wyatt said.

★ ★ ★

'Do you remember me?' Glad said. Michael Law turned and looked at him and shook his head. Glad drove slowly as the car turned out of the Presidio and headed downtown. The young man seemed distant, and Glad wasn't sure that he hadn't gone too far with him.

'What's your name?' Glad asked him.

'Michael.' The voice was mechanical and tired. The kid's eyes were bloodshot.

'*We're going to kill someone.*' Glad shouted it, almost screaming, because it was the volume that would set him up and clear any resistance. Michael Law nodded his head slowly.

'All right,' Michael said. Glad nodded, satisfied. It was amazing what you could do to people, Glad thought. He reached over and turned on the radio. He rolled through the channels until he found some rock music. He turned it up. The car pulled onto Turk Street and slowed, the music loud. 'You're going to kill some men in a hotel room. Just follow my instructions . . . ' Glad said.

★　★　★

The girl was standing inside the doorway on Turk Street a few doors up from the Edwards Hotel. For a moment, Michael thought about another girl who was further down the block. 'Take the first one you see,' Glad had said before he got out of the car. *The first one you see.* The girl was pretty, very young, maybe eighteen, tall and broad-shouldered, a dishwater blonde. She had on a very short black skirt and some kind of tie-dyed blouse. She smiled at him. Michael, his eyes a blank, didn't smile back. The girl had smoked a joint and was already so high that she didn't notice the empty look he gave back to her. She did notice he was good-looking, and she was tired of tripping with fat, ugly men. She gave him the 'wanna-date?' look. He got closer.

'I want to go over there,' Michael said. He turned around and pointed at the Edwards Hotel in the middle of the block.

'Anywhere you want, baby.'

'How much?'

'You want a suck or a fuck?' she asked.

'Everything,' he told her in a flat voice. *He's stoned too,* the girl thought. *So what, probably won't even be able to get it up. Easy money. Cute.* She stopped leaning on the drugstore window and stood up straight. She was even taller now, almost six feet.

'Suck and fuck is seventy-five.' Michael took out a handful of twenties he'd been given. 'Not yet,' she said, surprised. He dropped a twenty-dollar bill on the sidewalk and didn't bother to pick it up. 'Hey . . . honey.' Michael looked at the girl for a moment and then grabbed her by the arm. 'Don't you want the money?' she said. 'Jesus!' They walked into the Edwards Hotel.

There was a kind of cage around the desk. The clerk behind the cage recognized the girl as one of the hotel's regulars. Another day, another dollar, he thought. She was prettier

287

than most, tall and kind of big, the way he liked them.

'I want a room on the fourth floor,' the young man with her said. His voice was a little strange, flat-sounding. Usually when they were this age, they were self-conscious. This john was looking at him straight in the eye, fixing him for a moment with a strange look. The clerk noticed the girl scrounging in her hand bag. She was rummaging around for a condom, found one of several she carried, and fished it out. She winked at the clerk crinkling the package as she held it up.

'Sixty dollars,' the clerk said. He got a key from one of the scores of dark cubbyholes behind him. Michael took the tarnished key with its black plastic tag from the old marble counter.

'I'll be right there,' Michael said in a strange-sounding voice. The girl took the key from him and started up the stairs to their left. Michael began counting out the money on the counter in a slow, childish way. The clerk was watching the girl climb the stairs. He knew he could look up her dress at just the right moment, it was one of the perks of the job. 'That's just for two hours now,' the desk clerk said, not looking at the kid. He kept his eyes cocked to the 'sweet' step, waiting for the money. He watched her ankles and then her white thighs as she climbed. He leaned forward and he saw the dark panties and her crotch.

Michael pushed the bills toward the opening. The clerk reached for the money. *You'll kill the desk clerk first. You don't want him to stop you on the way out in case someone calls down an alarm.* Glad's instructions played back to him as he reached between the bars and grabbed the clerk's shirt, yanking his face into the bars of the cage. He let go of the shirt and got his hand behind the clerk's head, then slammed his face down on the marble counter. Still conscious, the clerk struggled to stand up. Michael had him by his greasy hair. He brought the head down a second time, harder on the sharp edge of the marble counter. The man buckled. Michael took the gun Glad had given him from the small of his back, a Colt .45 automatic, with silencer. He reached through the bars and placed the end of the barrel on the center of the man's lacerated forehead and fired once. The shot knocked him backwards against the key box. The bullet left a burnt-looking dime-sized hole just above the bridge of his nose.

★　★　★

Michael followed the girl up the stairs. She had stopped on the second floor landing and waited until he'd caught up with her. For some reason, she'd kissed him in the darkness of the landing. She pressed her lips onto his. It was, she thought, moving her lips away from the handsome face, like kissing a cold iron slab. She'd tried to put her tongue in his mouth for the fun of it, but he hadn't budged. All right, it was going to be slam-bam-thank-you-ma'am. *So much the better*. They walked the rest of the way up the stairs in silence. The bit of blood he'd gotten on his finger from the clerk's face he was able to wipe off on the back of the girl's dress when she'd stopped to kiss him.

Michael heard the music as they stepped into the hallway. The girl kept walking but he stopped her. She said something but the music was starting to reach him now, the way it had with the doctor. He was hearing the same song. Things in his head went hot. The girl's face came closer. She saw the smear of lipstick she'd left on his lips. The girl was asking him something and took hold of his arm, laughing. He shook off her hand and looked up at the ceiling. He saw the filthy light fixture above him. *LOUD, TOO LOUD*. He leaned over, putting his hands on his knees, and tried to think.

Kill the men in 455. Kill the men in 455.

But he couldn't move. His body started to jerk. He was in the tank again. Yes, yes. *Who are you supposed to kill?* The music seemed to fill up his insides. *OHHH OHHH.* The blare of a guitar. *Doctor?* He was screaming. The girl backed away from him. *Kill the men in 455, Kill the men in 455.*

After a moment, he got hold of himself and stood up, wiping his face with his hand. 'Do you like this song?' he said. 'Do you like this fucking song? This song!' Michael grabbed the girl by the arm. She had been backing down the hall, terror growing in her eyes.

'Listen man. You're sick.' She managed to push him back. He felt her strength and heard the music blaring behind her. He put his palms against his ears, screaming at her.

'I ASKED YOU A QUESTION!' The girl turned and started to run down the hall. Michael fell to his knees, his palms still over his ears, the music driving everything from his head now but the desire to kill. The words burned on his tongue as he dove and just caught the heel of the girl's shoe, just two fingers digging in and pulling it hard. She stumbled. His hand moved up to her calf and yanked. This time her whole body crashed in front of him onto the floor.

'I ASKED YOU AND YOU WON'T SAY.

WHY WON'T YOU SAY? DO YOU LIKE THE MUSIC?' Michael crawled over her, feeling the girl's strong legs kicking, trying to kick his face. He pulled on her calves until he was even with her, climbing up her body, feeling her bigness. Her begging face was a blur, and the music was so good. The volume was the way he liked it — LOUD — the way they had made him like it. FULL VOLUME.

He started to sing: *Babe, I'm gonna leave you, babe babe.* She stopped struggling. She was looking at him, suddenly frozen, realizing now that he was a maniac, the kind of freak that killed girls. He was too strong for her. He covered her mouth and told her to stand up. They got up together slowly. 'Don't kill me, please,' she begged. He held her arm, twisting it behind her back, then ran full speed suddenly, ramming her into the door of room 455 face first.

★　★　★

'*Open the fucking door!*' Michael was banging the girl's forehead on the door, bouncing it off the wood like a knocker.

Bowles had barely heard the first bang. Helen looked at the door. It was shaking, but she could just barely hear the banging over the music. An organ solo started in even

292

louder, the people in the other room turning it up as loud as it would go now. Why hadn't the desk clerk done something about this noise, Helen thought. Bowles reached for his gun and turned to the door. He motioned Helen to get up and move into the corner of the room by the window, pushing her back. He quickly opened the revolver and checked the cylinder. It was full. He had a speed loader on the bed; he picked it up and clipped it over his belt. It wasn't Alex, he was sure of that. A drunk probably . . . He started toward the door.

★   ★   ★

Blood splattered onto the door from the girl's forehead. She passed out and he held her full weight, clenching the back of her blouse to keep her standing. Michael Law hadn't felt so good in a long time. *Why do I feel so good? Because we know who we are going to kill.* The door still wasn't opening. He backed up, the girl a limp dancing partner now, her blood warm on his hand. He backed, holding the girl up, all the way to the other wall, then stopped for a moment to make sure he had his gun barrel clear. He took off running, pushing the girl's big loose body full force into the door, smashing it off the hinges.

What Helen saw she would never forget. The door came crashing down. The girl's bloody face and body hurtled toward them. Bullets slammed into the girl's torso, then chest from Bowles' gun. Michael, his eyes wide, fired at Bowles from the end of the bed. Bowles' gun clicked emptily. A bullet hit Bowles in the head knocking him back into the window. Helen could hear the sound of her own screams.

★ ★ ★

Alex scanned the opposite side of the street looking for Wyatt's men. He knew they were out there somewhere in the city. He knew it was possible that they were onto the Edwards. The street was crowded with people — down-and-outers, prostitutes, bag ladies, winos. They were the reason why he had been trained to gravitate to the seedy parts of town. When the suits came, they stood out. Street people had a look that was impossible to forge. Alex looked now among the derelicts and pimps for that clean-cut face that would give them away. If he was lucky, they'd send the FBI. They were always the easiest to spot — like Jehovah's Witnesses in a brothel.

An older black prostitute in gold hot pants and tank top stood outside the Edwards, her midriff sloppy over the top of her pants. Alex studied her closely, reminding himself that the days of the all-white agency were over. But the ugly, streetwise face, stupid from booze, and the blue mascara said it all. He focused on the porno shop to the right of her, its yellow papered window was two doors down the street. Two white men, their arms covered with jailhouse tattoos, stood talking in the doorway. He let his eyes wander to the apartment windows above street level. Most were dirty, a few with curtains. Nothing. Then down again to the crowded sidewalk. An old white woman wearing a heavy coat was almost completely bent over and clutching a plastic bag in her gloved hand, trying not to be noticed. He moved again, this time letting his glance go to the traffic slowing for a traffic light. But something wasn't right, some sixth-sense made him hold back and kept him from going across the street to the hotel. *What is it?* He could almost feel the danger. He kept his back to the street and used the reflection from the drugstore window to show him the scene. He pretended to be studying the display of cheap radios. Midway up the block, there was a parking garage and a man with a mechanic's uniform talking to the ticket taker, real grease on the coveralls. Alex moved along the street. His eyes stopped at a used bookstore where bins out in front were piled high with paperbacks. He noticed a man inside browsing through the books. He almost went on, but it was the way he was doing it, *the way he was doing it*. A tour bus came down the street, stopped at the traffic light, and was sitting between him and the bookstore now. Alex glanced at the traffic light. The prostitute had gone out into the crosswalk and fallen. He watched her get up, sway slightly, and curse the traffic in front of her. The light turned green, but she was still in the crosswalk, cursing. A cacophony of horns started, first a few, then a steady increase. Alex moved into the street along the rear of the tour bus, putting his hands on its smooth metallic sides and stepping up on the big tire to look into the window. A young girl and her mother were looking at him, startled, but he didn't pay them any attention. He was looking at the man in the bookstore through the bus windows. *Something about him. If the store's windows weren't so filthy . . . .* The bus started to move and his foot rolled off the tire. He fell back to the street.

Damn it. A car switched lanes, the driver honking, and just missed him. A black cloud of exhaust came from the bus as it pulled forward. He almost stumbled into the path of another car. He managed somehow to avoid the car's front fender. *I know that person.* The traffic started to move around him now. He'd lost his cover and was in the middle of the street. He glanced again at the figure in the book shop for just a second; the sun glinted off something inside, almost like a mirror shooting the sun into his eyes. Alex squinted. Another horn. *Yes . . . careful.* Squinting now, he felt for his gun and moved back across the street, turning his back on the bookstore. *I know that person.*

★   ★   ★

Glad had seen the bus. He'd kept his eyes on the street and on the entrance of the hotel. The bookstore, with its sweet smell of rotting paperbacks and the sound of a coffee machine, had been the perfect place to wait for the kid to come back out. He'd parked in a white zone but could easily handle a police metermaid. He'd watched the commotion at the intersection, pretending to read Madonna's sex book. The proprietor, an old East Indian, anticipated a good sale.

When Glad saw the cloud of smoke from the exhaust, and then the cars, he had almost not looked, thinking they were still honking at the whore, but there had been the horn that had blared after the others had stopped. When he saw Alex in the middle of the street, Glad let the book slide to the floor, and its aluminum cover had glinted like a mirror.

'Alex.' He'd said the name out loud. For a moment, the two were looking at each other. Alex's hands were in the pockets of his trench coat, and his expression was blurred by the store's dirty window.

Alex. Glad ripped the gun out of his shoulder holster. Should he fire from inside the store? And if the kid came out? He lifted the gun anyway. Something powerful, hate, made him raise the gun and aim through the dirty window, his finger on the trigger, the ramp sight just below Alex's chin. He waited for the front bead to catch the sight . . .

Then someone shoved his shoulder. *No, damn it. Damn it.* 'You pick up book. Pick up book, you crazy?' The little Indian, who was hectoring Glad, froze when he saw the gun. The image on the gun sight jarred. Alex was moving now up the street. Someone opened the shop door, setting off a string of bells tied to it. Glad spun on the Indian, smashing him in the face and knocking him into the bookshelves. It was a knockout punch. His hand caught the little man full in the mouth and picked him up like a piece of cloth. Whoever had been coming through the door had left when he'd seen the gun. Glad looked back out the window, but Alex had vanished. Glad moved toward the door. He had to get the kid. They weren't finished yet. *Fucking Alex.*

★   ★   ★

Michael watched Red Bowles's body tumble out the window. The head knocked twice on the brick wall as it fell the four stories into the garbage-strewn courtyard. The music had stopped. He turned around. The woman? He'd seen a woman. His hands and face were smeared with blood. He took his shirt-tail out and wiped his face off. A young man stared at him from the doorway, long hair, stoned out, terrified, then he was gone. Michael looked down at the prostitute's body. Glad had been right. She'd been the perfect battering ram and shield. The other woman? He'd seen her somewhere before. An old woman was standing in the doorway screaming. As he started to move, Michael tripped over something, then he was out the door. He pushed the old woman, a stick-like figure, into the wall as she tried to get out of his way.

★   ★   ★

Helen ran blindly at first, not able to think. *Just get down the stairs.* The first flight had been a kind of blur. Going down the second flight, something had gone wrong with her shoe and she realized she'd been in heels. She kept running down to the last flight, her body shocked by the hard jarring, trying not to stumble.

She ran down the steps and from the last landing looked down at the cage, desperate for help. The dead clerk stared up at her. A man pushed open the lobby door. 'Help me. Help me,' she screamed.

'Grab her!' Glad said as Helen felt Michael's hand reach around her waist.

★   ★   ★

Alex pulled open the door to the hotel's back entrance, following the route the night manager had shown him days before. He trotted back through a long narrow service tunnel, then through another door to a small dirty office with a metal cot and black-and-white TV. He went through a swinging half door to the Edwards' desk. The clerk he'd paid off a few days before was lying on the floor, a single, dime-sized hole at the bridge of his nose. Alex stepped over the body of the dead clerk, and pulled his forty-five from the holster at the small of his back.

The automatic banged against his knee as he ran up the stairs. Two doors were open on the second floor. A frightened black man peered from the slit of an open door as he went by. He ran on to the next set of stairs. A siren began to wail somewhere outside on the street.

'You the police?' A skinny white woman came out on the top of the fourth-floor landing and looked down at him as he came up. 'They threw somebody's ass out the window, man. Fucking out the window . . . In there.'

'Yes, I'm the police,' Alex lied, out of breath.

'Out the window, man. Ain't that a *bitch?* Out the fucking window.' He pushed past her and ran down the hall to the shattered doorway and through the splintered door frame. He stepped over the door lying on the floor inside the room and saw the bullet-torn body of a girl halfway on the bed, mouth open, facing him. He went to the open window. Alex saw Bowles lying in the trash-covered courtyard four stories below, his arms twisted under him. He was too late. Alex turned around, saw a purse on the floor. *Where was Helen?* The sirens were growing louder, the sound echoing through the courtyard. He went out the door toward the fire escape at the end of the hall.

25

At five in the afternoon, Glad got off a municipal bus at the main entrance to 3Com Park. He wore a new Giant's cap, a T-shirt that said Shit Happens, new black Levi's and a pair of Nikes. You couldn't see what he was carrying in the fanny-pack strapped to the front of his waist, where he could get to it quickly. He queued up at one of the ticket-vending machines, then made his way inside the stadium to the main concourse. He bought a hot dog, a large Coors, and ate standing against a wall, casually looking at the early arrivals, mostly men in small groups. When he was finished eating, Glad walked down to the field and watched the Giants take batting practice. Occasionally, he would glance at the workers who were hurriedly finishing the presidential box just behind the Giants' dugout.

★　★　★

An hour later the fog was just coming over the dirty gold hills behind 3Com park. The park's famous wind was blowing in from the

302

ocean. Long gray streamers of fog were pushing over the freeway toward the top of the stadium, then vanishing like smoke in the wind. Michael Law got out of a taxi, took his new backpack out of the cab's trunk, paid the driver who had brought him, and started walking toward 3Com's VIP entrance across the huge parking lot. The stadium's main parking lot was filled with families and young couples having tailgate parties. A fireworks company had set up its equipment, rocket tubes and floodlights, in a corner close to the stadium's main entrance. A score of workers were busy preparing for the annual fourth of July fireworks show. No one paid any attention to the young man in baggy shorts and T-shirt as he crossed the parking lot; just another fan making for the stadium. At the VIP gate, Michael handed a security man his skybox passport and was waved through to a special elevator that took VIPs straight up to the skyboxes at the top of the stadium. As he stepped into the elevator, a test rocket was fired from the parking lot. The fireworks shot over the top of the stadium and burst red and gold over center field.

★ ★ ★

303

Michael switched on the big screen TV as soon as he got into the Law family's skybox. He stood transfixed in front of the images from MTV. He pretended to hold a guitar, moving with the riffs, shaking his head just like the rock and rollers on the screen. *We know who we have to kill*. One of the band members seemed to look up at him and speak. *We know who we have to kill*. Then he was back to his guitar, the music screaming. *We know who we have to kill*.

When the commercial came on, Michael went to the bank of windows and hit the electric switch that opened the curtains. He looked at his watch. It was six-fifteen. *You know who to kill*. He repeated the mantra Glad had taught him. He watched the field being groomed below. A big mower turned around at second base and headed for the outfield. The mower made perfect contrasting stripes across the field. Here and there, he could see fans starting to take their seats in the stands.

He turned toward the workers putting the finishing touches on the President's special box set up just above the Giants' dugout. The box was built on a platform that raised it above the surrounding seats. Workers were carrying folding chairs up for the expected dignitaries who would sit with the President.

Michael took out the binoculars he'd brought and carefully examined the clear bullet-proof partition around the box. They had told him the presidential box was exactly a hundred and twenty-five yards from where he stood.

He went across the room to a control box and turned off the speakers that brought in the live organ music from the stadium. It was quiet again in the room except for the TV. He went to one of the closets and found the laser-guided TOW rocket that they had put there for him. He picked it up and carried it to a table. The rocket had been designed to blast though the latest tank armor. What it would do to plywood and flesh was predictable.

Michael took the video cassette out of his backpack and slid it into the VCR, the way he'd been instructed by Glad. 'Michael, you have exactly an hour left.' Michael nodded at Glad whose face had appeared on the television screen. The doctor was seated at a desk, shot in tight close-up. 'Now I want you to tell me. Who are you going to kill?' Michael answered carefully, then the video cut to a presidential look-alike sitting in a replica of the presidential box. The look-alike waved to an imaginary crowd, got up and shook his hands above his head. A computer generated red dot started to blink, a countdown clock flashed in the upper right hand corner of the screen, and then, in slow motion, a TOW rocket's laser-guided system locked on the target, and the laser light hit the look-alike. The rocket came into the picture on the right, just like Michael had seen on TV during the Gulf War. The blast incinerated the box and everything in it.

'We don't want to hesitate, do we, Michael,' Dr. Glad said. The young man shook his head. His lips formed the word NO. 'You only need to arm the rocket, touch Neal White with the laser light, and fire,' the voice on the video said. Michael knelt down and watched the TV screen fade back to a music video, featuring a young girl dancing in black and white. Michael started to move his shoulders to the beat.

★ ★ ★

Alex's cab took the 3Com Park exit off the freeway. The traffic going to the stadium was heavy. His cab came to a stop still many blocks from the stadium. Alex paid the driver, got out and started to jog between the stopped cars toward 3Com Park.

Alex queued up with the throngs of excited fans going through the turnstiles into the stadium. He tried to think clearly. The

306

running had exhausted him and sweat stung his eyes. He'd had to stop twice to catch his breath. He cursed himself for being so out of shape. *I have to think.* He felt the crowd of people pushing against him. It was seven forty-six, less than fifteen minutes before the President was scheduled to appear and throw out the game ball. Alex made his way into the stadium's main concourse past the food concessions and program hawkers and stopped for a moment under a huge orange and black Giants banner. He knew the only hope he had was disrupting the program before Neal White took the stage. He would have to get up there with the President and somehow stop the show. He stopped one of the program hawkers and asked him where the President would be sitting.

A *cordon sanitaire* had been set up around the presidential box. A line of police officers in blue helmets and jumpsuits stood shoulder to shoulder. Beyond them was the bulletproof box, and in between were Secret Service men walking the no-man's land of empty orange seats. TV reporters and a dozen press photographers had been allowed in the buffer zone with them. Alex looked at his watch. It was ten to eight. He was going to fail. Once the President was out in the open, there was little he could do. The stadium's organ started up and played 'Hail to the Chief.' Alex fished out Helen's press pass and stepped into the roped-off no-man's land. A policeman immediately stepped forward.

'Chronicle,' Alex said matter-of-factly. The policeman, his face obscured by the plastic shield over his helmet, glanced at the pass. Alex held it with Helen's picture covered and kept walking, not sure what would happen. A balloon of adrenaline seemed to burst in his chest as he walked through the cordoned-off area and up into the bleachers past the photographers who barely noticed him. A half dozen Secret Service men surrounded the bunting-draped dais behind home plate where the President would watch the game.

'You're Helen's husband,' a startled voice said behind Alex. Alex froze and fingered the pass as he turned around. 'You have about five seconds to explain where Helen is and what's going on,' Merriwether said. He'd recognized Alex from the article Paulson had sent him. 'Where is she? Is that her press pass?'

'Yes,' Alex said.

A Secret Service man walked past them speaking into his lapel mike within earshot of Merriwether. Alex moved his hand to his trenchcoat pocket. A fireworks rocket exploded almost directly above them, a burst of red and gold showering incandescently over the stadium.

'Where is she?' Merriwether asked again over the sound of the fireworks. 'What's going on?' Merriwether looked down at Alex's pocketed hand that was motioning him away. Alex fingered the trigger of his pistol. He would have no choice but to shoot the man in front of him if he motioned to the Secret Service.

'She's sent me,' Alex said, not knowing what else to say. 'Who are you?'

'I'm her boss.' Merriwether looked at the Secret Service agent as he passed. The agent had moved to one end of the presidential box and stepped in to examine the interior carefully. Merriwether made for the clear bullet-proof wall and knocked on the glass. Alex stepped up behind him and put the pistol against Merriwether's back.

'Are we still on schedule?' Merriwether asked the Secret Service agent. The agent looked at him through the glass carefully, nodded abruptly and then went on with his inspection. 'I'll give you one more chance to tell me what's going on,' Merriwether whispered, not turning around.

'There's going to be an attempt on the President's life,' Alex said. 'I want to stop it. If you don't do what I say, I'll kill you.'

'I told Helen that this morning. I told her something was screwy,' Merriwether said as he turned around excitedly and faced Alex.

'Will you help me or do I kill you?' Alex whispered. The Secret Service man came out of the booth and looked at the two of them. Alex put his arm around Merriwether suddenly and smiled. 'I haven't seen you since Afghanistan,' Alex said, and began slapping Merriwether on the shoulder, shoving his gun hard into Merriwether's side as he did. The Secret Service agent stopped in front of them.

'I'll have to ask you gentlemen to stay back now, please,' he said.

'Kabul, wasn't it?' Merriwether said. The two of them walked down the steps from the dais to a walkway right above the dugout, Alex still unsure about what Merriwether might do.

'Something's happened to Helen, hasn't it?' Merriwether said as soon as they stopped. 'I tried to warn her. They didn't want me to be here tonight,' Merriwether said.

'Yes,' Alex said. 'She found out.'

'How did you get her pass? How do I know you aren't part of it?'

'You don't,' Alex said. 'And there's no time to explain. The President will be here in a few minutes.' Merriwether took out a package of cigarettes and lit one. He was shaking slightly.

'OK, what do we do? We aren't exactly an army.'

'I'm not sure,' Alex said looking across the stadium. 'Where's the President now?'

'He's waiting in a limo under the grandstand, last I heard. They're just waiting for a signal to drive him out.' Merriwether tried to light the cigarette but couldn't because of his shaking. He threw it onto the roof of the dugout below.

'Can we get close to him with these passes?' Alex said.

'Maybe,' Merriwether said. Two more fireworks rockets streaked across the sky and burst over home plate.

The crowd began to clap and roar their approval as the fireworks burst above them. *I'm going to fail*, Alex thought, realizing what it would mean for everyone as he scanned the stadium. How stupid he'd been to think he could stop them. Across the stadium, at center field, Alex caught a glimpse of a limousine emerging from a tunnel under the grandstand. 'We've got to stop him from coming up here,' Alex said. Merriwether looked at the slowly emerging limousine. Alex turned and went down the stairs to the field. Merriwether followed.

Thousands of people stood and applauded

spontaneously as they saw the first of two limousines leave the tunnel and drive onto the field. Then Alex saw it, a small square of blue light coming from his family's skybox at the top of the stadium. He started running, leaving Merriwether behind him. *I'm not going to make it, not going to make it . . .*

Merriwether stopped, his face bright red from his short run onto the field. The limousines, fifty yards in front of him, were closing in quickly, the lead limo just entering the infield. He didn't understand where Helen's husband was running off to, but he was going in the wrong direction. *Go on. Just get in front of the damn car and stop it yourself. You can do it.* Merriwether turned and looked at the lead limousine as it drove past second base. He dashed out into the infield. Merriwether ran toward the first limousine at full speed, his arms waving wildly in the air and then suddenly, clutching his chest, collapsed, dead.

★   ★   ★

Sunset. Michael Law looked at his watch; it was almost eight. The pills he'd taken were working, and his heart was beating slower now. Calmly, he knelt and turned the volume up on the TV. Ignoring the sound of the fireworks outside, he put his sweaty palm on the cool glass of the big screen. A small shadow of fear passed over him; he shook it off.

'Time now. Time now.' The music stopped playing. Glad's face came back on the screen. Michael turned away from the TV and dragged the table away from the bank of windows. 'Time now. Time now.' Michael made sure all the lights were turned off, went to the middle window and slid it open as far as it would go. The noise from the fans and the fireworks filled the dark room. He went to the table and picked up the rocket and crouched in front of the open window, standing back enough so he couldn't be seen. He looked through the laser sight and watched the two black limousines move over the brightly lit infield.

⋆　⋆　⋆

Glad stepped into the room. He'd seen the limousines coming out on the field from outside. His orders were to detain Michael and wait for the authorities to arrest him after he'd killed the President. It was a few minutes past eight when he entered the skybox, his Nikes soundless on the carpet, and locked the door behind him. Across the room, in the darkness tinged with blue light, he could make out Michael's form in position by the window. His own voice was still coming from the TV. The electronic beeping of the armed rocket was loud enough for Glad to hear over the sound of the crowd outside.

He could see the presidential box below framed by the window, the ribbons of red, white and blue bunting in the flood lights. A squad of Secret Service men huddled around the President as they hustled him from one of the limousines up the steps and into the safety of the box. The whole Giants team in the dugout was watching, on their feet now, clapping. Some of the players reached up and tried to shake the President's hand. A fireworks missile sailed over the rim of the stadium and exploded, then another and another. By the time Glad had come within a few feet of Michael, Neal White was safely inside the box, waving to the cheering fans. He stepped up directly behind Michael Law and looked at the compact rocket tube resting on his shoulder.

'Arm your weapon, Michael,' Glad ordered. Without looking at him, Michael hit the rocket's safety. Immediately the volume of the beeping increased. 'All right, let's blast the son-of-a-bitch,' Glad said.

★ ★ ★

Alex rested the barrel of the forty-five flat on the dead bolt and blew it off the door. The sound was covered by the concussion of fireworks. He kicked the door open and walked into the skybox. A fireworks rocket timed to go off at the exact moment the President reached his box came over the edge of the stadium. There was a loud OOOOOOOOH from the thousands of fans. A huge and perfect American flag burst onto the night sky.

Alex heard the big screen TV playing as he crossed the darkened room. He glanced at the face of Glad on the TV screen, who was talking some kind of gibberish. 'Enemies of the country deserve one thing. God is country and country is God,' Glad said. Alex turned away from the TV screen and walked further into the room. He heard the beep, beep of the armed rocket. He got closer. The red-white-and-blue fireworks light suddenly painted on the walls of the dark room the outlines of two figures . . .

Alex saw a shimmering mask from the fireworks on Glad's face, and the outline of a man kneeling, holding something on his shoulder in front of the window. Glad's eyes were completely without fear. The strange light began dying almost as quickly as it had come on, and the ghost-like images faded back into the darkness of the room again. Alex raised the forty-five, his night vision destroyed by the fireworks.

'Michael. Don't!' Alex, blinking, tried to see and fired.

'I know who I have to kill,' Michael said, looking at his father now, the last of the strange light of the fireworks in his eyes.

'Michael, don't do it!' Alex said. Glad turned and looked at Alex.

'DO IT. DO IT,' Glad screamed. Michael stood up. He turned the barrel of the launcher and pointed it at Alex. He centered the rod of laser light on his father's forehead.

'I know who I have to kill,' Michael said.

'You stupid fuck!' Glad moved toward Michael. Alex fired, but Glad's thin kevlar vest absorbed the bullet. Glad uncoiled the garrote and felt its wooden handles against his palms. The loop of the garrote came over the top of Michael's head. In an instant, it was over, and Michael was pushed aside, his arms flailing in agony. The wire had cut through to the bone. Alex ran to his son and tried to pull the wire out from his bleeding throat. He turned to look at Glad who had gone to the window.

Glad knelt and picked up the rocket

launcher and turned it toward the window. He kept his eye on the President, found the rocket sight; the laser's light touched the President's face. Glad hit the fire button. He felt something hit the barrel of the rocket as it was launching from the tube. 'Fuck you!' Alex had thrown something. The rocket launched following the blue rod of laser light.

Alex watched the rocket's smoking tail emerge from the tube, then accelerate in mid-flight, tracking, descending, gaining speed, and slamming into one of the empty limousines on the field. The limousine's armor plate blew open, and chunks of burning car catapulted into the air. When Alex looked up, Glad was looking at him and Michael was dead.

'Well, aren't you going to shoot?' Glad said. Alex ran at him and picked him up. The adrenaline and hate made him scream. He ran to the window. He could feel Glad struggling as he let him go.

26

Tijuana, Mexico

Helen opened her blouse and lay across the unmade bed. She tried to think of cool safe places; it was too hot in the room to do anything else. 'Would you like a swim?' Wyatt asked. He unlocked the door to the bedroom he'd kept her in since they'd arrived and tossed a two-piece bathing suit he'd bought in San Diego at her. The orange-colored suit landed on her stomach, a big paper tag still attached. Helen picked it up and let it drop on the floor, nonplussed. She slid her legs over the side of the bed. Drowsy from the heat, she felt nauseated and her head hurt — even the linen on the pillow felt warm to her skin.

'I'd like to at least have the windows open,' she said. She tried to appear unafraid of him, but she *was* afraid of him. She couldn't look at Wyatt without thinking about what had happened at the hotel, and about the way Glad had spoken to Michael in the car, getting him to describe the murders. She clutched the pillow and told herself she had to act as if *she* were in control. 'And how about telling me where I am and why you've brought me here and where my son is . . . '

'Sorry, can't do that,' Wyatt said. He stepped inside the bedroom but left the door open behind him. The smell of suntan lotion followed him into the room. Helen looked at the freckled face that was sweaty and smiling at her. He'd come in straight from the pool and was wearing a black Speedo swim suit and rubber sandals. There wasn't any fat on his big muscular body. The hair on his chest was red and she saw that he had freckles on his upper shoulders that were turning dark orange from lying in the sun. It was hard to believe she'd had any feeling for him. He was looking at her body, getting an eyeful.

'How about a swim? No reason you can't enjoy the pool while you're here,' he said. Wyatt walked to the window that looked out on the pool and garden of the safe house. He ran his fingers around the window frame to make sure the lock hadn't been tampered with.

'Why would I want to do that?' Helen said. The smell of the sun lotion started to mix with his body odor and the nauseating smell of bug killer that had been used throughout the house. Helen started breathing through her mouth so she wouldn't smell it. Wyatt came away from the window and checked the empty closet. She watched him snap on the light in the closet then snap it off, satisfied that she hadn't been up to anything. Her drowsiness was giving way quickly to fear. She slid down the bed away from him. She'd been locked up only a day, and it seemed like a month already.

'Are you sure then? You don't have to stay locked in *this room*.' Wyatt turned around and faced her.

'Wyatt, let me go.' Wyatt shook his head and smiled. 'Then at least tell me what you did to my son?'

'I tell you what. You come out to the pool and I'll fix you a drink. What are you going to do in here, anyway? It's hot as hell in here,' Wyatt said. 'And I know you're thirsty.' He ran his hand down his stomach and knocked a glob of lotion and sweat onto the red tile floor. A cockroach ran out from under the bed and Wyatt immediately stepped on it with his rubber sandal. There was a crunching sound. He walked up to the edge of the bed, put one of his lotion-wet legs between hers and tore the pillow out of her hand.

'So tell me about Alex,' he said. 'How did he know about our plans?' Wyatt asked. His face had gotten suddenly ugly. Wyatt put his index finger on the inside corner of her bra and ran it down the inside edge. She started to tremble. She'd been brave up until the moment he touched her.

'I don't know what you're talking about,' she said. 'We're in Mexico, aren't we?' She turned her head toward the windows and looked out at the flat blue water of the swimming pool. She reached up and grabbed his hand and pulled it off of her.

★ ★ ★

When he was finished with her, Wyatt went back to the patio and read the *San Diego Herald* by the pool. The paper's banner headline read COUP FOILED. Wyatt read about a corrupt cabal inside the CIA. Alex's name didn't appear anywhere, but he knew somehow that Alex had been the one who had stopped them.

The men who had come with Wyatt to the safe house in Tijuana had left after they'd heard the news. Some of them would try to go back and pretend they hadn't been involved. Wyatt knew he could never go back. He would have to run. He put down the newspaper. He'd decided he would go to Africa. There were places there where nobody cared, and you were safe if you had money. For a long time he lay supine thinking, then he got up with a hunch and went inside, picked up the phone in the living room; he had a message for Alex. He had an ace in the hole and he was going to use it. 'I've got Helen . . . Corsican rules, old chum.' That was the message Wyatt left for Alex.

★   ★   ★

Tijuana, Mexico was its usual tangled mess of people and cars that Friday afternoon when Alex walked across the border from San Ysidro. Tourists from San Diego and LA were pouring into TJ for the afternoon dog races. Alex followed the crowds onto the downtown strip. The air smelled of car exhaust. Loud music came from the bars on the strip that catered to the American college kids. The sidewalks were filled with girls in shorts and young Marines in mufti in bands of fours and fives, already drunk, and anxious to take it out on someone.

By Saturday night, Tijuana's main drag had reached a frenzied pitch; the weather still balmy before midnight. Alex had come out of the crowd shortly after eleven, just the way he'd been instructed to do by Wyatt, and sat in the designated café. He watched a street photographer put a long-legged college girl on his donkey and take her picture. She was

322

drunk and had a bad sunburn, her arms and legs bright red. Every corner on the strip had a photographer with a donkey and big sombrero. For five dollars, you could have your picture taken sitting on the donkey. The photographer managed to pinch her on the ass as she slid off. Rap music was coming from a second-story night club across the street. In the summer, the night club removed its windows. You could see the twenty-something crowd inside dancing under green strobe lights. Wyatt had been watching the street from inside the club. He slipped out of the club onto the crowded sidewalk and into the café where he sat down at Alex's table. Wyatt was wearing a tourist get-up and sunglasses. He was tan, the freckles on his face had turned deep orange. His sunglasses had a blue tint to them and caught all the neon lights on the street. Wyatt's shirt was loud, brown with some kind of yellow flowers on it. A waiter appeared and Wyatt ordered a *Dos XXs*.

'Why Michael?' Alex had been waiting to ask the question since the moment he'd left the stadium. 'I want to know about Michael before we talk about anything else.' Alex poured the rest of his Coke out of the bottle and watched the brown liquid make a head. Wyatt took his cigarette lighter out. It was the same one he'd always carried, the one with the Hundred and First Airborne logo on it, the eagle's head. He turned it over once on the café table, took out a small cigar and lit it.

'It wasn't my idea . . . It was Penn's. He thought it would be the perfect story. Young son avenges his father's ignominious treatment by the US Government. Comes from a rich family. No one would care what happened to him. America secretly hates rich people,' Wyatt said. 'The kid wanted to be just like you.'

'What did they do to him?'

'The PSYWOP people did a number on him . . . Penn is from the old school — drugs, mind control, LSD. They wanted somebody that would be . . . pliable.' Alex didn't say anything. Wyatt's eyes met his.

'Look, the kid signed up. You know the game. He lost. You won. That's the way it's played, isn't it. You and I are still playing. I have Helen. I want out. I need money. You can fix it for me.' The waiter came back with the beer and put it down on the table. Alex paid him automatically without looking at him. He had to practice every bit of self-control not to kill Wyatt right where he sat.

'Where's Helen?'

'She's here with me in TJ.' Wyatt picked up

the beer and took a drink, put it down and wiped his lips. 'I want $15 million. I want half a million in cash tomorrow, the rest you can wire to this numbered account.' Wyatt tossed him a card with the name of a bank in Switzerland. 'You do that, and I'll give you Helen. If you don't, I'll kill her and disappear. I'll make sure it's slow, too, because I'm pissed off. You know me, I'm good at it. Are we on or not?' Wyatt wiped the top of the bottle off and took another drink. The crowd on the street was reaching a critical mass of tattoos and short-shorts, middle-aged white couples and young Latino gangbangers.

'How do I know she's still alive? I'll have to talk to her.' Alex reached over and picked up the card, looking at the name of the bank.

'She'll call you. Where are you staying?' Alex gave him the name of the Hotel Roosevelt in San Diego.

'Let's say she calls you at midnight at your hotel. The wire transfer should be done first thing tomorrow morning. It shouldn't be any problem for someone who owns a bank. I want the cash tomorrow in small bills.'

'If Helen's alive, I'll get you the money,' Alex said.

'There's a municipal bus that leaves the

border for the bull ring tomorrow at three. Take it. Have the money with you. If you come after me, or anyone does, she'll be dead. Do you understand? I just have to pick up a telephone. So no amateur high jinks, like people trying to follow me.' Wyatt put down the beer, got up and disappeared into the crowds on the sidewalk.

27

When Butch knocked on the door of the hotel room, Alex was relieved to see him. For a moment, Butch, in blue jeans and a sweatshirt, stood there grim-faced; then they embraced. Butch walked with a slight limp from the leg wound he'd gotten in Lisbon. He went over to the mini-bar and took out a beer. The two men looked at each other for a moment from across the room. Butch offered him a beer but Alex shook his head, he hadn't had a drink since the day he'd left Helen.

'I'm sorry about Michael,' Butch said. He'd read about it in the newspaper. 'I tried to call you.' Alex nodded his head and watched Butch strip the cap off the beer bottle.

'Butch, Wyatt's holding Helen hostage in Tijuana; I need your help to get her back.'

Butch took out a cigarette, lit it, and took the smoke deep into his lungs as he looked over the expensive antiques in the hotel suite. 'You know, for a couple of days, I didn't want to live without Patsy. I didn't. I didn't see the point,' he said. 'I still don't, really.'

'Glad's dead, if that makes any difference,' Alex said.

'I should have killed him in Cuernavaca,' Butch said. There was a long silence then. Nothing Alex thought to say seemed right.

'I'm going to meet Wyatt tomorrow, Butch. I want you to cover me.' Butch nodded. Alex took some money out of his wallet. Butch waved it away and sat on the expensive yellow couch and stared at him for a moment. It was an odd look. Alex could only guess what he was thinking, what he wanted to say. Instead, Alex asked him what he planned to do now.

'I've been thinking of going back to Cuernavaca,' Butch said finally. 'Do you think that's a good idea? It's funny how it is; you want to go back and see it. See where . . . '

'I don't know,' Alex said. 'I think maybe you shouldn't. Start fresh, maybe.' Butch studied him a moment.

'They've offered me a job, head of Clandestine . . . There's been a wholesale shake up at the agency. I'll need a good man to help me run it,' Alex said.

'Do you think much about what we did all those years, and about the pain we caused people? Now that we know what it's like.'

'Now I do, yes,' Alex said. Alex walked to the mini-bar and looked at the closed door as if it were calling him, then he turned around.

I'm finished with all that, he told himself.

'You know, the funny thing is, I still can't talk to regular people. You know, civilians. They just seem like children to me,' Butch said. 'I have to be around our kind . . . ' He smiled, finally. There was something indefatigable in the smile. 'I'll take the job. Old dogs and all that, what else would we do?'

★ ★ ★

Sunday, at three in the afternoon, Alex boarded a municipal bus just across from the main border crossing. It had rained overnight, but it was clearing now and humid. The bus splashed through the big puddles and took the back streets toward the center of Tijuana. Alex held the money he'd gotten from a Western Trust office in San Diego. He'd taken the money from his own account and had the bank's New York office wire the larger sum to the numbered account Wyatt had given him in Zurich. The red gym bag Alex had crammed with cash was almost too small for the half-million dollars. More and more Mexicans got on the bus as it moved into town. Tough-looking *hombres* eyed the tourists who had gotten on with Alex. He put the gym bag between his legs and tried to appear relaxed.

Alex didn't see Wyatt get on the crowded bus. Wyatt had pushed his way through and was standing next to him. He was wearing jeans and a white *guayabera,* his hair slicked down with something so that it was darker, but he wore the same sunglasses with the deep blue lenses as the night before. Wyatt told the kid sitting next to Alex to move in Spanish, lifting his shirt and showing him the gun in his belt at the same time. The kid got up hurriedly and squeezed through the standing crowd. The bus driver closed the doors at the front of the bus and they started moving again, the roar of the diesel engine loud. Wyatt sat down next to him. For a moment, neither one of them said anything.

'Where is she?' Alex said.

'There's time for that. Do you have the money?' Alex nodded as he picked up the bag and put it back on his lap. Wyatt made him open it. Alex looked around. People were looking at them. He unzipped the bag, and Wyatt, unconcerned, dug his hands in, turning over the bundles of cash. Wyatt zipped it up and moved the bag to his lap. Then, carefully, he lit a small cigar with one hand. He seemed very relaxed for a man with half the police forces of the world looking for him.

'We don't have much time. I got the

deposit. Good work. Two stops from now, she'll be allowed to board the bus *if* I get off . . . Only if I get off, you understand?' Alex nodded. 'Good. I doubt we'll ever see each other again,' Wyatt said.

'I wouldn't bet on that,' Alex said.

'Don't bother looking. You won't find me.' Alex turned away to the window. They'd come into the center of town now. A bullfight poster on a shop window caught Alex's eye.

'Did you love Helen at all?' Alex said, looking out the window. It was strange that he asked the question, but somehow he wanted to ask it.

'I don't know; maybe. At first I just wanted to take her away from you because I knew you did love her. You had everything, it never seemed fair to me. I hated you because you had too much,' Wyatt said. The bus came to a stop. More people got on. Someone called to the driver in Spanish to keep the back door open.

'Time's a funny thing. In combat it goes by so fast. Now a few blocks go by so slow,' Wyatt said. He took a puff of the cigar then moved it to the corner of his mouth.

'Why the drug cartel? Why?' Alex said.

'Money. What other reason is there?' Wyatt looked at Alex and then did something strange — he reached across and wanted to shake Alex's hand. 'For old time's sake . . . I know you want to kill me. Now you know how it feels to hate someone,' Wyatt said.

'You won't get away, you know that. Tomorrow or the next day, I'll find you,' Alex said. Wyatt looked at him and smiled.

'They want you back, don't they? I always said you'd end up running the place. I bet you will, now. Like I said, time's a funny thing,' Wyatt smiled broadly. 'Do you remember what you said to me the day we met on the pistol range at the farm? You shook my hand and said *Vive la mort, vive la guerre*. That's all we were ever good for wasn't it, Alex. Nothing really changes. Well, this is my stop.'

Alex turned away toward the window. He could see the stop coming up as Wyatt got up from the seat. The driver called out the next stop in English for the tourists: *Bullring*. Most of the tourists stood up and crowded into the aisle, their colored shirts and shorts in contrast to the drab poorly dressed Mexicans who quickly took their seats.

Alex got up and started pushing toward the front of the bus, past the big shoulders of the North Americans who were moving toward the door. The foreign passengers were getting off here. Alex saw Helen waiting to board. He pushed past the last few passengers, stepped

332

off the bus, and grabbed her by the shoulders. He turned, looking for Wyatt in the crowd of tourists, and saw him moving toward the bullring.

'Alex, oh God, Alex!' Helen threw her arms around his neck. 'Alex, oh God. I was so afraid he was lying about you.'

'Is there anyone watching you?' Alex asked holding her.

She shook her head. 'There was someone. I think he's gone.'

'Stay here. *Don't move.*' Helen nodded, her eyes frightened. Alex started to move up the street. He felt for the gun in his coat pocket as he picked up speed in the crowd.

★   ★   ★

The good taste of the cigar was still in his mouth. Wyatt let the Blunt slip from his hand. The weight of the money felt good. Africa, he told himself, was a very big place. Wyatt was pushing people out of his way on the sidewalk. He'd left a rental car in the parking lot of the bullring. He would drive straight through to the port of La Paz. Anyone could get out of La Paz if they had money. He turned around for a moment and scanned the street. Would Alex be that stupid? *I'd kill him now.* The game was over. He could have killed him on the bus, why hadn't he? He got to the intersection across from the bullring. The traffic light turned red. Wyatt glanced behind him and saw Alex coming up the street after him. He wasn't even trying to hide himself. He could see the wake Alex was making as people cleared out of his way.

Wyatt dodged through the traffic on the wide boulevard in front of the bullring. He felt the sweat and gun metal at his stomach and heard the car horns blare at him as he trotted across the street in the afternoon heat. The sound of bullfight music filled the air in front of the bullring. Wyatt queued up with the crowd and showed his ticket to the ticket takers, passing by the scruffy musicians.

★   ★   ★

Alex lost him for a moment at the turnstiles; too many tourists had gotten in his way. Alex looked at the crowd streaming into the plaza, then he saw the red gym bag and Wyatt passing through the turnstiles ahead. He began to feel the panic of losing him. He threw a wad of bills at the ticket man and felt the turnstile release him. He ran into the shade made by the massive stone arcade that circled the bottom of the bullring, brimming with people now. Inside, in the penumbra, a fine gold dust from the floor was suspended in the air, illuminated by the sun that shot through the grandstands above.

Alex scanned the masses of people. He was losing control of his emotions. The idea of losing Wyatt now was too much. A young American woman in the crowd stopped and screamed unexpectedly. Her boyfriend had been pushed aside and cursed as he was showered with his own beer. There was the flash of the blue lenses. Alex saw the *guayabera*, wet with beer. Wyatt was running along the sun-dappled stone wall of the arcade. Alex could see the gun hanging at his side and began frantically pushing people out of his way as he ran after him.

⋆ ⋆ ⋆

Butch Nickels limped quickly into the section reserved for the matadors at the *barrera*. He saw the young matadors in their *trajes de luces* standing waiting for the music to start from the bandstand. Members of the various *cuadrillas* were unfolding their heavy pink capes for the *veronicas* that would come first. The men unwrapped them and swung them out, shaking them and making test passes. Butch saw the swords lined against the *barrera* wall in their flat leather scabbards. He

335

went to the edge of the *barrera* and slid one out. Then he made his way along the *barrera* to the press box and out through one of the two long passageways under the bleachers back into the crowd, limping faster now, keeping the sword against his bad leg.

★ ★ ★

Alex passed from the cool dark arcade into the blinding sunlight and the metallic hell of cars in the parking lot. It took his eyes a moment to adjust. The windshields and car tops glinted vision-shattering light. He could hear the bullring music start up with the trumpet solo followed by the snare drum. Wyatt was in front of him, still running with the red bag of money at his side. Wyatt stopped, keys out, and opened the door of one of the parked cars.

'You're a stupid son of a bitch, Alex!' he yelled over his shoulder. Alex stopped between two cars, a few car lengths away. Wyatt was holding his gun out under the bag. There was a roar from the fans in the bullring as the matadors walked out on the sand. The sound of the crowd rocked the parking lot.

Wyatt hesitated a moment. Alex saw Butch step out from behind the car. A sword punched through Wyatt's shirt at the sternum as he opened the car door. Butch stepped in closer and drove the sword to the hilt, at the same time ripping the gym bag out of Wyatt's hand. Standing there for a moment, Butch cursed him. Then he limped back toward the plaza with the money. Alex watched the horror-pain on Wyatt's face as he hung onto the open car door. Wyatt looked down to see what had happened to him. He managed to get his arm up and fire blindly at Butch. A car window exploded next to him. He tried to fire a second time but couldn't manage it. Alex watched him fall to his knees and saw the full profile of the sword, red and silver in the sun, as he approached. Wyatt tried to pull himself up and crawl into the car. Alex walked up closer. Wyatt stopped struggling and faced him. He tore his sunglasses off his face and then doubled over from the pain. Wyatt held himself up for a moment, still on his knees, the sword protruding from his chest, and looked up at Alex, reaching out and saying something as his gun dropped, clattering, on the ground. His mouth opened and closed grotesquely. His eyes were riveted on the sword.

'Alex? Help me . . . Are you there? God help me.'

Alex stepped forward. 'I'm here,' Alex said. 'I'm here.' He watched Wyatt try to stand up.

The gun jerked in Alex's hand. He heard Wyatt's body fall but didn't look. He turned away immediately.

Music from inside the bullring started up again, and Alex could hear it as he made his way back along the row of parked cars and into the cool arcade which was almost empty now. The cold and beautiful sound of a trumpet sounded first, then the snare drum. You could tell by the silence of the crowd that the first matador had walked out into the center of the arena. It was exactly four in the afternoon. Alex put the gun in his pocket after having held it for a long time without realizing it. He saw Helen running down the center of the arcade through the dust and shade coming back to him.

THE END

We do hope that you have enjoyed reading this large print book.

Did you know that all of our titles are available for purchase?

We publish a wide range of high quality large print books including:
Romances, Mysteries, Classics
General Fiction
Non Fiction and Westerns

Special interest titles available in large print are:
The Little Oxford Dictionary
Music Book
Song Book
Hymn Book
Service Book

Also available from us courtesy of Oxford University Press:
Young Readers' Dictionary
(large print edition)
Young Readers' Thesaurus
(large print edition)

For further information or a free brochure, please contact us at:
Ulverscroft Large Print Books Ltd.,
The Green, Bradgate Road, Anstey,
Leicester, LE7 7FU, England.
Tel: (00 44) 0116 236 4325
Fax: (00 44) 0116 234 0205

Other titles in the
Ulverscroft Large Print Series:

STRANGER IN THE PLACE

Anne Doughty

Elizabeth Stewart, a Belfast student and only daughter of hardline Protestant parents, sets out on a study visit to the remote west coast of Ireland. Delighted as she is by the beauty of her new surroundings and the small community which welcomes her, she soon discovers she has more to learn than the details of the old country way of life. She comes to reappraise so much that is slighted and dismissed by her family — not least in regard to herself. But it is her relationship with a much older, Catholic man, Patrick Delargy, which compels her to decide what kind of life she really wants.